Deadline to Love

About the Author

Lesley Dimmock is an Australian author, who began "properly" writing about fifteen years ago, when she finally stopped talking about writing a novel and actually sat down and began one. She now has two independently published books under her belt—*Out of Time* and *The Ganden Gambit*. Both feature much-loved characters, Lindsay Griffith and Kate Spencer. A third Lindsay and Kate adventure is in the pipeline.

During the Covid lockdown, Lesley discovered an online watercolour painting tutorial and discovered she was quite good at painting little birds. This fast became an excellent way of avoiding writing. Her other writing avoidance tactics include reading, watching the cricket and footy, birdwatching, photography, going camping with her wife, crocheting and travel.

Deadline to Love is Lesley's first lesbian romance.

Deadline to Love

Lesley Dimmock

BELLA BOOKS

Copyright © 2025 by Lesley Dimmock

Bella Books, Inc.
P.O. Box 10543
Tallahassee, FL 32302

All rights reserved. No part of this book may be used or reproduced or transmitted in any form or manner or by any means, electronic or mechanical, including photocopying, or for the purpose of training artificial intelligence technologies or systems without permission in writing from the publisher.

This is a work of fiction. Names, characters, businesses, places, events and incidents are either the products of the author's imagination or used in a fictitious manner. Any resemblance to actual persons, living or dead, or actual events is purely coincidental. The publisher does not have any control over and does not assume any responsibility for author or third-party websites or their content.

First Edition - 2025

Editor: Medora MacDougall
Cover Designer: SJ Hardy

ISBN: 978-1-64247-619-4

PUBLISHER'S NOTE

The scanning, uploading, and distribution of this book via the Internet or via any other means without the permission of the publisher is illegal and punishable by law. Please purchase only authorized print or electronic editions, and do not participate in or encourage electronic piracy of copyrighted materials. Your support of the author's rights is appreciated.

Acknowledgments

This novel was written on the lands of the Jagera, Yuggera, and Ugarapul peoples in what is now known as Ipswich in South East Queensland, Australia, and I pay my respects to Elders past, present, and emerging.

While I am not the most active of members, I am very thankful for the online group, Southern Cross Sapphic, a great bunch of women, who offer generous and enthusiastic support to all members.

I'd also like to thank my friends, family, and followers who have cheered me on throughout the three years it took to write this book.

Massive thanks go to Bella Books for seeing the potential in *Deadline to Love* and matching me up with editor extraordinaire, Medora MacDougall, who helped me bring that potential to light and made the novel so much better.

And, of course, it goes without saying that my biggest thanks go to my wife for her continued support and putting up with me disappearing into my study day after day.

Dedication

To Carmel, as always.

Content Warning

This book is written in Australian English and employs Australian English spelling and punctuation. This may look odd to US readers, but they are not errors or typos.

Also—Australians are a sweary bunch. As a result, there is a lot of swearing in *Deadline to Love*, which may shock a lot of readers unused to our casual use of profanities.

The story also contains some brief mentions of physical violence and alcohol abuse, however, these are not central to the story.

CHAPTER ONE

Frances Keating's hands tightened on the steering wheel, and she willed herself not to look as she crossed the street down where she used to live. It was hard enough coming back to Cannington after twenty years. She wasn't ready to see the old family home just yet. She winced as, unbidden, the words of an old David Cassidy song swam through her mind.

"Such a long way back, and this boy's lost track...You just can't go home again."

"Except I am, aren't I?" She continued driving along Cannington's main street, a sharp pang in her heart. God, it had been years since she last heard that song. It had been one of her mum's favourites, and while she used to sing along to its chorus, Frances had never imagined that it would ever apply to her. She was surprised at how easily the lyrics came back to her.

What was less surprising was how little the town had changed in the two decades she had been away. Cannington wasn't the largest town along Victoria's rugged southwest coast—that title belonged to Warrnambool, a hundred kilometres further west—but it claimed the bulk of the tourists that flocked to the region each summer. They were drawn by the pristine sands of Cannington's sheltered bay, its craggy coastline, and the town's proximity to two of the more iconic attractions along the world-famous Great Ocean Road—the Twelve Apostles and Loch Ard Gorge. While the January school holidays saw the town enjoying its peak tourist season, Cannington had always been a year-round favourite short-break destination for Melbournians keen to explore the region's natural beauty. Inevitably, as more people discovered the area, the more desirable it had become as a place to live. There were now housing estates where once there was farmland, a massive shopping centre squatted on the outskirts of town, occupying the site of the old woollen mill, and a cluster of midsized high-rise apartments fringed the esplanade that fronted Trelawney Bay. But the Trelawney Bay Hotel—the Lawney—was still there on the seafront. The shopfronts in the heart of town was still shaded by wide verandas, the civic buildings had retained their Victorian grandeur, and the offices of the *Cannington Clarion* looked just as run-down as they had when she had interned there as a high school student.

She swooped into one of the parking spaces right in front of the newspaper office. Marked as reserved for staffers, it was miraculously vacant, something that was not always the case during tourist season. She peered at the old place through the windshield of her Club Mini, overcome by a sudden wave of memories.

Batting away the unwanted reminiscences, she clambered out of the Mini, grimacing as her spine popped and cracked. The two-and-a-half-hour drive from Melbourne hadn't done her back any favours. Leaning back into the car to retrieve her satchel, she beeped the car locked and made her way past the neglected and unloved gardens fronting the building, pushed open the heavy timber-and-frosted-glass doors, and stepped into the reception area.

Christ, she thought to herself. *The place hasn't changed a bit.*

The same dusty rubber plant sat in one corner, while an armchair that looked as if it were last upholstered in 1973 sagged in the other corner. Running the width of the room, directly opposite the entrance, was a massive timber counter, its edges darkened and shiny from generations of elbows leaning against it. On the wall behind it, a clock ticked tiredly, while a ceiling fan circled lazily overhead. Frances was about to ding the little silver bell that sat on the counter when an inner door burst open and a woman who looked as if her sixtieth birthday was a distant memory bustled in, a mug of coffee in one hand and a plate with an enormous slice of chocolate cake in the other.

"Oh, my lord!" she exclaimed, catching sight of Frances. "You gave me a fright. You haven't been standing there long, have you, dear?"

Nope, nothing had changed at all. Frances grinned to herself before replying. "No, I've just walked in, Enid."

The woman frowned, then peered more closely at Frances. "Wait a minute. I know you, don't I?" A smile spread across her face as recognition dawned. "Frances! Oh, my lord, get in here, child!" She pulled open the door that separated her office space from the reception area and beckoned her into it. "We weren't expecting you until Monday," she said, enveloping her in a warm embrace.

"I know," Frances replied. "I just arrived in town and thought I'd pop in for a quick hello."

"Come on through. Everyone's going to be so excited to see you." Grabbing her by the hand, she dragged her into the newsroom.

"Look, everyone!" she hollered in a voice louder than it should rightfully be expected from someone with a frame as slight as hers. "It's Mick's girl!"

Several heads bobbed up from behind the partitions that divided the room into a dozen mini offices, each accommodating four workstations. Their faces broke into smiles as their owners came and gathered around Frances.

"Clarrie. Bob. Julie." Frances shook each of the journalists' hands, their names dropping into her brain as effortlessly as if she'd seen them just a few days ago instead of decades before. The delight on their faces did much to dispel the misgivings she had had about returning to her hometown. She still wasn't sure she'd done the right thing in accepting the job of editor in chief, but at least for now, no one seemed to resent her for it.

CHAPTER TWO

Spending the morning photographing politicians in hard hats and hi-viz vests was not really part of Kit Tresize's remit as the *Clarion*'s political reporter. But the newspaper's photographer had called in sick, so she had had no choice but to sign out a camera and take her own photographs of the groundbreaking ceremony for the new bridge over Canning River. It had been a frustrating few hours as she had grappled with the unfamiliar equipment, and she had been relieved to finally wrap up the session.

Her frustration had only worsened when she arrived back at the office only to find some idiot had parked in the space in front of the newspaper building that was reserved for *Clarion* staff. She had worked up a good head of steam during the kilometre-long walk back from where she had finally managed to park her Vespa. As if lugging a camera bag all that way wasn't bad enough, she'd also had to dodge an endless stream of mindless tourists all clogging up the footpaths and dithering over which café or gewgaw shop they wanted to go to. Yes, yes, yes, she knew tourists were the lifeblood of the town. Her boss, Clive, reminded her of that every time she grouched about them, and the recent Covid lockdowns had been a graphic example of what happens when the tourists stop coming to a town dependent on them. It didn't mean Kit had to be happy with the way the annual influx of summer visitors choked the town's streets and shops, though, did it? Thank goodness, there were only a few weeks of January left to get through before all the tourists packed up and headed home for the start of a new school year. Finally reaching the *Clarion* building, she glowered at the offending Mini, stomped up the steps, and shouldered her way through the front doors.

"Can you believe some out-of-town clown has taken my parking space! I've had to walk bloody miles to get here," she complained, striding into the newsroom. Only then did she register the knot of people standing in the middle of the room, which turned as one and stared at her as she dropped her bag with a hefty thump onto her desk.

"Oh, Kit, that's terrible," Enid sympathised. "At least now that you're here, come and meet—"

"The out-of-town clown," an unfamiliar voice said, cutting Enid off, as its owner stepped out from the group surrounding her. A faint smile twitched at her lips as she extended her hand toward Kit. "A.k.a Frances Keating."

Huh, so this is the daughter of the legendary Michael Keating that she had heard so much about, Kit mused. It had been twenty years since the man had died, but people still spoke in near-reverential tones of the "MK years." She appraised the woman who had been appointed to usher in a new Keating era. In her late thirties, with straight blond hair that brushed her collar, Frances Keating was taller than Kit expected the owner of a Mini to be. Despite the weariness around her dark-green eyes, the travel-crumpled casual shirt and jeans, the woman exuded an air of understated elegance that only made Kit uncomfortably aware of just how dishevelled she was in comparison. Her unruly mane of black hair was clinging in sweaty tendrils across her forehead. Perspiration trickled down the back of her shirt. Her hands felt hot and sweaty, and her feet hurt from the unscheduled hike. She would not have worn her brand-new Oxfords today if she'd known she'd be schlepping across town. All this made her even less inclined toward graciousness than meeting one's new boss would demand.

"Kit Tresize," she said, snatching her hand away after the most perfunctory of handshakes. "I guess I owe you an apology. You're not an out-of-towner after all." She knew she was behaving churlishly, but the woman's cool demeanour was really annoying her.

"No," Frances replied with a tight smile. "Although I've been gone for so long, I wouldn't blame anyone for mistaking me for an incomer."

Kit winced as the barb hit home. Okay, so it seemed Ms. Keating was not averse to tossing around an insult or two of her own. Kit didn't know how long a person had to live in Cannington before the long-term residents stopped considering them a newcomer, but after five years, she still had not lost the incomer tag. She suspected she would always be considered an outsider, never truly belonging like those born and bred in the town did.

"Lovely as this has been, I do have a story to lodge," she said, gesturing to her desk.

"Of course," Frances replied before turning to address the other staff. "Please don't let me hold you up. It's been lovely to meet you all and I'll see you all on Monday." She hitched her satchel higher onto her shoulder and made her way back through the office, with Enid fluttering at her heels.

Kit slid into her chair, watching Frances's departure from the corner of her eye while gathering her hair into a loose knot in an attempt to cool the back of her neck. She had once had it all cropped short but had been appalled at how her ears stuck out. Nowadays, even though it for some reason led everyone to presume she was straight, which constantly annoyed her, she kept her hair long, figuring it a smallish price to pay to be able to cover up her poppy-out ears.

"Could you at least have tried to be agreeable?" Kit's boss, Clive "Clarrie" Sturt complained, perching his not insubstantial posterior on the corner of Kit's desk.

"It wasn't my fault," Kit grumbled in reply. "I wouldn't have been so grumpy if she hadn't parked in the staff space and made me walk so far."

"Well, technically, she *is* staff," Clarrie pointed out. "So, you could say she was entitled to park there."

Annoying though it was, Clarrie was right, but Kit was in a mood and not ready to concede.

"Hmph," she grunted. "Just how much is her getting the job down to her name, I wonder."

"Careful, Tresize," Clarrie said, a note of warning in his voice. "I don't think anyone would deny her name played a part in her appointment, but I wouldn't go around insinuating nepotism had anything to do with her appointment. It's not the way to win friends and influence people. Not where the Keatings are concerned, anyway."

He lifted himself off Kit's desk, patted her on the shoulder, and ambled back to his own corner of the office. Kit scowled after him. He was such a hypocrite. He had acted in the chief editor role for the past six months, expecting his seniority would secure him the job permanently. When Frances's appointment had been announced, he had complained long and loud to anyone who would listen about how it was all about who you knew, not what you knew. Shaking her head in exasperation, Kit turned her attention to her computer.

"Let's see what the Internet has to say about Ms. Frances Keating," she muttered, jabbing at her keyboard.

"Okay," she grudgingly conceded fifteen minutes later after trawling through a LinkedIn profile of the *Clarion's* new chief editor that revealed that Frances Keating was more than qualified for the job. She'd studied journalism at Melbourne University, holding a double major in political science, worked for *The Age* for a decade as that paper's political analyst, moved to Brisbane for a few years, where she was political editor for the online *Brisbane Times*, before returning to Melbourne to lecture in journalism and media studies at the inner-city Royal Melbourne Institute of Technology prior to her appointment at the *Clarion*.

"Still, I bet it didn't hurt that she's the daughter of Cannington's favourite son and longest-serving editor," she muttered to herself, glaring at the profile picture of Frances Keating that smiled out at her from the LinkedIn page. She stuck her tongue out at the image, taking a small pleasure in the childish act as she shut the site down, then scowled at herself as a traitorous part of her brain acknowledged that Keating did have a rather cute smile. She was so not going there. In her experience, no good ever came from a cute smile.

CHAPTER THREE

"Well, that went well," Frances muttered to herself as she climbed into her Mini. "Already trading insults with the staff and I haven't even officially started the job!" She shook her head, trying to shake off the memory of Kit Tresize's cobalt-blue eyes glaring at her. "Haven't won myself any fans there," she said. Starting the engine, she manoeuvred the car onto the street and toward the Waverley Hotel.

That was another thing. Of all the hotels in Cannington, the *Clarion* had picked the Waverley to put her up in. Granted, it was the only pub in town that offered accommodation, and she could have ended up in one of the dozen or so soulless and tourist-jammed motels, so she supposed she should be grateful for that. But still, the Waverley…

The hotel was one of those faded beauties you can find in many Australian towns—all wrought-iron verandas throwing the frontage into deep shade, a corrugated iron roof and heavy timber-and-etched-glass doors and windows. With her laptop bag in one hand and trailing a smallish suitcase in the other, Frances pushed her way through the main doors and down a

Deadline to Love   11

dimly lit hallway to where a reception area was squeezed into a tiny nook opposite the doors to the main bar. Frances studiously avoided glancing into it as she passed.

"Hi, I'm Frances Keating," she said to the woman behind the desk. "I believe there's a room booked for me?"

"Keating, huh?" the woman said. "Any relation to—?" She jutted her chin toward the bar.

"Yep," Frances replied brusquely, not wanting to get into a discussion about her family tree. "The room?"

If she took umbrage at Frances's curtness, the receptionist didn't show it. Instead, she turned her attention to her computer screen, tapping at the keyboard for a few moments before turning to retrieve a key from the row of pigeonholes behind her.

"There you go. Room Three. Up the stairs. Turn right and it's the second door on the left. Let me know if you need anything."

Hoping to make up for her earlier unfriendliness, Frances peered closer at the woman's nametag. "Thanks, Nancy." Frances took the key with a smile, and, tightening her grip on her bags, climbed the stairs to her room. Dropping her luggage onto the bed, she surveyed what was now home for as long as it took her to find a place of her own.

As hotel rooms went, it wasn't bad. Aside from the expected queen-sized bed, it was also furnished with a plump armchair and a small round table with two accompanying dining chairs. A set of tall, narrow French doors, bracketed by matching windows on either side, opened out onto the veranda, giving her views of Trelawney Bay a few blocks away to the south. A kettle, tea and coffee supplies, a coffee plunger, and two mugs sat on top of the bar fridge, which held nothing other than half a dozen little pods of milk. A large flatscreen television was mounted on the wall opposite the bed. The ensuite bathroom was compact, but clean and well-supplied with fluffy towels, soap, and skincare products.

She stood in the middle of the room, irresolute. Should she unpack or go shopping for essentials like ground coffee, real

12   Lesley Dimmock

milk, cheese and crackers? A loud rumbling from her stomach reminded her she hadn't eaten in hours—seven, in fact, as a glance at her watch confirmed. So, food it was.

She ran a critical eye over her reflection, deciding her shirt wasn't too rumpled from the car journey. She dragged a comb through her hair and tucked it behind her ears. She'd have to do. After all, it wasn't as if she was planning on dining at the Savoy, Cannington's poshest, if unimaginatively named, restaurant.

No, what she had in mind as she retraced her steps down the stairs and out onto the street, was much humbler—a souvlaki from what had been her favourite fish and chip shop as a teenager—Theo's. Her friends had mocked her for preferring it over good ol' Aussie flake and chips, but she had always been hungry for the world beyond Cannington and its predominantly Anglo-Australian traditions. As she stood on the street getting her bearings, a map of the route to Theo's unfurled in her mind. Funny how quickly the memories came back, even after twenty years. She set off, crossing her fingers that the shop was still in business.

Turning into Kinross Street, she sighed in relief at the sight of the old familiar blue-and-white sign proclaiming Theo's Takeaway. She pushed her way through the heavy plastic strips hanging in the doorway, grinning to herself as she spotted the same scarred Laminex tables she used to sit at. Also unchanged was the hand-painted menu board above the deep fryers, still with the same spelling mistakes—"hambruger," "sanwitches," and "sause"—that had made her giggle as a kid. The prices were different, though, as were the people behind the counter. Theo's grandkids? Frances wondered. Was the old bloke even still alive? To the teenaged Frances, he'd appeared an old man even then, although as she thought about it now, he was probably only in his fifties or so. His daughter, Zoe, had been one of Frances's classmates.

"You ordering or what, love?" The old man standing at her elbow gestured toward the teenage girl who stood with pen poised over paper.

"Sorry, sorry," she murmured. "Yes, I'll have a souvlaki, please. With garlic and hummus, please." She did a mental eye roll at the second "Please," but the kid taking her order didn't seem to care.

"Any drinks?"

Frances thought for a moment, torn between a meal down at the shore or washing it down with a glass of wine. Alcohol won out. She shook her head.

"Seven fifty," the girl said. "That'll be about ten minutes," she continued, handing Frances her change before adding her order to the row of orders already lined up along the counter. Frances nodded, pocketed the coins, and sat down at one of the vacant tables. The old man placed his order, then shuffled over and took the seat opposite her, even though all the other tables were unoccupied.

"You new in town?" he asked.

"Yes and no," Frances replied. She didn't really want to get into a conversation with the man but couldn't bring herself to give him the cold shoulder. He was just being friendly, after all. "I grew up here but moved away a long time ago."

"Huh." The man squinted at her. "Do I know you?"

"I don't think so." Frances shook her head.

"You look kinda familiar," the man said, frowning in an apparent effort to remember where he might know her from. "You remind me of someone."

Frances had a good idea who he might be remembering, but she wasn't going to volunteer any information. Luckily, her order was ready, and she was able to evade further questions. She muttered a hurried goodbye, grabbed her food, and scurried out of the shop before her identity could dawn on the old man.

She called in at the bottle shop attached to the Waverley and chose a chilled bottle of pinot gris from one of her favourite boutique Yarra Valley wineries. The South West was just about the only region in Victoria that did not have its own wine industry, but the spectacular wines coming out of the hills to Melbourne's east more than made up for it. Besides, the artisanal cheeses now being created in the Cannington district were compensation enough for the lack of local wines. Making her way back into the hotel, she paused at the reception desk, where Nancy was still on duty, and asked for a wineglass.

"Just ask Rob," she said, gesturing toward the doors to the main bar. "He'll fix you up."

France made a mental grimace. She would really prefer not set foot in the bar. Not unless it were absolutely necessary.

"I'd rather not go in with all this," she said, holding up the food and wine, thankful for the plausible excuse. Nancy gave Frances a shrewd look before nodding.

"All right, I'll fetch you one. Won't be long." She ducked under the counter flap and crossed the hallway into the bar, returning several moments later with two wineglasses.

"Here you go."

"Thanks, Nancy," Frances said, juggling the souvlaki and wine bottle to take the two glasses from her. "I appreciate that. Have a good night."

"You too, love," Nancy called as she traipsed up the stairs.

Once inside her room, she poured a glass of the straw-coloured wine, giving the crisp, melon-y flavour a nod of approval before recapping the bottle and putting it in the little refrigerator, and settling into the armchair to eat the still-warm souvlaki. She was about halfway through it when her phone rang from inside her satchel. She lunged across the bed and rummaged through it, retrieving the phone and swiping the answer button just before it went to voice mail.

"Abs, how's things?" she said, wiping a smear of garlic sauce from the corner of her mouth as she spoke.

"Frances!" The voice of Abby, her best friend, boomed from the phone. "So, how's Cannington? You've been welcomed back to the bosom of your hometown? Parades down the street for the return of the prodigal daughter? Keys to the city and all that?"

Frances laughed. "Not quite. They've put me up in the Waverley. Probably thought I'd be chuffed to be staying at the old man's local."

"And you're not? Chuffed, that is?" Abby asked. She might have known Frances for close to twenty years, but her childhood was one thing Frances rarely talked about.

"Not likely," Frances replied. "Let's just say I'm not my father's biggest fan." She chewed another mouthful of souvlaki before continuing, "Oh, and I called in at the paper, just to say hi, you know? And managed to get on the wrong side of one of its senior reporters. So yeah, off to a flying start. Can't wait until the staff meeting on Monday. That's going to go down a treat."

"Oh dear," Abby said. "What did you do? Break their favourite mug?"

"Not this time." Frances laughed. "No, I inadvertently parked in a space reserved for staff, causing our political reporter a bit of a hike to the office."

"Well, technically you are staff," Abby said, rising to her friend's defence.

Frances laughed again. "I don't think Ms. Tresize saw it quite that way," she said. "Called me an 'out-of-town clown.'"

"Points for the rhyme," Abby cut in, giggling.

"Yes. I had to work hard at not grinning at it, myself," Frances said. "And, in fairness, she didn't know it was me she was calling a clown. She did look somewhat abashed when she discovered she'd just insulted her new boss. Apologised for calling me an out-of-towner."

"Ooh, left the clown insult standing, huh?" Abby said. "Pretty gutsy."

"Yeah," Frances replied. "I got her back, though, by implying she was an incomer."

"Dastardly of you." Abby laughed. "I bet that hurt!"

"She flinched. I definitely saw her flinch," Frances said. "So, it's one all at the end of Round One. Anyway, that's enough about me. Tell me what's been happening with you." She wriggled back into her armchair, getting comfortable and finishing her meal while Abby regaled with tales of her latest thrift shop finds. Abby loved second-hand stores and the thrill of chasing a bargain. It was where the two women had first met, after Frances—lonely, miserable, and unable to find her

feet in the unfamiliar surroundings of the big city campus—
had taken refuge in a local thrift shop to browse the used book
collection, only to be approached by the bubbly tawny-haired
veterinary student demanding Frances's opinion on the bright-
red overcoat she had just discovered.

"Oh, I, um…" Frances had stammered.

"No, you're right," the woman had said. "The colour's
totally wrong for me. But it's just perfect for you, don't you
think?" She held it against Frances. "You should buy it. In fact,
as a thank-you for saving me from a massive fashion faux pas,
I'm going to buy it for you." She thrust the coat into Frances's
hands, ignoring all her protests and handed a ten-dollar note to
the bemused shop assistant. Frances and Abby had been the best
of friends from that day, and Frances still had the coat.

CHAPTER FOUR

Frances groaned as her alarm went off. She groped on the bedside table for her phone and fumbled to switch the irritating sound off. Despite looking forward to starting in her new role, Monday had seemed to come around way too fast. Even after spending most of Sunday going over her notes and plans, as well as studying a dossier on the newspaper's employees, she still felt unprepared for the day ahead. Her brain, turning in endless circles, had kept her awake most of the night. She was tempted to pull the sheets back over her head and try for some more sleep, but turning up late to her first day on the new job probably wasn't the best look.

A long, hot shower had her almost feeling her normal self, and once she had pulled on a pair of tan slacks and a plain white business shirt, she figured she at least looked the part of a professional, even if she wasn't feeling it. She stared at her reflection, wondering what her eighteen-year-old self would make of the woman in the mirror. Would she be aghast that not only had she returned to her hometown, but that she had stepped into the shoes of her father? What would *he* have thought?

18   Lesley Dimmock

Frances shook that thought away. She didn't really care what her father would have made of this career move. Although, given their rocky relationship, he would probably be surprised at her choice of profession. Not her mum, though. Contrary to people's assumptions, she'd inherited her love of words from her English-teacher mother, not him. She became a journalist in spite of her father, not because of him, after his job showed her the power of telling people's stories.

One thing she could be sure about. That eighteen-year-old self would be proud of the successful, competent, and confident woman she had grown into. Not that she was feeling particularly confident right now. The nerves roiling in her stomach put breakfast out of the question, so with one final check in the mirror and a deep breath, she slung her satchel over her shoulder and let herself out of her room.

The *Clarion* building was only a ten-minute walk away from the hotel, so she decided to stretch her legs and use the time to calm her mind.

"At least I won't get on the wrong side of anyone by taking their parking spot this time," she mused to herself as she made her way along streets already thickening with holidaymakers. The end of summer may be fast approaching, but cafés still teemed with families poring over breakfast menus, while clumps of teens slouched along the footpaths, beach towels and boogie boards tucked under their arms, ready for a day on the sand.

She found Enid waiting for her in the reception area, pacing nervously.

"Oh, good morning, Frances," Enid gushed, rushing over and taking her hands in her own and gently wringing them. "I'm so glad to see you. I was worried you'd changed your mind." She gave a little titter, peering anxiously at Frances's face. "You haven't, have you?"

She freed herself from Enid's grasp and shook her head.

"No, Enid, I haven't changed my mind." She smiled gently at the older woman.

"Oh, that is such a relief! It's just that it's such a big challenge, breathing new life into the poor old *Clarion*. You wouldn't be the first person to decide it's all a lost cause. Change has been slow to come to this part of the world, I'm afraid. Although, the last editor did manage to convince everyone that tablets and mobile phones were respectable tools of the trade and that it was perfectly acceptable to use the Internet for research purposes. But you don't need to hear me wittering on. Here's your security card," she said, handing Frances a slim plastic card on a lanyard. "Now, can I show you to your office?"

"I think I can remember the way," she said, smiling slightly. "Unless, of course, the place has undergone a major refurbishment in the last twenty years?"

Enid gave a derisive snort. "This place? Frozen in time," she said. "The only things that get changed around here are the light bulbs."

"I guess I'll have my work cut out for me, then," Frances replied, grinning at the office manager.

"Would you like me to bring you a cup of coffee, dear?" Enid said, trotting behind Frances as she strode to the "Staff Only" door.

"No, thank you, Enid," Frances replied. "You're the office manager. It's not your job to wait on me, or anyone else." Ignoring Enid's protests that she didn't mind making the coffee, she swiped her new security card against the sensor, pushed the door open and stepped through it and into the open-plan office area. The majority of desks were already occupied, and a chorus of greetings trailed after her as she made her way to the office that was once her father's.

She stood in the doorway and gazed around the room. Although the office looked nothing like it had thirty years ago, she was overwhelmed by a vision of her father leaning over his scarred old desk and roaring at a hapless reporter. So vivid was it, for a moment she became her seven-year-old self cowering in the doorway. She squeezed her eyes shut.

"Is everything all right, Frances?"

Frances's eyes flew open again, and she whirled to find Enid peering anxiously at her.

"You look like you've seen a ghost, dear," Enid said, her eyes creasing with worry.

"No, no, I'm fine," she replied, casting a surreptitious look over her shoulder. Relieved to see the office was once again filled with empty bookshelves and anodyne prints on the wall rather than the sporting memorabilia and trophies her father had decorated the room with, she forced herself to smile.

"Perhaps I will have that cup of coffee, after all," she said. "Oh, and could you let everyone know there'll be a staff meeting in fifteen minutes? Thanks, Enid."

She grinned as the office manager scurried from desk to desk to relay the message about the meeting. Evidently, she had yet to grasp the concept of the group email. Taking a deep, steadying breath, she entered her office, dropped her satchel onto a corner of the desk, and sank into the executive-style chair. Swivelling around, she took in her surroundings. Nothing remained of her father, of course, but someone had also cleared the room of any evidence of its most recent occupant, who after eight years at the helm, had retired six months ago to devote himself to his golf, leaving the place a clean slate upon which to impose her own presence.

Apart from a sleek monitor, with matching wireless keyboard and mouse, the desk was bare. On pulling out the desk's two narrow drawers, Frances discovered they were fully stocked with stationery items. Gel pens in red, blue, and black ink, Post-it notepads in a range of sizes and hues, a stapler and boxes of staples, sticky tape, pencils, white-out liquid, and a packet of AAA batteries—presumably for the mouse and keyboard. There was also a small stack of Moleskine-branded A6 notebooks. She ran her fingers over the cover of the topmost notebook. She always found a blank notebook alluring, despite using a tablet and computer for all her writing. Something about all those empty pages…

"Sorry to intrude, dear." Enid spoke from the doorway. "But everyone is now gathered in the meeting room."

"Oh, right. Yes. Sorry." She glanced at her watch as she scrambled to her feet. Grabbing her tablet from her satchel, she made to leave her office, then turned back and picked up one of the Moleskine notebooks and a gel-tip pen. Slipping them into her satchel, she followed Enid across the newsroom and into the packed meeting room. All but two of the dozen chairs around the large oval table that dominated the room were occupied, and another dozen or so people stood along the walls, shifting uncomfortably from foot to foot whilst thumbing at their mobile phones. The quiet murmur of conversation that had buzzed around the room fell into a tense silence as everyone watched her progress across the room to the empty seat at the head of the table, where a steaming mug of coffee sat. The mood wasn't exactly hostile, but it wasn't particularly welcoming either. Sliding into the seat, Frances could feel wary eyes upon her. She gave a nod of thanks toward Enid, who, taking the seat next to her, flipped open a legal notepad, poised to minute the meeting.

Her mouth suddenly dry, Frances took a grateful gulp from the mug of coffee before speaking.

"First of all, thank you all for coming," she began. "I'll try not to let this go on longer than it has to. I know a lot of you are probably nervous about what my appointment might mean for your jobs, so let me straight up assure you all that no one is losing their job. Well, not as a result of any restructure anyway." A few nervous laughs greeted her last words, but the majority of people continued to watch her in wary silence.

"Of course, a newspaper doesn't change hands and its new owners appoint a new chief editor without expecting some changes to take place," she went on. "In the *Clarion's* case, this means going digital."

"What, again?" someone snorted from the back of the room. Frances searched her memory for the man's name.

"Andrew, isn't it?" she asked, then continued as the man reluctantly nodded. "Yes, I am aware that it's been tried before and that the whole venture was an abject failure. But this time will be different. We'll be starting from a much stronger standpoint, with proper buy-in from the paper's new owners."

She raised her hands, making patting motions in the air as a hubbub of voices broke out around the room as people reacted to the news, calling out questions.

"Okay," she said, once she had regained their attention. "I'll be going into more detail about what this means as I meet with individual teams, but no, it doesn't mean the end of a printed *Clarion*. The digital edition will be in addition to the paper edition. The new owners are fully on board with this and while they haven't exactly given me a blank cheque, we'll have everything we need to get this thing up and running. The one thing they haven't given me is a lot of time. They want to see the digital edition launched on March first."

"But that's, like, just a few weeks away!"

"Six weeks," Frances said. "It's not that much time, so we need to get cracking. Obviously, the most important task right now is establishing our web development team. To that end, I have appointed Nick Davies as the web team manager. Nick is a former colleague from the *Brisbane Times*. He will take up his position here in a week's time, when he will assist me in recruiting the remainder of the team. Those roles are open to all current staff. The job descriptions will be on the intranet by the end of the day and applications will close on Friday. So, if a change of career appeals to you, I strongly encourage you to apply. Enid, we'll need to discuss the necessary office refurbishment. My office in ten minutes? Clarrie, can the news team meet back here in an hour?"

"Sure, boss." The man nodded, ignoring the muted objections from his team about having stories to write and file.

"Great, thanks," Frances said. "Okay, that about wraps it up for now. I just want to say I know this going to be a challenging time for everyone, and anytime any of you feel the need to talk, my door is always open. Always. Okay?"

She allowed herself a massive sigh of relief as the room emptied. "That's the first hurdle crossed," she muttered to herself as she gathered up her coffee cup and tablet. "Now, I just need to eliminate gambling advertising revenue, shake up the content of the print version, and introduce a new staffing structure. And try not to get run out of town."

CHAPTER FIVE

"Now look, calm down, the lot of you," Clarrie said, looking at the circle of anxious faces crowded around his desk. "I don't know any more than you do about what all this means, but I'm sure we'll all find out shortly."

"Digital!" Bob Currie spat. "Waste of bloody time. Might be all right for wanky city hipsters, but out here?" He shook his head in disgust and stomped off to his own desk.

"Oh, I don't know," Kit said. While her role at the *Clarion* was as the paper's reporter on all things political and having to do with economic development, she also took a keen interest in developing trends, especially in the tech world. "I reckon it would appeal to heaps of people. I know I prefer my news digital. I like the idea."

Her mind was already racing with the possibilities. A column about cryptocurrencies perhaps? Or maybe she could write about the growing use of AI. Regular profiles of the local cheesemakers? And hadn't a new brewery recently set up business in nearby Port Haven? Maybe she could even slip in some articles about birds and the environment.

Julie Huxton, the *Clarion*'s reporter on community news, looked worriedly from Clarrie to Kit. "It's all right for you, Kit. You're young. Same for you, Simon and Caitlyn. But what about us older journos? What if we can't adapt, learn the new skills? What does the union have to say about all of this, Clive?"

"I think you're getting a bit ahead of yourself there, Julie," Clarrie said. "She said no one's job was at risk."

"Pftt! They all say that," Julie replied, her tone dismissive. "Just you wait and see. Six months' time and those of us over forty will be getting a tap on the shoulder."

Clarrie shook his head at Julie's doom and gloom. "It won't come to that, Julie. But, if it makes you feel better, I'll give the union a call. See just what our rights are, okay? Now, how about you all get back to your desks? Don't you have stories to file? Go on!" He shooed them away.

He was right, Kit thought. She did have a story to file, but it was difficult to focus on the council's new Community Development Plan with Julie continuing her low-level grumbling from the other side of the partition that divided their workstations. After fifteen minutes of banging away at her keyboard, she pushed it away from herself in frustration.

"I need some fresh air," she said, getting to her feet.

"But the meeting…" Julie said, worry etched onto her face.

"I'll be back for that," Kit replied, shoving her tablet into her satchel.

"Okay, but can you bring me back one of those custard cannoli from Angie's?" Julie said.

Nodding, Kit slipped her bag onto her shoulder and slipped out of the office and past Enid's reception desk undetected. She made a beeline for one of her favourite places—the nearby Botanic Gardens. There was one little corner she loved and not just for the stunning lemon bottlebrush tree that grew there. It was also home to a dozen or so Superb Fairy-wrens and—apart from the gorgeous blue of the males—the way they hopped and bounced around never failed to make her smile. After all the Chicken Little thinking in the office this morning, a dose of these cute little birds was just what she needed. She never had understood why some people always jumped to the worst possible scenarios whenever a change was proposed, then spent so much time and energy worrying about something that never eventuated anyway. Julie was a frequent victim of this kind of thinking, and the endless, and ultimately pointless, conversations she had with the woman trying to alleviate her fears did Kit's head in. Much easier to let her get on with her catastrophising and escape from the office while she did so.

Today, the Fairy-wrens let Kit down. When there was still no sign of them after ten minutes of sitting on the grass in the shade of the bottlebrush, she sighed, stood, and brushed herself down.

"Julie's not the only one in need of a custard cannoli," she muttered to herself as she set off toward Angie's Bakery.

"Oh my god, that was sooo good," Julie murmured half an hour later as she licked a dusting of icing sugar from her fingers. "I feel so much better now."

"There's not much that custard cannoli can't fix," Kit said, balling up her empty paper bag, lobbing it toward Julie's wastepaper bin, and missing by a mile.

"Except your aim," Julie laughed. "Come on, time for our reveal-all meeting with K2. It's what we used to call Frances when she interned here as a teenager," she explained in response to Kit's confused expression. "To differentiate her from her father."

"Oh, right, I forgot you've been around that long. It must be weird having her as your boss, having known her as a kid."

Julie shrugged as she collected her notebook and pen and walked toward the meeting room. "All I know is that she has big shoes to fill," she said over her shoulder. "We all loved Mick. It was a huge loss when he died. Things just haven't been the same at the paper since."

Kit would have asked what things, but they had arrived at the meeting room, where the rest of the news team, and Frances, were waiting.

"Sorry," Kit said, sliding into a seat next to Caitlyn. "I didn't realise we were late."

"Right on time, actually." Frances beamed at her. "It's just that the rest of us got here early. Right, so shall we get started?" She shuffled the pile of papers in front of her, then continued, "As I announced this morning, we're going to launch a digital version of the *Clarion*. Are any of you familiar with the *Guardian Australia* or the *Brisbane Times*?"

Bob and Clarrie shook their heads, Clarrie growling that he liked his news in print, but the others all nodded.

"Good, so we'll be going for a similar concept. Obviously, all the content that the *Clarion* currently produces will also be available in the digital version—all the news and sport, anyway. The classifieds are being hived off onto a separate website. So, the first bit of good news is that more of your news stories will be able to be published instead of being spiked because of lack of room.

"But we'll also be looking to include new content, content that we just can't fit into the print version. So, there'll be an Opinion and Analysis section. A Travel section. Culture and Lifestyle. Those are the sections we'll start with. Others will be added later, once we've got the thing well established."

"That sounds like a lot of extra content that needs to be generated," Simon Peters, the still-new sports reporter, cut in.

"Exactly." Frances nodded at him. "And that's where you all come in. As well as writing pieces in your current area of expertise, you'll have the opportunity to write articles for any and all of the new sections as well. And not just you, the whole team will be able to contribute. Barbara from Sales has already put her hand up to curate recipe articles. This is your chance to expand your writing skills into other areas and subjects you're interested in."

Frances stopped speaking and looked around the group but was met by silence and frowns. Realizing perhaps that it was a lot to take in, she gave them a few moments to gather their thoughts.

"Okaaay," Kit said, just as the silence was becoming uncomfortable. "It sounds intriguing, but where do we find the time to write all this extra material on top of the stories we have to file for the print version?"

"Very good question!" Frances grinned. "We haven't worked out all the details yet, but the thinking is that for every article you write outside of your regular assignments that gets published on the site, you'll be paid one hundred dollars."

"So, in essence, we'll be writing on our own time?" Kit pressed.

"And getting paid for it." Frances nodded. "Remember, none of this is obligatory. If you don't want to or are unable to contribute more than you already are, that is perfectly okay."

"Sure. You say that now." Clarrie glowered from his end of the table. Simon and Julie shot him alarmed looks.

"They wouldn't, would they?" Simon asked in an agonised stage whisper. "Sack us I mean if we don't write those extra stories?"

"They're management," Clarrie growled, his inner union shop steward finally coming to the fore. Bob Currie rolled his eyes and winked at Kit. They'd both experienced Clarrie's antimanagement tirades over the years.

"People, please!" Frances had to raise her voice above the growing muttering. "No one is sacking anyone, okay? Look, I know this is a lot to take in. Let's leave it here and meet again in a week. You'll have had the time to digest what this might mean for each of you by then, and we can talk then about how we take this forward. Meantime, as I said at the earlier meeting, my door is always open if you have any questions or want to talk more. This really is an exciting project, and there's nothing to fear from it, I promise you."

No one looked very convinced. They watched in silence as she left, a fierce, whispered conversation breaking out behind her. Kit looked on as her colleagues argued among themselves. Frances Keating had certainly managed to put the cat amongst the pigeons, she thought. And this was only her first day. This was going to be fun.

CHAPTER SIX

Kit had been skeptical when Frances had first outlined the plan for the new digital version of the *Clarion*. Typical of management, she'd thought, to expect people to work in their own time. But the more she had thought about it, the more she was liking the idea. And now an idea for an article was rattling around her head and she couldn't wait to get home to start getting to work on it.

Home was a tiny cottage out on Brewster's Lane, a dirt track that petered out into a sandy wasteland on the western fringe of town. The cottage nestled into a ridge of sand dunes that backed onto Marnoo Cove. Although sheltered at its eastern end by Tumbledown Point, the sea here was notoriously rough, with messy waves crashing onto a rock-strewn beach. Unappealing to swimmers and surfers alike because it required a long scramble over the sand dunes from the road, Marnoo Cove was pretty well deserted all year round. Which was just the way she liked it. She found the constant roar of waves, punctuated with the cries of various seabirds, the perfect soundtrack to unwind to after a day at the *Clarion* offices.

She steered the Vespa into the narrow driveway that flanked the house and rolled it down to the little, ramshackle wooden shed at its end. Heaving the doors open, she wheeled the scooter inside, then followed a stone path to the back door of the cottage.

A sinuous grey cat greeted her with a plaintive yowl as soon as she stepped indoors.

"Hey, Marvin." She stooped to tickle the cat under its chin. "How was your day? Did you get the ironing done? And the dishes?" She grinned as the cat just blinked owlishly at her. "Tell me you got dinner ready at least!"

Ignoring her words, Marvin wrapped himself around Kit's ankles and meowed again, demanding she get his dinner ready. She picked him up and smooshed her face into his fur, laughing as he squirmed out of her grasp and jumped to the floor with a loud thump that belied his slight build.

"All right, all right. I get the message!" She laughed as she reached into the pantry for a tin of cat food and spooned it into Marvin's bowl. He gulped it down as if he hadn't eaten for a week rather than just eight hours ago.

"You little pig!" she said, ignoring his pleas for more. Preparing herself a plate of cheese, crackers, and fruit, she carried it into a living room into which she had managed to squeeze a two-seater settee, an armchair, and a coffee table. An unkind observer might describe the room as cramped, but she preferred to see it as cosy. Returning to the kitchen to retrieve her satchel, she settled into a corner of the settee and pulled out her tablet.

Having connected it to a compact Bluetooth keyboard, she was soon engrossed in crafting an opinion piece about a proposed development in nearby Coniston that threatened a protected wetland. The only sounds in the room were the clicking of the keys as she typed, Marvin's rhythmic purring as he lay curled up at her feet, and the distant roar of the ocean.

Increasing discomfort from a full bladder eventually forced Kit to stop working. Clambering to her feet, she was startled to find the room in darkness, illuminated only by the glow from her tablet's screen. She reached for the switch to the corner

30   Lesley Dimmock

lamp and flicked it on, sending its pool of warm, yellow light spilling across the settee. Looking askance at the remnants of her earlier meal, she went to the bathroom, then made her way into the kitchen and fixed herself a mug of chai tea and raided her stash of Cherry Ripe bars before returning to the lounge. Despite the late hour, she settled back down on the settee and, unwrapping the chocolate bar and biting into it, began to read over what she had spent the last three hours writing.

"Pretty good, even if I do say so myself," she said to Marvin, poking him with a toe. "Let's hope our illustrious new leader thinks so too." Marvin's only response was an irritated twitch of his tail.

Never normally one to doubt her own journalistic abilities, it nevertheless took Kit most of the next day to screw up the courage to send the article to Frances. Was she pro-development, loath to offend local developers? Or would she welcome the controversy? Kit had no idea, although, given the enthusiasm with which she had embraced what was in effect a disruptor role at the paper, Kit rather suspected the latter. So, she had crossed her fingers and hit Send and then spent a nerve-wracking hour waiting to hear what her response might be. She used most of that time to compose the arguments she would use to rebut the inevitable rejection.

When the message summoning her to Frances's office finally pinged on her screen, Kit's heart rate shot up. Trying to look as nonchalant as possible, she ambled over to the editor's office and slouched in the doorway, her sweaty hands shoved deep into her trouser pockets.

"This is great." Frances looked up from her screen. "Just the sort of thing we're looking for."

"Really?" Kit's tone was skeptical. Having convinced herself Frances would reject the article out of hand, she was waiting for the "But…"

"Yes, really," Frances said, gesturing for Kit to take a seat. Trying not to let her surprise show, Kit sat down quickly, before her knees could buckle and betray just how nervous she had felt.

"If you could add some photographs, it'll make it perfect. Have a chat with Jake and set up a time to go out to the wetlands with him. Show him the sorts of shots you'd like. It's great work and the first-rate standard we're looking to achieve for the digital edition." She leaned back in her seat and smiled at Kit.

"Right, yeah. Okay." The unexpected praise reduced Kit to an inarticulate mutter, for which she mentally berated herself. "Um, ah. Actually, I'm kinda into photography myself. Would it be okay if I took my own images?"

"I think that would be okay." Frances nodded. "Do you have any more material like that?" she asked. "It doesn't have to all be on the environment. I'd be interested to see anything you have."

Pulling herself together, Kit shook her head. "Not right now, but I have some ideas. Give me a couple of weeks and I'll put a few more pieces together."

"Great!" Frances got to her feet and extended her hand. "I look forward to it."

"Yeah, right, okay." Kit shook Frances's hand and got out of her office as fast as she could. God, the woman must think her a complete idiot, unable to string together an intelligible sentence!

"She's making it really hard to dislike her," she complained to squash buddy and friend Hilary, as she whacked a ball with pleasing ferocity against the court wall that night. "And she's been making some surprisingly good changes around the office. She's introduced this idea of an editorial board, giving the team managers a bigger role in decision-making. Clarrie started off moaning about how many more of her friends and colleagues she was going to impose on us all. Soon as he joined the inner circle, he hasn't stopped extolling her virtues as the most collaborative editor he's ever worked with!"

"Who'd have thought," Hilary replied, swatting the ball back at Kit. "A new editor charged with making changes turns out to be good at her job!"

"Yeah, yeah." Kit grunted as she lunged at and missed the ball. She went over and retrieved it from the corner of the court. "So, I may have been wrong with my first impressions of her."

32   Lesley Dimmock

Hilary stood and gaped at her. "I'm sorry. I think my hearing's going. Did the great Tresize just admit to being wrong?"

"Very funny." Kit scowled. "You going to keep making fun of me or play another round?"

CHAPTER SEVEN

Fridays at the *Clarion* office were always a little more light-hearted than the rest of the week. The day's paper was already out, and it was up to the weekend shift to produce Monday's edition, so people were relaxed, slouching over the partitions between their desks and chatting about their weekend plans. Today, the mood was even more laid-back as the Australia Day long weekend loomed.

Not for Kit, though. She was one of the unlucky few whose scheduled weekend shift fell on this particular weekend. Not that she was bothered by it. It meant she got to avoid all those crowds of boozed-up, flag-wearing idiots thronging the beaches and streets as they celebrated not just the national holiday, but also the virtual end of summer. For the next three days, there would be a frenzy of partying as tourists wrung the last few drops of fun out of their summer holiday. By Tuesday, though, all the holidaymakers would be gone, returning to their jobs and a new school year. With a population close to thirty thousand people, Cannington could hardly be described as a sleepy country town, but beginning next week life would definitely become quieter. The cafés, bars, and restaurants would bear the brunt of the reduction in trade, relying on weekend visitors to get them through the long weeks until the Easter break.

Kit worked through the afternoon, waving distractedly to her colleagues as the office slowly emptied and quietened. By five o'clock the only sounds in the office were the clicking of her keyboard and the buzzing of one of the overhead lights as it flickered intermittently. As the assigned copy editor for the weekend, it was her job to proofread all of the stories submitted for Monday's edition before sending them on to the editor in chief for final approval. She was keen to get through as many as possible tonight as Sunday would bring all the weekend news, sports results, and stories from the weekend celebrations.

An hour later, she had had enough. She had four more articles to proof, but they could wait until Sunday. She shut down her computer, stood, and draped her bag across her shoulder. As she made her way through the deserted newsroom, she was surprised to see the lights still on in Frances Keating's office.

"You know even chief editors get to go home on a Friday, don't you?" she said, leaning against the doorway.

"Eh?" Frances peered up from her screen. "Oh, hello. Yes, well, I should be out celebrating the successful conclusion of my first week in the job, but someone keeps sending through proofread articles for my approval," she said, her expression deadpan.

"Well, I guess in that case it behooves me to shout you a drink then," Kit replied, surprising herself. "Just as long as you don't order anything from the top shelf. My humble reporter's salary doesn't quite stretch to shots of Johnny Walker Blue Label."

Frances looked just as surprised as she mulled over Kit's invitation.

"All right then," she said finally, pushing herself away from her desk and grabbing her satchel. "So, what's your recommended watering hole?" she asked, gesturing for Kit to lead the way out of the office.

"I don't really have a favourite," Kit replied as they stepped outside into a balmy evening. "But the Waverley is probably the closest."

"Ugh, please." Frances shuddered. "Anywhere but the Waverley. You haven't been there, have you?" she went on in response to Kit's quizzical look.

Kit shook her head. "Not for a long time. It's a bit too sports-themed for my taste, but I didn't think it had that bad a reputation."

"It's not its reputation that's the problem," Frances said. She paused for a moment, as if mentally wrestling with herself, then made a decision. "Okay, it's easier if you just see for yourself," she said, walking with determined steps along Helier Street toward the Waverley, forcing Kit to break into a jog to keep up with her.

"After you," Frances said when they reached the hotel. She held the door to the main bar open and gestured Kit inside. Taking a deep breath, she followed her in, watching Kit's reaction as she took in the surroundings.

"Mick Keating in all his glory," she said quietly, gesturing at the display that filled the wall alongside the bar. "Cannington's own footballing hero." She struggled to keep the bitterness from her voice as Kit moved forward to study the collection of framed photographs, signed jerseys, and newspaper headlines. She hadn't set foot in this room since her father's wake and had forgotten just how overwhelming it was to be surrounded by his image beaming down from the wall. A sudden tightness in her chest made it difficult to breathe. Reaching out to steady herself against a chair, she took in several deep lungsful of air.

"Actually," she said when she could speak again. "Do you think we could go somewhere else?"

Seeing the look of alarm on Kit's face as she turned to face her, she waved away her concern.

"It's just that I don't think I could enjoy a drink with his face staring down at me," she explained. Kit nodded.

"Sure," she said. "The Criterion's only another block away."

The ten-minute walk to the Criterion was conducted in silence. Frances was grateful that Kit seemed to be resisting her natural reporter's curiosity to interrogate her about what had just happened. She knew if the situation were reversed, she would have subjected the younger woman to a barrage of questions.

"Right then, take two," she said, pushing open the doors to the Criterion bar. "How about I find a table while you fetch the drinks?"

"Sure," Kit said, nodding. "What'll you have? Beer? Wine?"

"Surprise me," Frances replied. She watched Kit thread her way through the crowd toward the bar for a moment or two, then looked around for a free table, sidling across the room to where two men in business suits appeared to be leaving.

"All yours, love," one of them said, grinning boozily at her. She rolled her eyes and muttered a thank-you as she slid into the now vacant booth. Spotting Kit glancing about, she raised her arm in a wave until she caught sight of her and wove her way through the Friday night crowd.

"Here you go, a cheeky little on-tap pinot gris," Kit said, sliding into the seat opposite Frances and putting a glass streaked with condensation in front of her.

"Thanks, and cheers." Frances tilted her glass toward Kit before taking a large sip from it. "Mmm, not bad."

"Bit of a wine connoisseur, are you?" Kit asked after taking a long drink from her own glass.

"Hardly!" Frances gave a short bark of laughter. "But I do like a crisp, dry white and this is that. What about you?"

"Well, I know a riesling from a chardonnay, but if you lined up a chardy, pinot gris and sav blanc and asked me to pick which is which, I couldn't do it," Kit replied. She paused for several moments, as if weighing up her words. "Tell me if it's none of my business, but what happened back there?"

Frances shrugged and toyed with her glass for several long minutes while she debated opening up to Kit—a complete stranger, a subordinate, and a woman who had begun their working relationship by insulting her. Admittedly, since then she had been nothing but polite and friendly. Sod it, she told herself. I could do with a friend. Nothing ventured and all that.

"It's not the reminders I struggle with," she said. "It's the bloody hero worship. I mean, on one level I can understand it. He took the Cannington Cougars to their first footy premiership in forty years. And against our archrivals, Warrnambool, too. Then did it again the following year *and* the year after that. I'm surprised they didn't bloody canonise him. But he was no hero in our family. Made our lives a misery, in fact. Especially after the knee injury that ended his football career. To the outside world, he was this big man, everyone's mate, best bloke in the world, etc., etc. But at home, he was just an angry bastard who was too fond of using his fists when he'd had too much to drink."

"What, he hit you?" Kit interrupted, aghast.

"No, he never went that far." Frances shook her head. "He'd punch the walls, smash stuff. Mum and us kids were terrified of him. We lived in fear of setting him off. And anything could set him off. Samantha and Patricia giggling too loudly. Pork chops for dinner instead of a steak. Stupid stuff, really. He got even worse after Mum got sick. Like that was just one more thing cursing his life. She'd be in hospital getting treatment and he'd be at home getting stuck into the whisky and feeling sorry for himself. Course, the whole town had nothing but sympathy for him. Poor Mick Keating losing his footy career and now with a sick wife and three girls to look after."

She stopped talking and took a deep drink from her glass, avoiding the look of pity she knew she'd see on Kit's face.

"Bloody hell! I had no idea," Kit said. "He is always spoken of in such glowing terms down at the *Clarion*."

"I know," Frances said, nodding. "That's partly what made it all so hard to bear. He was like Cannington royalty as far as the town was concerned. Their golden boy. My sisters were already at uni by the time Mum died, so then it was just Dad and me," Frances went on. "He wasn't quite so violent those days, but the damage was already done. I hated him. Hated him for his self-pity, his complete self-absorption during Mum's illness. Even when she died, he still managed to make it all about himself.

I suppose we lived in a kind of cold war, him and me. Then he died, just a few weeks after I began university. I came back for the funeral and that was the last time I saw Cannington."

"And now you're back," Kit said.

"And now I'm back," Frances agreed.

"Does it feel weird? Being back and following in his footsteps?"

"Yeah, it does. The being back bit anyway. I know everyone thinks I've chosen to follow in his footsteps, but I don't feel that way. It's been twenty years since he died. How many chief editors has the *Clarion* had in that time? Still, I can't deny the legacy the Keating name carries, but I'm determined to put my own stamp on the paper." Frances gulped down the last of her wine and reached for Kit's now empty glass. "Same again?"

"Yeah, sure, but how about I get them?" Kit collected both glasses and stood.

"Okay, but I'm buying this round," Frances said, giving Kit a twenty-dollar note.

"So, the house wine, is it?" Kit said. Frances gave her a chagrined look as she scrabbled in her wallet for more cash. "No, it's all right, I'm just giving you a hard time." Kit laughed. "The twenty will cover it fine," she said.

Frances watched Kit make her way to the bar, a wry smile on her face. She may have been the target of Kit's humour just now, but she appreciated the woman's quick wit. She was also thankful for Kit's quiet acceptance of her story. She had felt a weight lift off her shoulders when she realized she wouldn't have to defend her portrayal of her father. It probably helped that Kit was a relative newcomer to Cannington and therefore not so invested in protecting the image of the town hero.

"Penny for your thoughts," Kit said, returning to the booth with two fresh drinks and sliding back into her seat.

"Pfft, they're not even worth that much." Frances made a dismissive motion with her hand. "I just wanted to thank you for listening to a stranger's sob story."

"Pfft yourself," Kit replied. "I'm sorry you had such a tough childhood, but it's bit of a relief. I always struggled to believe that Mick Keating was as wonderful as everyone makes him out. I mean, seriously, no one is that fabulous, are they? Now I've heard your story, I feel better about resisting the Kool-Aid."

Frances burst out laughing. "Kool-Aid! I like that. And it's just how it feels in this town sometimes. It's good to have an ally."

"Allies, huh?" Kit cocked her head. "Yeah, okay. Cheers to that." She raised her glass in a brief salute and drank.

CHAPTER EIGHT

"Two-one to the hotshot journo." Frances laughed into her mobile phone when Abby rang later that evening. She had just fixed herself a light snack of Camembert cheese on water crackers—all that she had in the little bar fridge—and poured herself a glass of wine when her phone had rung and Abby had greeted her with a breezy, "How's it hanging?"

"Asked me out for a drink, didn't she," Frances went on, stretching out on the bed and popping a cheese-laden cracker into her mouth. "I was so surprised, I just blurted out a yes!" She spoke around the mouthful of food. "I think she was a bit shocked that, one, she asked and, two, I agreed!"

"Ha!" Abby barked. "So perhaps two-all, then?"

"Mmm, maybe," Frances replied, taking a long sip from her glass of wine.

"So, how was it?" Abby pressed.

Frances took a few moments to answer, replaying the evening in her head.

"Actually, it was really nice," she said eventually.

"Nice," Abby repeated. "That's it? It was 'nice'?"

"Okay." Frances laughed. "I had a lovely time. There, is that better?"

"Marginally," Abby said. "Come on, Frankie! I'm dying here. Tell me more! What's this hotshot reporter really like? Obviously, she's not as obnoxious as she first appeared, else she wouldn't have asked you out. So come on, spill!"

"All right, all right," Frances said. "But first, I need to go fill up my wineglass. Be right back." She tossed her phone onto the bed and made her way across the room to replenish her drink.

"Okay, I'm back," she said, shuffling herself into a comfortable position against the pillows and picking up the phone. "So, we ended up deciding to have drinks downstairs, in the Mick Keating tribute bar."

"Oh, awkward," Abby said. "You couldn't suggest somewhere else?"

"I was going to, but then thought I may as well get it over and done with. But then, seeing all those photographs, jerseys, and newspaper articles all over the walls really shook me and for a few minutes, I could barely breathe. Had to get out of there. Luckily, Kit agreed, no questions asked. Must have seen something in my face. We went to the Criterion, where I told her my version of the great Mick Keating. Turns out Kit isn't a member of his fan club either. Referred to it as 'drinking the Kool-Aid.'"

"Drinking the Kool-Aid!" Abby spluttered. "Oh, that's good."

"Yeah, I thought so too," Frances said. "She's actually pretty funny. And smart."

"Cute too?" Abby cut in.

"I haven't really thought about it," Frances said, thankful this wasn't a video call as she felt her face growing hot. Because actually it had occurred to her over the course of the evening that Kit Tresize was exceedingly cute.

"Uh huh, so what does she look like, this woman who may or may not be cute?" Abby's voice took on that tone she always used whenever she thought Frances was hiding an attraction to someone. It was kind of annoying the way she switched into interrogator mode and tried to make Frances 'fess up. Well, not this time. Mainly, because there was nothing to confess.

"Oh, I don't know," Frances harrumphed. "She's in her thirties, I'd guess. A bit shorter than me, so about five feet, six inches. You know that singer, the one with the big hit that you loved so much. Oh god, what was it called…'Royals'! That's it!"

"You mean Lorde? Your reporter looks like Lorde? Sheez, Frankie, that's a whole other level up from 'cute.' That's hot!"

"Okay, so she's not 'my' reporter," Frances said. "And no, I didn't mean she looks like Lorde. Just that she has the same wavy dark hair and blue eyes."

"That's still pretty hot," Abby said. "So, did you invite her up to your room for a nightcap?"

"Would I be talking to you right now if I'd done that?" Frances shook her head in exasperation.

"Ha! No, I guess not," Abby giggled. "But you set up a second date, yeah?"

"Okay, so first off, this wasn't a date. It was just a couple of drinks. But yes, we will be seeing each other again." She winced and held her phone away from her ear as Abby whooped and hollered on the other end. She waited until she had quietened down before speaking again.

"Yeah, we're both rostered onto the weekend edition shift, so we'll see each other in the office on Sunday," she said, biting the inside of her cheek to stop herself from laughing.

"That is so not what I meant!" Abby remonstrated, her voice squeaking in indignation.

"Maybe not, but asking an employee out on a date a week into the job is just a step too far, don't you think?"

"Yeah, maybe. But you are going to ask her out, aren't you?"

"I'm hanging up now, Abby. It's been great chatting. Love you. Bye!" She grinned as she pulled the phone away from her ear, cutting short Abby's repeated urgings that she ask Kit Tresize out on a date.

As if that were ever going to happen.

CHAPTER NINE

Kit had to concede she'd had a good time Friday night. Frances was good company. Witty and engaging, with a warm, easy, and generous laugh. And she had laughed a lot as their conversation roamed across a diverse range of topics, including a discussion on the best souvlaki in town.

"Theo's, hands down," Frances had declared in a tone that brooked no argument.

"Isn't his the only souvlaki in town?" Kit had asked.

"There you go, then. No contest!" Frances had laughed. She gulped down the last of her wine and got to her feet.

"Fun as this has been, it's time for me to call it a night," she said, gathering up her belongings.

"Oh, right." Kit had scrambled to do likewise, surprised at how disappointed she was that Frances was leaving. "Do you have far to go? Perhaps we could share an Uber," she said, following Frances out of the bar and onto the street.

"No," Frances had said, her eyes shining with amusement. "I'm just down the road. At the Waverley." She'd rolled her eyes.

"What?" Kit looked at her, aghast. "They put you up there? Well, I guess it would never occur to them that you'd be anything less than thrilled to stay there."

"No, I suppose not," Frances had said. "It's comfortable enough, but I'm pretty keen to find a place of my own. Anyway, see you on Sunday." She stuck out her hand.

"Sure thing," Kit had replied, feeling ever so slightly dismissed. She'd given Frances's hand a perfunctory shake, watched her disappear into the Friday night crowd, then pulled out her phone to summon an Uber ride. With a few glasses of wine under her belt, she didn't want to risk being pulled over for an alcohol test.

Having left her Vespa in town on Friday night, Kit had to resort to another Uber ride on Sunday to get into work. She exchanged a guarded smile with Frances when they met at the coffee machine, but apart from a mumbled "Hello," neither woman spoke as they waited their turns. The racket from the bean grinder made conversation all but impossible anyway, but there were far too many flapping ears in the room, especially those belonging to Samira, the paper's accounts manager. If she got word that Kit and Frances had met outside work, it would be all over the office in a nanosecond. That wasn't something Kit wanted spread around the workplace.

"Have a good one," she murmured, her customary long black firmly in hand as she sidled past Frances, taking care not to jostle her in the confined space.

"You too," Frances replied distractedly, already focussed on the mechanics of getting the coffee machine to produce her macchiato.

Her favourite mug in hand, the one that depicted "Writer Snoopy" at his keyboard, Kit wandered back to her desk and was soon absorbed by her work. She liked these weekend shifts as there were fewer people in the office, so less of a distracting buzz about the place and fewer interruptions from colleagues stopping by for a chat. She spent the morning working her way through the pile of sports reports that Simon had sent through, tweaking a phrase here and there for readability. He was young, just out of university, and this was his first job as a reporter. He had only been here for five months and was still in his probationary period. Keen to prove himself, he often got a bit carried away. He was prone to adopting a breathless, TV-commentator style when recounting key moments in a game. She remembered being just as keen to impress at his age too. She pared his sentences down to the basic facts, then sent the articles along to the design team, so that they could set the sports pages.

She was about to tackle the collection of articles reporting on the various Australia Day celebrations held around the region when a chorus of ragged cheers broke out at the front of the office. Peering around her partition, she saw a young guy hidden by a teetering stack of pizzas make his way into the room, followed by a beaming Frances.

"In celebration of my first weekend shift, lunch is on me," she exclaimed. No one needed to be asked twice as everyone descended on the aromatic boxes. As big a fan of pizza as the next person, Kit wasted no time in joining the melee, quickly snaffling herself a slice each of feta and beetroot, mushroom, and four-cheeses pizzas. Stepping back from the crush, she found herself standing next to Frances.

"Nice one," she said, and then gesturing to Frances's empty hands. "Not having any?"

"Oh, I'll wait until the scrum dies down," Frances replied. "I might have over-catered," she went on, nodding toward the table where at least three of the twenty pizzas sat untouched.

"Oh well, that's your dinners sorted for the foreseeable future then," Kit replied. "Although I'd be happy to take some of it off your hands. Especially if there's any of that beetroot-y one left."

"Help yourself." Frances grinned. "Partial as I am to leftover pizza, I don't think even I could get through that lot."

Having eaten their fill, people began drifting back to their desks, snagging final slices of pizza as they left. Kit grinned at the bemused expression on Frances's face as she surveyed the carnage.

"They're like a bunch of gannets where a free feed is concerned," she said. "Here, I'll help you clean up." She picked out half a dozen different slices of pizza for herself, very happy to see there was lots of the feta and beetroot one left over, and wrapped them in several layers of paper towels.

"You don't want any of these?" Frances asked, gesturing to the meat-laden pizzas that remained.

"Nuh uh," she said, shaking her head. "I'm vegetarian. This lot will do me."

She helped Frances consolidate the remaining slices into three boxes and took them to the staff kitchen for people to help themselves to later. Stacking the boxes of untouched pizzas, she handed them to Frances.

"There you go, that lot's yours," she said. "They'll just end up getting chucked out," she went on, forestalling Frances's protest. "At least, you can freeze them for another day."

"If I had a freezer, yeah," Frances replied. "Conversely, you could help me eat at least one of them." She peered into the top box. "That's if you're partial to a veggie supremo. Seems like it's not quite to everyone's taste."

"Oh yeah, I forgot about your living arrangements," Kit said. "Speaking of which, I may be able to help there."

"Really?" Frances's face lit up with surprise. "Well then, you definitely have to come over tonight. You can tell me all about it while we eat our way through these!"

"Oh, um, er," Kit mumbled, taken aback by the offer.

"Sorry, sorry," Frances said, mistaking Kit's hesitation. "You've probably already got plans. Forget it."

"Actually, I don't." Kit shook her head. "So, er, yeah I can come over."

"Great. That's great," Frances said. The two women stood awkwardly staring at each other, Frances with her arms filled with the stack of pizza boxes and Kit with her paper-wrapped pile of slices.

"Right then," Kit said eventually. "So, until tonight then. Around six?"

"Uh huh."

CHAPTER TEN

"Uh huh?" Frances marvelled at how inarticulate she must have sounded as she watched Kit make a rapid escape from the room. Had she just asked Kit out on a date? Would Kit think she had? Does inviting someone around to your room constitute a date? Abby was going to have a field day with this once she found out about it.

Of course, I could always not tell Abby, Frances mused, then gave a derisory bark of laughter. As if she could get away with not telling Abby anything. That woman had an uncanny knack of worming out her every secret.

Frances carried her pile of pizza boxes back to her office and dumped them on the desk. She tried settling in to working through the afternoon but couldn't focus. By four o'clock, she gave the whole thing up as a bad joke. She'd just come in early in the morning and whiz through any approvals for stories that came through between now and then. She sent an email out letting the rest of the staff know she was leaving, then logged off her computer. Stuffing her tablet and phone into her satchel, she hoisted it onto her shoulder, grabbed the pizza boxes, and managed to get out of the office without dropping any of them.

Once in her room, she rushed around in a frenzy of nerves tidying away her clothes, straightening up the bathroom towels, kicking her dirty laundry into a corner of the wardrobe, and washing and drying the two wineglasses she'd blagged from downstairs the other night.

"Wine!" she blurted and dashed down the stairs and out to the bottle shop. She spent fifteen minutes in an agony of indecision over which pinot gris label to buy, finally settling on a bottle from the Coombs winery in the Yarra Valley. At thirty dollars, it was a little pricey, but she was counting on Kit's lack of wine knowledge stopping her from thinking she was trying to impress her. Racing back up the stairs, she shoved it into the little fridge. Great. Now as well as feeling anxious, she was dishevelled and sweaty. Could she get away with a quick shower?

She had just redressed in a clean T-shirt and a pair of linen-blend shorts when there was a knock at the door. She gave herself a quick examination in the mirror, took a deep breath, and pulled the door wide open.

"Hey, come on in," she said with a cool calmness that belied her jangling nerves.

CHAPTER ELEVEN

Kit hovered on the landing outside Frances's door, clutching a bottle of chardonnay. She had grabbed the first bottle she had seen in the bottle shop's fridge. It had only cost fifteen dollars, so she hoped it didn't turn out to be too nasty tasting. Taking deep breaths to calm the nerves playing havoc with her stomach, she told herself, "It's just pizza with the boss. Nothing weird about it at all." Shoving her misgivings into a tiny corner of her mind, she rapped on the door before she changed her mind.

"Not too early, am I?" she asked as the door was flung open. "I brought wine." She flourished the bottle at Frances.

"Oh, what? No," Frances said, looking as nervous as Kit felt. "Come in," she said. Kit handed Frances the wine and sidled past her into the room.

"Right, uh, so just take a seat," Frances said, "and I'll open this."

Kit's eyes skittered around the room, as she tried to ignore the enormous bed that dominated it. She had been wrong. Stepping into what was the very intimate space of her boss was

50   Lesley Dimmock

as weird as it got. Thankfully, the bed wasn't the only furniture in the room. She crossed quickly to a little dining table and sat.

"So, I see we spared no expense putting you up then," she said, hoping a touch of humour would lighten the atmosphere.

"Well, it's not exactly the Ritz," Frances said, handing Kit a generously poured glass of wine and sitting down opposite her. "But it'll do. At least in the short term. And it's close to work, so there's that."

"Hmm, well, if it's proximity to the *Clarion* you're after, the place I'm thinking of might not be for you," Kit said, swallowing a mouthful of chardonnay, relieved that it had a light, fruity flavour. "It's a bit out of town."

"Define 'a bit,'" Frances replied.

Kit leaned down to retrieve her bag, which she had dumped on the floor beside her chair when she sat down. She pulled out her tablet and tapped at it for a few moments before sliding it across to Frances.

"It's probably about a fifteen-minute drive," she said as Frances picked up the tablet and peered at images of a small, whitewashed stone cottage. "It belongs to a friend of mine, who's looking to rent it out as she's got a job in London for the next two years. She's leaving in a fortnight, so she needs to get it rented pretty soon."

"It's very cute," Frances said. "I think I know it. The old Peterson place out on the Halsham Road. Just down the road from the Buttery."

"Yeah, that's the place." Kit nodded. "Leonie's been in there for going on ten years now, but everyone still calls it the Peterson place. Drives her nuts. Anyway, the rent's two-fifty a week, and it can come empty or furnished. Up to you."

"It looks ideal," Frances said, handing the tablet back to Kit. "But I'd have to look at it before making any decisions. Is that possible?"

"Sure," Kit said, reaching for her phone and tapping in Leonie's number. "Yeah, hi, Lee, it's me. Yeah, good, good. You?" She paused for a few moments, as the woman at the other end spoke, her lips curling into a smile as she listened.

"Yeah, look," she said, locking eyes with Frances as she spoke. "I've got someone—my boss, actually—who might be interested in your place. Tomorrow?" She raised an eyebrow at Frances, who nodded. "After work? Say five thirty?" Frances nodded again. "Yep, works for us." She fell silent, then snorted. "All right for some," she said, laughing, then hanging up. "Sorted," she said, smiling at Frances. "Says she might be a little late. Depends on how good the surf is."

"Great," Frances said, getting to her feet. "Well, you've kept up your side of the bargain. Now it's my turn. Pizza," she said in response to Kit's puzzled expression.

"No, really that's not necessary," Kit said.

"Nonsense," Frances replied in a tone that brooked no argument as she plonked the three boxes of leftover pizza on the table. "Besides, we had a deal. So, dig in!"

"Okay, okay!" Kit put her hands up in surrender. "Just a couple of slices, then."

They ate in a companionable silence for several minutes, the only sounds the clinking of their glasses as they replaced them on the table after each sip and appreciative murmurings for the food.

"So, what's the Kit Tresize story then?" Frances asked.

Kit shrugged and drained her glass. "There's not really anything to tell," she said.

"Oh, come on…You know all the sordid details of my past. It's only fair I get to learn something about you."

Kit shrugged again. "Okay, but I'm warning you. There really isn't much. Unlike you, I'm a city girl. Born and bred in Brunswick. Got a degree in journalism at Monash University, then went from job to job until I ended up here. That's it. That's me in a nutshell."

"Huh," Frances said. "So why here? It's a bit of a backwater career-wise."

"Says the woman who just took up a job here," Kit retorted, reaching for another slice of pizza.

"Yeah, but becoming chief editor is a step up for me," Frances replied. "You're in the prime years. You should be looking for bigger gigs than the *Clarion*."

"Guess, I'm just not that much of a go-getter," Kit said. "To be honest, after about five years in the bright lights and glitz of a city paper, I'd had enough. The job had become my whole life. There was never any time left over for me. Here, I have time to pursue other passions, like photography. And I like the work, the connection to the community that working in a smaller paper gives me."

"Fair enough," Frances replied.

"Right then, that's my lot," Kit said after devouring the last slice of supreme vego pizza. So much for "just a couple of slices." She really was hopeless when it came to pizza. She leant down to grab her bag, then got to her feet.

"You won't stay for just one more drink?" Frances asked, scrambling to her feet. Kit shook her head.

"I can't," she said, making her way to the door. "I'm on the Vespa."

"A cup of tea then? Or coffee?"

Kit shook her head again, smiling gently. "Sorry. It's been a long day already and I've got an early start again in the morning."

"Of course, of course," Frances said, her tone all brisk and light. "Well, thanks for coming over and showing me that house."

"No worries," Kit said, standing aside as Frances reached for the door handle.

Instead of opening it, though, as Kit expected, Frances leaned in and kissed her.

CHAPTER TWELVE

"On the lips!"

Frances's first response after a shocked Kit had fled the room was to ring Abby and tell her about her faux pas. A howl of laughter greeted her horrified words.

"You should have seen her face. I tried to get her to wait, but she couldn't get out of here fast enough. Oh my god," Frances whimpered. "How do I face her tomorrow?"

"Ha ha ha!" Abby couldn't stop laughing.

"It's not funny," Frances wailed. "She could do me for sexual harassment or something."

"Oh my god, Frankie, you're killing me," Abby gasped. "How long have you been in the job? A week? Ha ha! I can see the headlines now. 'Chief Editor Booted After A Week For Hitting On The Staff'! Tell me, though," she said, suddenly serious. "What was it like, the kiss? Worth losing your job for?" She burst into more hysterical laughter.

"If all you're going to do is laugh, I'm hanging up," Frances said in a huff.

Phoning Abby was turning out to be an even worse idea than kissing Kit Tresize had been. Why she thought Abby would offer some consolation and sympathy was a mystery. Not that she would admit it to Abby, not in a million years, but the kiss had been very enjoyable actually, and she had found Kit's lips soft and eminently kissable. So much so that she rather fancied repeating the experience.

"Sorry, you're right." Abby's contrite words broke into her reverie. "But I could see this happening from a mile off."

"What, that I'd accidently kiss one of my reporters?" Frances retorted with just an edge of sarcasm.

"Well, maybe not so clumsily, but you're always talking about her. It was just a matter of time before you acted on the attraction."

"Attracted to Kit? I'm not attracted to Kit!" she replied indignantly.

"Right, that's why she's always the first thing you bring up whenever we speak," Abby said. "The first thing you told me about your new job was the clash you had with her. And then you couldn't wait to tell me all about Friday night's date. I've hardly heard a word about how the job is actually going."

Frances opened her mouth to argue, then closed it again. Abby was right. She did talk about Kit a lot. But that was because she was annoying. Smart and cute, yes, but also annoying.

"Yeah, but that doesn't mean I'm attracted to her," she said.

"So why did you kiss her then?" Abby countered.

"I don't know!" she wailed. "Oh god, what am I going to do?"

"Well, I suppose you could pretend it never happened," Abby suggested.

"Yeah, that's never going to work," Frances said morosely.

"Or you could just apologise and promise to never do it again," Abby said, giggling.

"Thanks, Abby, you've been a big help," Frances said, stabbing the End Call button and flinging the phone onto the bed before scooping it up again. She should text Kit, apologise.

"Bloody hell, what do I even say?" she muttered to herself, tossing the phone aside again and pulling a pillow over her head. "How the hell did I get myself into such a predicament?" She moaned. "If only I could wake up in the morning and find this has all been a horrible dream."

CHAPTER THIRTEEN

"Kit, wait!"

Ignoring Frances's plea, Kit fled down the stairs and out to where her Vespa was parked by the kerb. Her mind was reeling. Frances Keating had just kissed her! Her *boss* had just kissed her! Even more unsettling, though, had been the flicker of desire she had felt when Frances's warm lips had pressed against her own.

She fumbled her keys and dropped them as the thought of the kiss caused another jolt of desire.

"Christ, Tresize, get a grip!" she admonished herself, finally retrieving the keys and getting the scooter started. Jamming her helmet onto her head, she glanced briefly up at the rectangle of light that shone from Frances's room, shook her head, and then pulled out into the traffic.

She arrived at her cottage with no memory of the journey, her brain going round and round as she tried to make sense of what had just happened.

"She bloody kissed me!" she said to a startled Marvin, who, until Kit came in and tossed her helmet onto the settee, had been blissfully curled up in a ball and sleeping there.

"No friendly peck on the cheek, either," she went on. "Nope, it was right on the lips!" She plumped down next to the cat and pulled him onto her lap. "Shocking, right?"

Marvin's only response was to blink his yellow eyes at her and yawn.

"And, as if being hit on by the boss isn't bad enough…" Kit went on, undaunted by her cat's lack of outrage. "Turns out, I wouldn't mind if it happened again. What do you make of that, then?" Marvin twitched an ear, stretched out a paw, and started purring.

What do *I* make of that? Kit silently asked herself as she sat slowly stroking Marvin's back. "You're right," she said to the sleeping cat. "Nothing. An attraction to Frances Keating? Not one of my greatest ideas, hey?" She sat lost in thought, idly caressing the cat, long into the night.

CHAPTER FOURTEEN

Kit finally roused herself around two in the morning. Marvin had abandoned her lap for his corner of the settee long ago. She took herself off to bed and managed a few hours of fitful sleep before the alarm went off. It took three espressos, drunk in rapid succession, before she felt in any condition to face work.

As she pushed her way through the front doors of the *Clarion*'s office, she was greeted by a cacophony of power tools. She'd forgotten that the renovations to the reception area and the remodelling down in the design area had been scheduled for today, to take advantage of fewer people being around because of the public holiday. Luckily, the noise was also not conducive to prolonged conversations; she would be able to tackle the jobs that were piled up in the system, awaiting her attention, with few interruptions.

Seeing the lights on in Frances's office, she gave it a wide berth, taking a roundabout route through the office to her own desk. She slid into her chair and booted up her computer. As she did so, her phone buzzed with an incoming text. She froze. Shit! Had Frances spotted her coming in? She'd half expected a text or something from her last night and had been relieved that none had come. She hadn't been ready to address what had happened. Not then. She wasn't sure she was ready now. Holding her breath, she thumbed the screen awake, her shoulders slumping in relief when she saw it was just a reminder that her library books were due in three days.

Although conscious of Frances sitting only a few dozen metres away, she managed, with the help of an ambient sounds app playing bird songs through her earbuds, to focus on her work. Mostly. As the morning went on, thoughts of Frances kissing her gave way to the job in hand. Clicking Send on the fifth article, she stretched her back and shoulders, then froze as she caught sight of the editor heading in her direction.

"Shit!" she swore under her breath. "Now what do I do?" She was tempted to make a run for it. Pretend she hadn't seen Frances and just get out of there as fast as she could.

"Uh, Kit..."

Too late. Kit glanced nervously around the office, checking there was no one in hearing distance. She really didn't want this conversation and she sure as heck didn't want anyone listening in.

"Frances," she said, plucking a bud from her ear and scooting her chair to the far side of her cubicle as Frances paused at the edge of her desk.

"Look, I'm really, really sorry about last night," Frances said in a low voice.

"It's okay," Kit replied, keeping her eyes fixed on her computer screen. "There's nothing to apologise for."

"I swear it will never happen again," Frances went on.

"Like I said," Kit replied with a tight smile, fervently wishing this whole conversation would just stop. "It's nothing, really." She gave Frances a tight smile.

"Okay. Thank you. And once again, I am really, really sorry." Kit's shoulders sagged in relief as Frances began to walk away, only to stiffen again when she stopped and turned back.

"Are we still on for this afternoon?"

Hell, no, Kit said to herself. She could think of a thousand reasons to cancel, but instead she nodded. "Unless you've found somewhere else to live already," she said.

"Cool," Frances replied. "See you out front about five then?"

Kit nodded, stuck her earbud back in and watched Frances's retreat before turning her attention back to her screen. After reading the same sentence five times, she realised she was never going to get any work done. Not now. Not after that conversation. All she could think about was Frances promising never to kiss her again—and how disappointed she felt about that prospect.

CHAPTER FIFTEEN

Back in her office, Frances sighed in relief. That hadn't gone as badly as she had feared. At least she had cleared the air and could now get on with doing some work. That was the theory, anyway. In reality, that brief encounter had only served to strengthen her desire to kiss Kit again. By the time five o'clock came around, all she had been able to achieve was a heightened state of agitation. A state that only worsened when she walked outside and saw Kit standing beside her Vespa. She eyed the scooter's seat with alarm. There really was not much room for two people on that thing. She would have to sit far too close to Kit for comfort.

"Hop on," Kit said, tossing Frances a helmet and straddling the seat.

"Oh, uh, um, wouldn't my car be better?" Frances said, hugging the helmet to her stomach.

"Is it here?" Kit asked, peering through the visor of her own helmet at her.

"Uh, no." Frances shook her head. "It's at the Waverley."

"Well, then, I guess we go with this. Come on." She patted the seat behind her. "It's perfectly safe," she went on, responding to Frances's hesitation.

There was nothing for it, but to climb onto the scooter. Frances pulled the helmet onto her head, fastened its strap, swung her leg over the seat, and slid in behind Kit. She felt along the back of the seat, her heart sinking when she realised there was nothing there to cling to. She would have to put her arms around Kit's waist. She gingerly stretched her arms around Kit, trying her best to not make contact with her body.

"Hold tight," Kit said, grabbing Frances's left arm and pulling her close. Ignoring the frisson of desire that the contact elicited, she clutched at Kit's shirt as she started the scooter and took off up Marchant Street toward the highway.

The journey couldn't end fast enough for Frances. For the whole ten minutes—which felt like an eternity—all she could think about was the way her breasts were pressed against Kit's back and how their legs slid against each other. When they finally stopped, Frances couldn't scramble off the scooter quickly enough, almost losing her balance in her haste. Luckily, Kit was too occupied with taking her helmet off to notice. Composing herself, Frances fluffed up her helmet-flattened hair, handed the helmet back to Kit, and followed her down the short crazy-paving path to the front door.

"Leonie should be here soon," Kit said, glancing at her watch. They stood in silence, studiously keeping their distance from one another for several excruciating minutes before Frances couldn't stand it any longer and cracked.

"Listen," she said. "What I said this morning. About not kissing you again—"

"I wish you would," Kit interrupted.

"What?" Frances wasn't sure she had heard right.

"Kiss me," Kit said.

Frances didn't need to be asked again. She pulled Kit close, her head swimming as Kit responded to her kiss. Their lips mashed together, then opened as their tongues sought each other. Kit's tasted faintly of coffee and aniseed, Frances noted before losing herself in the kiss.

"Not interrupting anything, am I?"

CHAPTER SIXTEEN

They tore apart from each other, gasping and blinking at the woman who stood grinning at them from the gate. They'd been so engrossed they hadn't even heard the car pull up.

"Could have saved myself a trip to the beach," the blonde said, coming down the path and propping the surfboard she carried under one arm against the veranda post. "Seeing as how all the action's going on here."

Kit and Frances flashed sheepish smiles at each other before Kit collected herself and made the introductions.

"Leonie, Frances. Frances, Leonie."

Dressed in a faded blue T-shirt and palm tree-patterned board shorts, Leonie was the archetypal surfer, complete with long, damp, sun-bleached hair, bright blue eyes, and deeply tanned skin.

"Figured as much," Leonie said, grinning broadly as she shook Frances's hand. "Although," she said, turning to Kit, "I didn't realise this is what was meant when people talk about a close working relationship!" She laughed uproariously at her own joke.

"Oh ha ha," Kit said, flushing furiously. "Can we just see the house, please?"

"Sorry," she mouthed to Frances as they followed Leonie inside.

"It's fine," Frances replied, giving Kit's hand a small squeeze. "It really was rather funny, don't you think?"

Kit rolled her eyes. "Don't encourage her!" she hissed. "I'll never hear the end of it as it is. Thank goodness it's not long before she heads off to the UK."

"All right then, you two lovebirds," Leonie said, flinging open the door on the left of the hallway. "The living room. Excuse the mess. It's all half packed up." They crowded into the room behind her. Packing boxes sat scattered around the room but didn't obscure the whitewashed walls, gleaming floorboards, and blackened cast-iron fire grate that shone in the sunlight streaming from two windows that were set into the foot-deep walls.

"What a lovely room," Frances said.

"Bedroom," Leonie said, opening the door on the other side of the hall to a room that was the mirror image of the living room. Frances nodded again.

"Just imagine how cosy you'll both be snuggled up in here with the fire going," Leonie said. "What?" she went on as Kit glared at her. "I'm only saying what you're both thinking anyway." She smirked at their reddening faces before leading them down the hallway to the kitchen, waving toward the two other doors leading off it as she went. "Bathroom. Second bedroom. And finally, the kitchen."

The kitchen was galley-style, running the full width of the house. A classic ceramic farmhouse sink sat under a large window that looked out into the back garden. The stove sat at one end of the room, while the other end was filled with a small dining table that could sit four people.

"I love that pantry," Frances said. "Never had one of those before. The whole place is great. I'll take it. That is, if you'll have me as a tenant."

"Whoa, you haven't checked out the bathroom yet," Leonie said. "That could be a deal breaker!"

"I don't think so," Frances said, following her to the room. "It's gorgeous!" "It" was a claw-footed bath that filled one end of the room. A vintage-style pedestal basin and toilet complemented the bath. "I can just see myself taking long, luxurious baths in here!"

Images of a naked Frances relaxing in a bubble-filled bath leapt into Kit's mind. Her face grew hot at the thought of being in that tub with Frances. Thankfully, both Leonie and Frances were too engrossed in studying the bathroom's features to notice how flustered she had become.

"I'm glad you like it." Leonie grinned, peering over Frances's shoulder into the room. "I did it all myself. You should have seen what was in here before. It was a nightmare!"

"I love the place," Frances said. "Where do I sign?"

"Excellent." Leonie clapped her on the shoulder.

Kit took the opportunity to escape out onto the veranda to compose herself while the two women spent a few minutes discussing the details.

"Okay," Kit said, once Leonie and Frances had shaken hands on the deal and joined her outside. "We'll let you get on with your evening. Let me know when you're up for some farewell drinks, yeah?"

Leonie nodded and waved as Kit led Frances back along the garden path and out to the Vespa.

"Hop on," Kit said, passing Frances a helmet. She grinned to herself as Frances climbed aboard and snuggled against her back, then steered the scooter onto the road and headed back into town. This was not quite how she imagined the day would turn out, but it felt good, right even, having Frances there behind her.

Frances was startled when Kit drove straight past the Waverley and headed toward the eastern outskirts of town, but she realised quickly where Kit was taking them as she wound their way up through the residential streets that flanked Cannington's highest vantage point.

"Beacon Hill!" she said, once Kit had cut the engine. "God, I haven't been up here in years!" She clambered off the scooter and removed her helmet as she wandered over to the safety barrier to take in the view. Cannington lay sprawled out around Trelawney Bay, whose waters at this time of evening had turned to a glittering pewter.

"We need to talk," Kit said, joining her.

Frances turned her back to the view, perching against the railing, and looked up at Kit, whose face was creased with concern.

"Okay," she said slowly, not sure where this was going. Her heart raced at the thought that Kit was about to end things before they had even begun. That she was about to launch into the "This was all a big mistake and can we put it behind us?" speech.

"So, ah, this whole thing has come as bit of a surprise," Kit said.

"Here it comes," Frances muttered to herself. She stared at Kit, who looked away, shoved her hands deep into her pockets, and scuffed her boot at the loose gravel. She was so ill at ease, it could only mean one thing. Frances braced herself, while at the same time marshalling her counterarguments.

"And it's all been a bit quick," Kit continued. "But, if it's all the same to you, I'm keen to see where this goes." She gave Frances a searching look, a look of doubt growing on her face as Frances stared at her in open-mouthed surprise.

"Okay, right. Forget I said anything," Kit said into the growing silence. Her words snapped Frances out of her stupor. She sprang to her feet and caught hold of Kit's wrist, stopping her from walking away.

"Sorry, sorry," she said. "It's just that I was so convinced you were about to call this, this…" She flailed around, searching for the word that described whatever it was that was happening between them, then gave up. "Call it off," she went on. "It took a while for what you actually said to sink in. Sorry," she said again. "So…yes, let's see where this goes."

CHAPTER SEVENTEEN

Kit dropped Frances off at the Waverley, lifting her hand in acknowledgment as Frances waved and smiled before disappearing through the front doors. They'd both agreed that they each needed some space right now to think about what had transpired. And boy, did Kit have a lot to think about. Like how she had gone from deciding to pretend that nothing had happened to willingly snogging her boss in less than twenty-four hours. And after knowing the woman for barely over a week! And how, barely an hour after saying she wanted to see where this went, she was now having second thoughts about the whole thing. The speed of it all was scaring her.

"What?" she said to Marvin, who stared up at her owlishly from his end of the settee as she came in the door. "Can't a woman change her mind?" She slumped down next to him and scooped him onto her lap, ignoring his irritated, "Mreow."

"It was all her fault. She shouldn't have kissed me in the first place. Then I could have quietly ignored that I was attracted to her. And then I wouldn't be in this mess at all."

Marvin's only response was a deep reverberating purr that vibrated against Kit's thighs.

She was no clearer in her mind about Frances when she walked through the doors of the *Clarion* the next day. She nodded in appreciation at the foyer's fresh new look. Smoky grey carpet tiles replaced the old worn-out carpet. The walls shone under a new coat of pearly-looking paint, while a pair of funky armchairs created a welcoming little space to one side. The only thing that hadn't changed was Enid. Kit waved to the older woman as she swiped her card and pushed her way through to the newsroom. The renovations over in the design corner were ongoing, with new workstations being installed amid much hammering and drilling.

Kit shoved her bag under her desk, booted up her computer, grabbed her mug, and headed straight to the kitchen. Her heart skipped when she spotted Frances in a small knot of people clustered around the coffee machine and peering at its innards.

"Problem?" she asked.

"I think it's given up the ghost," Clarrie replied, giving the machine a disgusted whack with his hand. "Piece of cheap shit. It's always doing this. We should have just forked out for a more expensive one to start with. Right, who's coming to Bean Worx with me?" he said, referring to the coffee bar attached to the nearby art gallery. He headed out, followed closely by Julie, and Susan Winters, the advertising accounts manager.

"Okay?" Frances asked Kit as the door swung closed behind the trio.

"Yep." Kit nodded. "You?"

"Yep." Frances smiled in reply. "So, do you want to catch up for a bite after work?"

"Sorry, I can't. I've got a squash game with my mate."

"No problem," Frances said. "Another time, hey?"

"Sure," Kit replied. "That would be nice."

"Nice? Is that the best one of our brightest reporters can come up with?"

70   Lesley Dimmock

"Okay, it would be great. Fantastic. Wonderful. Lovely. Is that better?" Kit said, grinning despite herself and feeling a warm glow in her gut at the "brightest reporters" comment.

"Much." Frances nodded, grinning back at her. "Now, how about we follow Clarrie's example and head to Bean Worx? My shout this time."

That was an offer too good to refuse. Kit dashed back to her desk to grab her sunglasses, then met Frances as she was coming out of her office, her satchel dangling from her shoulder. As they made their way through the newsroom, Enid bustled toward them, intercepting them before they could reach the foyer.

"Frances, there you are! There's a Nick Davies in reception for you. Shall I bring him through?"

"Oh, right. Thanks, Enid." She turned to Kit. "Sorry, looks like I'll have to renege," she said before disappearing back into her office.

Not knowing whether to feel relieved or disappointed, Kit continued on her way out of the building. God, she really needed to get her head sorted out regarding Frances. Coffee would help with that. And a *pain au raisin*.

Fifteen minutes later, she was back, juggling cup and paper bag as she swiped her way through the newsroom door and cursing to herself, yet again, at the clunky technology. If only there was a way that doors could recognise people as they approached and open automatically for them. It would certainly solve all those problems of people losing or forgetting their swipe cards that the facilities manager was always complaining about.

"Hmm, that might make a good topic for an article. The pros and cons of facial recognition," Kit mused as she sat down at her desk. She tapped out a note on her phone to research the topic later, then plucked the pastry from its bag. The spiral-shaped, raisin-filled sticky pastry was one of her favourites and she bit into it with relish, letting out a little moan of appreciation.

Apart from a short interruption when Frances brought Nick Davies around to introduce him to the news team, the rest of the day went in a blur, spent in fact-checking, making phone calls, and pulling together a story on the state government's plans to increase housing in regional areas and what it would mean for Cannington. It was only when Bob Currie, the paper's crime reporter, asked Kit if she was planning on pulling an all-nighter as he passed her desk on his way home that she realised it was past five o'clock and she was late for her squash game with Hilary.

"Shit!" she swore, grabbing her phone with one hand and shutting her computer down with the other. She rapidly typed out a message to Hilary, grabbed her bag, and raced out the door.

"About time!" Hilary said as Kit ran into the squash centre, red-faced and short of breath fifteen minutes later. "We're on in five minutes!"

"Sorry, mate," Kit said. "You go grab the court and warm up while I get changed. I'll be right there." She dashed into the changing room and hurriedly kicked off her shoes and stripped out of her slacks and shirt. She almost overbalanced while trying to pull her shorts on at the same time as stuffing her feet into her sneakers but managed to complete the wardrobe change and get out to Court 12 without mishap.

"Again, sorry about that," she said, entering the court, where Hilary was busy whacking a ball around its walls.

"No worries," Hilary said, catching the ball and tossing it up and down in her hand. "You ready for another thrashing?"

"Huh, in your dreams," Kit snorted, taking up a position at the back of the court in readiness for Hilary's serve.

Things weren't going well for her. She was two games down and trailing by six points in the third. Her timing was off, and she couldn't seem to land the winning shot. She desperately needed something to unsettle Hilary and wipe that increasingly smug smile off her face.

"So, I kissed Frances yesterday," she said, returning Hilary's serve.

"You what?" Hilary slid to a halt, letting the ball bounce unheeded past her, and gaped at Kit.

"Well, she did kiss me first," Kit said, retrieving the forgotten ball and squaring up to serve. "11-6. You ready?"

"Wait, what? No! Forget about the game! I want the whole story right now!"

"Ohmigod!" Hilary squealed once Kit had finished recounting the events of the past few days. "You sly dog! So, what, you're dating now?"

Kit shrugged. "I really like her, but I'm not sure it's really a good idea to get involved."

"Are you kidding me?" Hilary said. "A woman, who you readily admit is gorgeous, throws herself at you and you think it's a bad idea?"

"Yes. No, hear me out," Kit said, holding up a hand to forestall Hilary's objections. "First off, I know nothing about her. I don't even know if she's out."

"Is that a problem?"

"It could be if she isn't. I dated a closeted woman once ages ago. It's really hard. I couldn't even hold her hand in public. I don't want a relationship like that again."

"Fair enough," Hilary said. "I don't reckon I could handle something like that either. Okay, say she is out. What's stopping you?"

"She's my boss! How's it going to look to everyone at work if I'm dating the boss? And after only knowing her a week?"

"Okay, that is a good point," Hilary said. "There's something else, though, isn't there?"

"It's all happening so fast," Kit admitted. "Too fast. It just feels like it's Cassie all over again." She whacked the ball into the corner of the court.

"Oh, mate." Hilary put her arm around Kit's shoulder. "So, what are you going to do?"

Kit freed herself from the hug and shrugged again. "I don't know. But I need to figure it out fast. Before one of us gets hurt."

CHAPTER EIGHTEEN

Frances's disappointment at missing out on the coffee date with Kit was tempered somewhat by seeing Nick again. She grinned as he ducked through her office doorway. She had forgotten how tall he was. At six foot five and with a shaved head, Nick bore an uncanny resemblance to Peter Garrett, the gangly former frontman of the rock band Midnight Oil.

"Nick! How are you?" she said, coming out from behind her desk with her arms held wide.

"Great, Frances. Just great," Nick said, his voice a mellow baritone. Releasing him from the hug, Frances gestured for him to sit in one of the office's two armchairs.

"Would you like a coffee? Actually, the coffee machine is on the blink, so we'd have to order some in. Unless you'd prefer tea instead?"

"No, no. I'm fine," Nick said. "I stopped for a cuppa on the way here, so I'm good for now."

"Okay," Frances said. "God, it's so good to see you again! How's Renae? And Charlie? He's what, three now?"

"Four, and keeping us on our toes," Nick replied. "Renae's pregnant again, with a girl this time, so that's exciting."

"Oh, congratulations!" Frances grinned at him, then turned businesslike. "You can't imagine how relieved I was when you agreed to take on this gig. We're going to have our work cut out getting it all done in the time head office have given us. So, the first order of business is finding you a team."

She reached across to her desk and picked up a pile of manilla folders, placing them on the coffee table between Nick and herself.

"We had four staff members expressing interest in the web team roles," she said. "I think two of them are really strong candidates. Do you want to see those first?"

"No, let's just work through the pile," Nick said.

"Okay." Frances picked up the top folder and flipped it open. "Ah, Siena. She's one of our finance officers." She passed the file to Nick, giving him a few moments to digest its contents.

"A coder, hey?" he asked. "That sounds promising."

Frances handed the next folder to him, watching as he read it and placed it to one side without comment. He did the same with the next application.

"I think you'll like this one," she said, smiling as she gave him the last file. "I was a bit shocked when I saw the application. Andrew Masters scoffed at the whole idea of a digital edition. Turns out he's been building and maintaining a website to showcase and sell the fishing lures he makes."

"Looks like we just found our web team," Nick said.

"I think so." Frances nodded. "I'll get Enid to set up some interviews with them for tomorrow, okay?" She glanced at her watch. "Now, how about I introduce you to everyone?"

The day had gone downhill after her meeting with Nick. She'd introduced him to all the staff, smothering a smile at the ill-disguised astonishment on people's faces as they registered Nick's height. More than once, someone made a comment about his resemblance to the famous rocker. Nick took it all in good grace.

After leaving him to get settled at his desk, she had had a quick lunch at her desk before meeting with the sales team to break the news to them that they would need to find alternative sources of revenue as the paper would no longer be accepting advertising from betting companies. That had gone over like a lead balloon.

It had been a relief to get to her room at the Waverley at the end of the day and shut the door on the world. She changed from her work clothes into a T-shirt and a pair of cotton drawstring pants, poured herself a glass of the pinot gris she had bought the other night but not opened, and curled up in the armchair with a copy of Margaret Atwood's *The Heart Goes Last*. She had just reached the bit where Charmaine meets her husband's Alternate for the first time when there was a soft knock at the door. She was almost tempted to ignore it and keep reading, but curiosity about her unexpected visitor won out.

She crossed the room and pulled the door open to find a sweaty, flush-faced Kit, clad only in shorts and T-shirt, and with a sports bag gripped in her hand, standing in the hall.

Frances couldn't help noticing how the shorts accentuated the lean, toned muscles in her legs, while the T-shirt revealed equally finely toned biceps and forearms.

"Sorry to turn up unannounced," Kit said.

"No problem. Jeez, you look hot in that," she said, standing aside to let Kit in.

"Nothing a long glass of cold water wouldn't fix," Kit replied, as she dumped her sports bag by the door, her eyes sliding past Frances as she entered the room.

"That's not quite…Never mind, one glass of water coming up," Frances said, following her into the room. If Kit wanted to play it cool, then so be it. She scooped up a tumbler and took it into the bathroom to fill.

"There you go." She passed the glass across to where Kit sat, stiff-backed, on one of the little chairs at the table. She took it wordlessly and gulped the whole lot down in one go.

"Thanks, I needed that," she said, plonking the empty glass down on the table.

76   Lesley Dimmock

"More?" Frances asked, but Kit shook her head, so she slid into the chair opposite her.

"So, good game?" she asked, scratching around for small talk when all she really wanted to do was lean across the table and kiss Kit.

"Not so much, no." Kit grimaced and shook her head. "Got beaten three nil. Hilary's going to be dining out on this for months. It's all your fault, though."

"Me? What did I do?" Frances's voice squeaked in indignation.

"Well, I couldn't stop thinking about you. Put me entirely off my game," Kit replied, a smile tugging at the corners of her mouth.

"All good thoughts, I hope," Frances said, trying to ignore just how kissable that mouth was.

"Well, mostly I was cursing you for stirring up emotions I wasn't expecting to feel or deal with," Kit said.

"Ouch, that's brutal," Frances said, leaning back defensively in her seat and nervously twisting the rings on her fingers.

"Well, if you can't have an honest relationship, then what's the point?" Kit said.

"Is that what this is? A relationship?" Frances's heart tripped wildly as she hardly dared think what Kit's reply would be.

"No." Kit shook her head. "Not yet anyway. Look, Frances"—she stretched an arm across the table and laced her fingers between Frances's—"I really like you. A lot."

"'Like.' That has such a reassuring ring to it," Frances said, trying to sound cavalier but not quite pulling it off. Her nerves were playing havoc with her stomach, and her chest felt like an elephant was sitting on it.

She inwardly squirmed as Kit stared silently at her with those deep-blue eyes for several moments before finally speaking.

"I'm attracted to you. Better?"

Frances nodded her head rapidly, a silly smile spreading across her face. She opened her mouth to speak, but Kit hadn't finished.

"The thing is," she said, letting go of Frances's hand. "I know I said last night that I wanted to see where this went—"

"I sense a 'but' coming," Frances said, her heart sinking.

"But"—Kit went on—"now I don't think it should go anywhere. I mean, we hardly know each other." She picked at a chip in the table's laminated surface.

"Easily remedied," Frances said nervously. Her smile, meant to be reassuring, felt fixed.

"Maybe," Kit replied, "but not so easily solved is the matter of you being my boss."

"So, we talk to HR at the head office," Frances said. "Keep it all above board."

"It's all happening too fast. I just feel like it would be a big mistake."

"So, we can go as slowly as you want." She heard the desperation in her own voice, tried not to sound as if she were begging. "We can work it out. Please, Kit. I thought we had something."

"I know," Kit said. "I'm sorry. I can't do this."

Frances nodded numbly as Kit picked up her bag and left the room, the door clicking quietly shut behind her.

CHAPTER NINETEEN

Frances barely slept all night. Her thoughts had tumbled over and over in her head, as she tried to make sense of what had happened. How had it all blown up so fast? One minute Kit was all for pursuing the romance. The next she was throwing cold water on the whole idea.

Sure, she got the hesitation about a workplace relationship. They were fraught at the best of times, but they could have worked something out. Couldn't they?

She wasn't looking forward to their first encounter since last night's events. Awkward wouldn't come close to describing it. But there would be no avoiding each other, as she had scheduled a meeting with the news team first thing this morning. She groaned at the thought of it.

She stared at herself in the mirror as she threaded a diamond stud into her pierced left ear, sighing at the shadows under her eyes. You can do this, she told her reflection before turning away, picking up her satchel, and letting herself out of her room.

She strode through the newsroom to her office, returning people's greetings with a distracted "Morning, morning." Falling into her chair, she sat with eyes closed for a few moments, collecting her thoughts for the coming meeting.

"Right, let's get this over with," she said, making her way to the boardroom, where the news team was already assembled.

"Good morning," she said, her gaze running around the room, lingering for a fraction of a second on Kit, who gave her a faint smile before dropping her eyes to the screen of her tablet. Frances slid into the chair at the head of the table, arranging her phone and tablet on the table in front of her and picking up her little notebook. Flicking through its pages, she found the list she had written out yesterday and cast her eyes briefly over it before turning her attention back to the seven people who were all looking at her with varying expressions of nervousness and anxiety.

"As you know, I wasn't appointed just to introduce a digital edition of the *Clarion*, but to also overhaul the print version," she began. "This meeting is to discuss the changes I have in mind." She glanced down at her notes again before continuing.

"So, the first thing is, I will not be writing any editorials."

"What?" Clarrie interrupted, his eyes widening in shock. "But that's what editors have always done!"

As a member of her newly created editorial board, Clarrie had been aware of most of her plans for the newspaper, but she had only come to the decision about the editorials the previous night, so his reaction was understandable.

"Not this one," Frances replied. "Why is my opinion more important than anyone else's in this community? I don't believe I should be able to influence elections or public policy just because of my position and nor should this newspaper. So, no editorials."

"Wow. Okay, so what else?" Clarrie asked, a wary expression on his face.

"We won't be syndicating Col Watson's column any longer."

"But he's one of Australia's most famous comedians," Bob protested.

"His material is also tired and out of touch. I would rather spend the money on someone local who has something to say about our community. Not some ageing bloke in Sydney whose column consists mainly of moaning about the traffic and how annoying he finds city hipsters."

"He's not the only one," Bob muttered, glaring at his colleagues as laughter broke out around the room. Frances allowed herself to grin, relieved as the mood lightened.

"Okay," she said. "Now on to what I do want to see. More arts and culture, more women's sport, more Indigenous content—"

"Women's sport gets covered," Simon interjected.

"Not nearly enough, Simon," Frances replied. "The only women's darts team in the entire region just won the championship and all it got was a one-inch story. And yet, a men's lacrosse team that only reached the semifinals got a half-page spread with photographs. We need to do better."

"You mean I need to do better," Simon said, looking and sounding like a sulky schoolboy. "And where are we going to find the room for all this extra coverage?"

He was bordering on insubordination, but Frances let it go. These changes were a lot to take in and she had to expect people would struggle with them.

"That was the next item on my list," she said. "The horse racing form guide and race results will be dropped."

"You're kidding, right?" He stared at her in disbelief.

"No, I'm not." She shook her head. "Look, I know this is a lot to absorb—"

She was interrupted by the ringing of her phone. "I'm sorry," she said, glancing at the screen. "I have to take this. Let's reconvene tomorrow same time, okay?" She hurried out of the room, her phone tucked against her ear, as soon as Clarrie nodded his agreement.

CHAPTER TWENTY

"What a bloody joke!" Simon burst out as soon as Frances had left the room. "Christ! Who thought appointing her was a good idea. Bloody ballbreaker!"

"Hey, that's out of line," Kit snapped, angered at his misogynist language.

"Huh, trust you to take her side," Simon replied. "All you bloody dykes stick together." His lip curled in a sneer.

"I beg your pardon," Kit began to say, her voice icy, but her words were drowned out by Clarrie.

"Peters! Out. Now!" Clarrie roared, his face a shade of puce Kit had never seen before. There was silence as Simon picked up his phone and tablet and stomped out of the room. Clarrie turned to the remainder of the team and jerked his thumb over his shoulder.

"The rest of you, too. Out! Except you, Tresize."

Caitlyn, Julie, Bob, and Bill almost fell over each other in their haste to escape. Kit could hardly blame them. She didn't want to be anywhere near Clarrie when he was this angry either.

82   Lesley Dimmock

She braced herself for a bollocking. Instead, he sank into the empty seat next to her.

"You okay?" he asked, with no trace of the anger of a minute ago.

She nodded, not trusting herself to speak. Simon's outburst had completely blindsided her. She'd thought he considered her sexuality no big deal. And maybe it hadn't been as long as it remained more theoretical than real.

"You want to make a formal complaint?" Clarrie went on. "Because Simon's behaviour was totally unacceptable. I won't have any of my team insulting another like that."

"No, it's okay, Clarrie," Kit replied. "I don't want to escalate the situation. I'm sure Simon will feel terrible about it once he's had a chance to cool off."

"Well, if you're sure," he said. "But I'll be having a private word with him. And I have to report the incident to Frances."

Kit groaned. "Nooo, do you have to?"

"She needs to know, Kit. Come on. Let's get it done now."

Sighing, knowing there was no way she was going to get out of this, Kit reluctantly followed him out of the boardroom. She kept her head down as they walked through the newsroom, convinced everyone was talking about the incident. About her.

"He said what?" Frances asked. Kit watched as shock and disbelief chased across her face as Clarrie related what had happened.

"Anyway, Kit doesn't want to take it any further, but I felt it my duty to inform you," Clarrie said. "I think she should have a couple of days off. But her decision." Kit gave him a wan smile as he left the room.

"My god. Are you okay?" Frances said, once he had gone. "I am so sorry that happened to you."

Kit's heart did a little flip at the tenderness in her gaze. She'd give anything to be wrapped in her arms right now.

"I'm fine. Really," she said instead. "It's nothing I haven't heard before." She gazed at Frances. "What about you? It was you he was insulting as well."

"As you said, it's nothing I haven't heard before," Frances said, a wry smile playing on her lips.

"Okay. Well. Ah, I best be getting back to some work," Kit said, getting to her feet before she said anything about last night. That was a conversation she did not want to have right now.

"You really should take some time off," Frances said.

Kit nodded. "I will," she said, reaching for the door handle.

"I'm not going to give up on us," Frances said, so softly Kit wasn't sure she had heard her correctly. She paused for a heartbeat or two, then left Frances's office without a word.

CHAPTER TWENTY-ONE

"What a trainwreck of a week!" Frances groaned to Nick later that day as they sat in the Nemo Café waiting for their coffee orders to arrive. "Half the staff hate me, and the other half are gossiping about whether I'm having it off with one of my reporters!"

"And you're not? Geez, you just can't trust the rumour mill, these days."

"Stop it!" Despite herself, Frances grinned at the mock indignation on her friend's face. She had missed Nick's laid-back camaraderie since moving to Melbourne. It was good to have him back. Apart from Abby, he was the only friend she had right now.

"Actually, I wish it were true," Frances confessed. "The rumour," she elaborated. "That's the other shitty thing about this week—"

Before she could say more, a server arrived with their drinks.

"One macchiato and one long black?" the woman asked. As Frances glanced up to claim the macchiato, the woman's eyes widened.

"Oh my god! It's Frances, isn't it? I heard you were back. Remember me? Josie?"

Frances frowned at the curly-haired woman, trying to place her. Finally, the memory clicked into place, and she smiled.

"Of course. Josie Beaton." She turned to Nick. "We were in the same class at school."

"Josie Beaton as was," the woman said, waggling her left hand at Frances. "I'm Mrs. Armstrong now!"

"So, you and Craig got married? He was the captain of the school football team," she explained for Nick's benefit. "Half the girls in the school wanted to be his girlfriend. Had eyes only for you, though, didn't he, Josie?"

"Uh huh," Josie said. "Twenty years and still going strong. Anyway, I'd best let you enjoy your coffees. It was really nice to see you again, Frances."

"You too, Josie," Frances said, watching the woman disappear behind the counter. They had never really been friends at high school. She had been too bookish to be included in the pretty girls' club but at least they had left her alone. Didn't pick on her like they did poor Bernadette Connolly, calling her "Moose" because of her heavy facial features.

"So, the other shitty thing you were talking about?" Nick's words jolted her back to the present.

"Nah, it's nothing," she said, batting away the topic with a dismissive wave. "Least of my problems at the moment. I need to find a way to improve morale and win back my team."

"Throw a party," Nick said. "Well, not a proper party. Drinks."

"That's a brilliant idea!" she said, grinning in delight. "I could kiss you!"

"Er, best not," Nick said. "We wouldn't want to start another rumour now, would we?"

CHAPTER TWENTY-TWO

After-work drinks was the perfect way to end what had been a stressful week for everyone, Frances mused as she walked to the newspaper building the next morning. As soon as she arrived, she corralled Enid and Phil, the building manager, and told them of her plan.

"So, beer, red and white wine, soft drinks, and juice should do it," she said. "And some finger food. Sandwiches, party pies, mini quiches—that sort of thing. Make sure to include things the vegetarians and vegans can eat."

"I reckon two hundred dollars should do it," she went on, handing her corporate credit card to Enid. "Let me know if there's anything else you'll need."

"Well, that was the easiest meeting I'll have all day," Frances muttered as they left her office. The next meeting—with the news team—would not go so smoothly if yesterday's interrupted one was any indication. She hadn't really been surprised at the negative reactions her announcements had triggered. It had been a lot for the team to absorb. She just hoped cooler heads would prevail today. At least Simon Peters would not be there. Clarrie had informed her that he had placed him on administrative leave without pay for the remainder of the week. She had been relieved at the news. She wasn't sure how she would react having to sit in the same room as someone who had called her a ballbreaker.

She glanced at her watch and swore. It was almost nine. She hadn't had her usual prework coffee yet and she wasn't going to get one anytime soon. She hurried to the boardroom, juggling her phone and tablet in one hand while she flicked through her little notebook and ran her eye over the notes she had scribbled there. Almost all the pages in the notebook were filled with her jottings and doodles. She had been surprised at how useful she was finding the little book. She'd need to start a new one soon at this rate.

The news team was already assembled around one side of the board table when she arrived. Including Kit Tresize.

"Kit!" she said, taken aback at the woman's presence. "Should you be here? I thought you were taking some time off?"

"I've already had that conversation with her," Clarrie cut in, the frown on his face making clear his disapproval. "Stubborn as a mule, that one."

"I took time off," Kit said, her frustration evident in the frown on *her* face. "Look, it was no big deal. Sure, what Simon said to me was pretty unpleasant, but it's not like he physically assaulted me or anything. I'm fine. Really!"

From the tone of her voice, Frances suspected Kit was well and truly tired of repeating those three words. She decided to let it go.

"Good. I'm very pleased to hear that," she said with a smile, gratified when Kit's face cleared and she smiled back.

"Now, I'm sorry I had to rush out of the meeting yesterday and that it had to be cut short before we could properly discuss all the ramifications of the changes I announced. I know that some of those proposed changes came as quite a shock to some of you and that they will have a profound effect on how you go about your work from now on. But now that you've had time to digest and think about the proposals, do you have any questions?"

"I've got one," Kit said after several moments of silence. "Are there any other sections or features that you are proposing be cut?"

"Let's see," Frances replied, glancing down at her notes. "Editorials, comedian's column, horse racing form guides and race results...oh yes, just one more column. The *Laughter Corner*. Its so-called jokes aren't very funny at all and border on being sexist. It doesn't belong in a modern newspaper."

"Good! I always hated that section," Caitlyn said. Frances was pleased to see her words were greeted by several nods, including those of Bill and Clarrie.

"So, what's going to replace all the dropped material?" Caitlyn went on.

"As I said yesterday..." Frances leaned forward and looked from face to face. So far, there were no scowls or closed body language. They all looked interested in what she was about to say. She relaxed into her chair and took a deep breath before continuing.

"I want to see more arts and culture, more women's sport. I want to see our Indigenous communities represented within our pages and not just in the crime section. I want more local voices. Dropping the editorial will make room for more letters to the editor, for example."

"That'll please everyone," Bill, the finance reporter, cut in. "We know how much people love to see their name in print."

"Exactly," Frances said once the laughter that greeted Bill's comment had died down. "So, that's it, really. None of these proposed changes are arbitrary or just change for change's sake. I really believe they will breathe much-needed new life into the *Clarion*. Any more thoughts, reactions before we conclude this meeting?"

A few shaken heads, but otherwise, silence.

"All right. Thank you for your time," she said letting out an audible sigh as the news team filed out of the room. That did not go as badly as she thought it might. They still looked dubious, but the hostility to the proposals was gone.

Oh goodie, she thought, as she checked her watch. She had just enough time to go to Bean Worx and get herself a coffee before her next meeting, if she walked fast.

Kit might have shrugged off yesterday's incident as no big deal, but it needed to be addressed, so she had emailed the staff requesting everyone's attendance at a meeting this morning. As she made the short journey back from the coffee shop, clutching a tall cup of lungo—an espresso on steroids—she rehearsed what she was going to say to the group.

"Can I have your attention please?" She raised her voice over the hubbub of conversations.

"Thank you," she continued as the noise died down. "As no doubt you are all aware, there was an incident yesterday morning that involved one staff member verbally abusing another. Behaviour of that sort has no place in this workplace. Of course, I don't expect that you will like all of your colleagues or always get along with each other. But I will not tolerate personal insults or name-calling, no matter what the purported aggravation. Ours is—or at least, I thought it was—an inclusive workplace culture, one based on respect and courtesy. Let's do better, people."

She looked out at the room, but everyone either stood or sat with their heads down, not making eye contact with each other or her.

"Okay," she said, after a beat. "On a lighter note, I am delighted to inform you that Andrew Masters and Siena Carson will be joining Nick Davies on the web team. Congratulations, both of you." She led the room in a round of applause. "Of course, that means we now have vacancies in the sales and finance teams. Let Enid know if you're interested. We will also advertise externally for those roles."

"Finally," she said after taking a sip of her rapidly cooling coffee. "I have one last announcement, and I promise it will be the very last one I make this week…"

She paused as a few titters broke out around the room.

"I know this has been a stressful and challenging week for everyone, so to show my appreciation for the professional way you all—well, almost all of you—have handled the curveballs

I've thrown at you, you're all invited to drinks tomorrow afternoon. Okay, that's all I wanted to say. Get back to work!"

She left the room feeling buoyed by all the smiles and excited chatter her drinks announcement had elicited. That was a definite improvement.

CHAPTER TWENTY-THREE

Frances was somewhat mystified at how Simon's outburst about dykes "sticking together" had morphed into rumours that she and Kit were in a relationship and even more mystified as to how to debunk them. It was not like she could stand up and declare that yes, she was a lesbian, but no, she was not in a relationship with Kit. That was hardly going to silence the rumour mill.

She may have made light with Nick of the gossip about Kit and herself, but she had not been immune to the sidelong glances and whispered conversations that suddenly halted whenever she moved through the newsroom. To be honest, she found the avid stares easier to take than the sullen, sometimes hostile, expressions that had been flung her way after her various pronouncements about changes to the newspaper. At least those had abated somewhat since yesterday's after-work drinks announcement. There were more smiles directed her way this morning, and the mood in the office felt lighter. Still, what with that and the bafflement she still was feeling at Kit's sudden change of heart about their relationship, the week had taken its toll emotionally.

It was a relief, then, to shut herself in her office and pour her energy into writing her very last editorial. It took several hours and five drafts before she was finally satisfied that she had struck the right note in detailing her vision for the newspaper.

"That's going to cause a stir over the cornflakes," she mused as she gave the article one last readthrough. It would be published in Monday's edition. A new week, a new era. The first real mark she had made on the newspaper as chief editor. She sat back in her chair as that realisation sank in. Beginning Monday, it would be clear that while there was again a Keating at the helm of the *Clarion*, this one was intent on doing things differently.

She also realized she had yet to make a mark in this very office. She had been in the job for two weeks, and yet there was not a single personal item in the room. None of the artwork reflected her tastes. The bookshelves remained empty. Time for that to change.

There were still a couple of hours until drinks. Plenty of time to do a bit of shopping. Besides, she hadn't had a break all day. Grabbing her bag, she set off toward the town centre, looking for a home décor store or a gift shop. Somewhere that would sell pretty little knick-knacks.

She found the perfect shop just a block away. It was filled with an eclectic mix of bric-a-brac, homewares, books, and handmade foodstuffs, and she spent over an hour, happily browsing its shelves. Picking up and putting down item after item until she came across a little bronze Highland cow. It brought an instant smile to her face, reminding her of a trip she had made to Scotland several years ago. She'd definitely get that.

She added a pale green ceramic planter in the shape of a whale—well, Cannington was on the whale migration route— and a boxed set of *The Adventures of Tintin* books. She'd loved reading those as a kid. That would do for now, she thought. It was a start.

She lugged her new purchases back to the *Clarion* and arranged them on the bookshelves. There, that looked better. Replacing the artwork would have to wait until she had her own possessions with her again. It was a bit clichéd, but she had a large, framed black-and-white print of a lighthouse surrounded by a surging sea that she loved. It would look good on her office wall.

The ping of the alarm on her phone alerted her to the fact it was three o'clock. Time to go help Enid set up the boardroom for this afternoon's drinks. She knew Enid would object, but this was her initiative and she wanted to play a bigger role than just handing over her credit card and letting others do all the work.

"But you're the boss. You shouldn't be in here mucking around with party pies and sausage rolls," Enid said, just as Frances thought she would.

"Well, okay," she responded. "You muck about with those while I organise the rest of the food." She picked up a platter of deli meats and cheeses and peeled away the plastic wrap, grinning to herself as Enid gave a disapproving "tut" before stalking off to the kitchen to heat up the pies.

People began drifting in as Frances was putting the finishing touches to the array of food that covered one end of the boardroom table.

"Come in, come in," she sang out, beaming at them. "Help yourselves to a drink," she said, gesturing toward several large ice-filled tubs that held cans of beer and bottles of white wine and soda. Leaving them to pick at the food, she hurried to the kitchen to help Enid carry the trays of hot pies and sausage rolls back to the boardroom.

By the time she had returned, the room was full of people and buzzing with conversations. She spotted Kit at the back of the room, chatting with Julie and Samira. Her first impulse was to make a beeline straight for Kit, but she forced herself to work the room, chatting for a few minutes with everyone in her path, until she finally reached Kit.

"Hello," she said brightly, including all three women in her smile. Julie and Samira smiled back, then sidled away murmuring about getting another drink and something to eat.

94   Lesley Dimmock

"Gotta give the lesbians some privacy," Kit said, rolling her eyes at their retreating backs. "Although the way everyone is gawking at us at the moment, there's precious little of that."

Frances could sense the surreptitious glances being thrown their way, but there was little they could do except ignore it all.

"They'll lose interest soon," she said. "Next week there'll be something new for them all to talk about. You'll see."

"I hope so. On a completely different note, this was a great idea." Kit gestured to the room at large with her glass.

"Yes, well, much as I would like to, I can't take the credit for it. It was Nick's idea. It's working a treat, don't you think?"

They both looked around at the little groupings of people scattered about the room, all chatting and laughing together. Half of the platters were empty and there was a growing collection of empty beer cans and wine bottles accumulating at one end of a credenza.

"Have dinner with me," Frances said suddenly, her voice pitched low to avoid being overheard. She fixed her eyes on Kit's face, seeing the indecision flit across her features.

"With Nick and me," she pressed, forestalling any refusal Kit might have been about to make. "Tomorrow night. He's been stuck in that motel room of his all week. A night out will do him good. And it'll be a chance for us to get to know each other a bit more."

It felt like an eternity before Kit responded.

"Okay. Text me." She put her now empty glass on the table and walked away. It was all Frances could do to contain the grin that threatened to spread across her face.

CHAPTER TWENTY-FOUR

Kit hadn't wanted to attend yesterday's drinks session. She'd had enough of the glances, smirks, and whispers over the past two days. But she also didn't want people thinking she was running away. So, she had gone, and, yes, people had stared. She had stood, irresolute and ready to flee. But then Julie had come up to her, shoved a glass of wine in her hand, and dragged her over to chat with Samira, and soon enough, people's attention turned to the food and drink and each other. She had relaxed and even started to enjoy herself.

Then Frances had walked over, her eyes shining as she approached and with that smile that felt it was meant just for her, and somehow Kit had found herself agreeing to have a meal with her. Tonight. Just thinking about it set her nerves roiling.

"Come on, Tresize, get a grip," she admonished herself. "It's just dinner with two colleagues. Nothing to get worked up about."

She decided the best way to not think about tonight's dinner engagement was to focus on writing some of those articles she had been thinking about for the paper's website. She opened the front door so that Marvin could bask in the sun, curled up in his favourite spot on the porch. Leaving the door open to let the sun's warmth into the lounge, she settled on the couch and flipped open her tablet.

She'd been engrossed in her work, unaware of the passage of time, when the sound of a snarling dog and then the yowling of a cat tore her attention away from the screen.

"Marvin!" she cried, leaping to her feet and racing out the door, where she was horrified to see that a large dog had seized Marvin by the neck and was shaking him from side to side.

"Get out of here!" she shrieked, grabbing a flowerpot and flinging it as hard as she could at the dog. Yelping as the pot struck its hindquarters, it dropped Marvin and ran off.

"Oh my god. Oh my god!" She knelt beside her inert cat, the blood oozing from several gashes in his body. She wrung her hands, afraid to touch him, before scrambling back to her feet and hurrying inside for a towel. Gingerly, she wrapped Marvin up and lifted him into her arms.

"Kit, what's happened?" John, her neighbour, peered over the fence separating their properties. "I heard the ruckus. Oh, no, is that your cat? Is he all right?"

Does he look all right? Kit wanted to scream at him. Instead, she shook her head.

"He's really badly hurt. Can you drive me to the vet? Please," she pleaded, seeing the hesitation in his face. "I can't take him on the Vespa."

"All right." The man nodded. "Give me a minute."

She hurried back inside, careful not to jostle Marvin, and scooped up her phone and keys. Locking the door behind her, she slid into the passenger seat of John's Volvo, cradling the cat on her lap.

"Thank you," she said, maneuvering herself and her burden out of the car once they had arrived. "I really appreciate it."

"Want me to stay?"

"No, you get back to Gwen," she said, shaking her head. She knew he was a carer for his wife and didn't want to keep him away from her longer than necessary.

She raced into the clinic, where the staff took Marvin from her and rushed him into an examination room. She collapsed into a chair, ignoring the sympathetic looks of the other customers scattered around the waiting room, and buried her face in her hands.

"Please, please, please make him okay," she whispered. Her anxiety ratcheted up with each passing minute. She glanced at her watch. Christ, was it only fifteen minutes since Marvin had been attacked? It felt like an eternity.

"Shit," she swore as she remembered tonight's dinner. She fumbled her phone out of a pocket and dialed Frances's number.

"Yeah, hi, look," she said when she answered. "I can't make dinner tonight. My cat was attacked by a dog."

"Oh my god, that's awful!" Frances cried. "Where are you now?"

"At the vet. They've taken him in to be examined. I'm just waiting for news."

"Tell me which one. I'll be right over."

"Grayson's, but there's really no need…" But she was talking to empty air.

CHAPTER TWENTY-FIVE

Frances burst through the doors of the veterinary clinic, frantically looking for Kit amongst the crowd that filled the waiting room. She finally spotted her in a corner, slumped in a plastic chair, and hurried to her side, her heart going out to her at the sight of her tear-stained face.

"Any news?" she asked, sinking down in the vacant chair next to her. Kit shook her head.

"What happened? I mean, I know what happened," she said. "But how did it happen?"

"I was inside, working," Kit replied. "Marvin was sunning himself in the garden. And then. And then—" She gulped and stopped talking. Frances reached out and squeezed her hand. "And then I heard a dog snarling and Marvin wailing and I rushed out and saw this big, black dog just shaking Marvin from side to side."

"Oh, that's just awful. Poor Marvin. Poor you," Frances murmured.

"I picked up the first thing I could find and chucked it at the bastard. Turns out a potted gerbera is a very effective weapon."

A glimmer of a smile flickered across her face, then faded as she kept talking.

"Marvin looked so helpless and frightened when I got to him. I was almost too scared to pick him up, in case I made it all worse. He just looked at me with so much pain in his eyes." Frances tightened her grip around Kit's hand, feeling a guilty pleasure when Kit's fingers squeezed back. She knew she was just reaching out for comfort, but god, it felt good. They sat hand in hand until the veterinarian entered the waiting room. She reluctantly let Kit's hand go as she jumped to her feet to meet him.

"How is he? Is he going to be all right?"

"He's going to be fine," the vet replied. "He had several serious puncture wounds and one of his lungs had collapsed. I've stitched him up and he's not in any danger, but we need to keep an eye on him for a few days."

"Can I see him?"

"Yes, but please don't be alarmed at his appearance. Come on, he's through here." Kit followed the vet from the waiting room. While she was waiting for her to return, Frances called Nick.

"Hi there," she said when he answered. "I'm really sorry, but dinner's off tonight." She quickly filled him in on what had happened, ringing off when Kit reappeared, looking a lot happier than when she went in.

"All right?" she asked, and Kit nodded. "Come on then, let's get you home."

"This isn't the way to my cottage," Kit said when she turned the car in the opposite direction.

"No, you're coming back to the Waverley," she said. "You don't want to be moping around your place, feeling Marvin's absence."

Kit looked like she was about to argue, but then her shoulders slumped.

"Fair enough."

Frances gave her a sideways glance, noting the worry lines around her eyes and her clenched jaw.

"He's going to be all right," she said softly. "He's in the best of hands."

"I know," Kit replied, turning to look out the side window. Frances took the hint and didn't speak again until they had reached her room at the Waverley and she got Kit settled in the armchair.

"Here, get that into you," she said, thrusting a glass holding an inch of amber liquid at her.

"Whisky?"

"Medicinal purposes," she replied, pulling out a chair from the little dining table and turning it so that she sat facing Kit. "For the shock."

"I see." Kit nodded at the glass in her own hand. "So, what are you self-medicating for?"

"Confusion and disappointment." The words were out before she could stop them. Kit's face clouded over.

"I think I should go," she said, getting to her feet and placing her untouched drink on the table. Frances grabbed hold of her arm, stopping her from leaving.

"Talk to me." She knew she should stand back. That Kit was emotionally fragile right now. But this could be her best chance to get her to open up. If she waited, Kit would have all her defences back in place and would be unreachable.

"Please. Just talk to me." She gazed into Kit's eyes, willing her to stay. Willing her to talk.

"I can't," Kit said. "Not today." She turned away from Frances and pulled out her phone. "I'll get an Uber home."

When then? Frances wanted to ask, but she knew it would be futile. Instead, she let her hand drop from Kit's arm and watched wordlessly as once again Kit walked away from her.

CHAPTER TWENTY-SIX

By the time she left work on Friday afternoon, Kit could confidently declare it one of the worst weeks of her life. It had started, of course, with her worry about Marvin. She'd hardly slept at all since his attack, and so she looked a wreck when she got to work on Monday. That led to Julie making an unwitting joke about her looking like her cat had just died.

She'd had to put up with glares from Simon Peters all week as well, but luckily, they had avoided getting into a verbal clash with each other. She wasn't sure what was worse—Simon's sullen animosity or fielding the constant solicitous comments about Marvin from everyone else, because of course Julie had told them all what had happened to him.

At least she had been able to take Marvin home on Wednesday. He looked rather bedraggled with his patches of shaven fur and one eye still swollen half-shut, but the vet had been happy with his progress.

"Just keep his fluids up, and don't let him exert himself too much," he had said as Kit carried him to the Uber she had organised. No danger of that, Kit had mused. The words "exertion" and "Marvin" never appeared in the same sentence.

She'd had a mountain of work to get through that week, too. It had felt like she had spent half the week on the phone, either on hold to the city planning department or trying to get the mayor's office to return her calls. There was the long and tedious council meeting to sit through and report on. Interviews with council staff about a refugee settlement plan. Chasing around trying to get a copy of the Regional Trails Strategy so that she could report on its recommendations. And that white paper on an air passenger service into the South West to read.

Then there was Frances. She'd only caught glimpses of her throughout the week, but there'd been no opportunity for even the most casual of chats. At least that also meant no awkward conversations while they skirted the massive elephant in the room. After the events of last Saturday, she had half expected a text from her, if only to ask how she was. Or Marvin. But there had been nothing. Not that she could blame her. She wasn't being fair to her, she knew that. She also knew she should talk to her. Explain what was going on in her messed-up head.

Sighing, she pulled out her phone and dialled Frances's number, her heart hammering with each ring and then hammering even harder when she answered.

"Kit?" The surprise in Frances's voice was evident despite the tinny quality of the call.

"Yeah. Hi. Um, I was wondering if I could call round this evening. Because you are right. We need to talk. I need to talk."

There was such a long pause she was beginning to think the call had dropped out, but then Frances spoke.

"I'm halfway to Melbourne to pick up my things," she said. "I'm moving into Leonie's place this weekend."

Shit, she'd forgotten about that.

"You could come around Sunday afternoon?" Frances said. "Say around two? I should have the bulk of my stuff unpacked and sorted by then."

Bugger. Now that she had set her mind to it, she had hoped to get the whole thing over this evening.

"That sounds perfect," she said out loud. "I'll see you then. Good luck with the move." She ended the call and tossed the phone on to the coffee table.

"Right, so now what am I going to do for the next forty-five hours, Marvin?" But the cat was fast asleep in his cat bed and didn't answer.

She was a jangled mess of nerves when she pulled up to Frances's new place. She drew out the whole process of getting the scooter up on to its stand, taking off and locking the helmet into the compartment under the seat, then running her hands through her hair, putting off the moment when she would have to go inside.

Frances must have heard her arrive, because she was standing just inside the open front door, leaning against the doorframe watching her approach, and smiling at her like her visit was no big deal. Kit eyed her baggy tee with its cut-off sleeves and long cotton pants and marvelled at how she managed to look effortlessly elegant even in the most casual clothes.

"Hiya," she managed to say. She would have smiled back but couldn't be certain it wouldn't turn into a grimace; she was that nervous and wound up.

"Come on in," Frances simply said, turning and walking into the front room.

"Oh, I like what you've done with the place," Kit said, following her and taking in the opened and half-empty packing boxes strewn around the room, while piles of scrunched-up newspaper littered the floor.

"Yes, well, I was striving for the anti-Kondo look. I think I've almost got it nailed. Here, have a seat," Frances said, sweeping a bundle of bubble wrap off a two-seater sofa. "Drink? I've got a sauvignon blanc I opened earlier that I picked up in Melbourne."

"Thanks, yeah, that would be great," she replied. Frances left the room, returning a short time later carrying two almost full tumblers of wine.

"Sorry, I haven't found the wineglasses yet," she said, handing her one of the glasses before lowering herself onto a nearby ottoman.

"No worries, I'm sure it will taste just the same," she replied. She took a large gulp of the wine, then stared down at the glass in her hand. She had spent the entire weekend rehearsing over and over and over again what she was going to say to Frances, but now that she was here, she was at a loss for where to begin. She took another swig of her drink and glanced up at Frances, who just sat in silence, an expectant look on her face.

Right, just start, she told herself. "So, yeah um the thing is…"

She paused, took a deep breath.

"The thing is, a few years ago there was this woman. Cassie. She was so charismatic and charming with a really cute smile. I fell for her really, really hard and really fast. So hard and fast that I was blind to her faults. Ignored the warning flags. Just thought the way she lapped up the attention of other women was because she was so outgoing and popular. Six months into the relationship, I found out I was just one of three women she was involved with."

"That must have been very painful," Frances said, her voice brimming with sympathy.

"Mmm, yeah. But now, here I am, falling hard and fast for another gorgeous, charismatic woman…" Her voice trailed off and she stared down at her feet.

"I'm not Cassie." Frances had moved from the ottoman and was crouching beside her, placing a hand on her knee. She forced herself to look at her.

"No, you're not," she said after a few moments silence. "But I could see myself repeating the same mistakes and it freaked me out."

"Okay," Frances said, clambering to her feet and taking a seat next to her. "Thank you for telling me all that. I think I get it. You know, we don't have to rush into anything. We can take all the time we need. I'm not going anywhere."

"Okay." Kit nodded and slumped back against the sofa, the release of tension after finally opening up leaving her drained.

"So, you really think I'm gorgeous?"

Kit burst out laughing. "That's what you took away from this?"

CHAPTER TWENTY-SEVEN

Kit stared at her wardrobe, frowning in frustration as she tried to decide what to wear. The black jeans or grey slacks? That new paisley-patterned brushed cotton shirt or her favourite collarless shirt with pale-green stripes? She'd had all day to sort out an outfit for tonight's dinner with Frances, who was due to pick her up in just fifteen minutes, and she was still dithering.

"For crying out loud, Tresize," she muttered to herself. "Get a grip. It's just dinner." She grabbed the jeans and paisley shirt off their hangers and pulled them on, tucking the shirt loosely into the jeans and rolling the sleeves up before slipping into a pair of black vegan leather Oxfords. There, that would have to do.

Of course, it wasn't "just dinner" at all, was it? The butterflies in her stomach were testament to that. It was their first official date. Their first romantic outing. They had not spent any time together outside of work since "that talk" last Sunday and their interactions at work had been strictly professional. She craved the spark of joy being in Frances's presence gave her, so when

Frances had phoned on Thursday to ask if dinner on Saturday was too soon, she'd had no hesitation.

"Yes! I mean, no. No, it's not too soon," she had babbled before collecting herself. "Dinner would be lovely."

She had just finished brushing her teeth and checking her appearance for the umpteenth time when she heard a car pull up outside. She took several deep breaths to calm her racing heart, scooped up her keys and wallet, and headed to the door.

"Wish me luck," she said to Marvin, who had resumed his customary position at the end of the sofa. His only response was a twitch of his tail.

"I'll take that," she said, yanking the door open and stepping outside. Frances was in the process of exiting her Mini and Kit suppressed a grin at the thought that she resembled an ungainly giraffe as she waved and began folding herself back into the car.

"No problem finding the place then?" she said, sliding into the seat beside Frances and buckling up the seat belt.

"Oh, yeah," Frances replied. "As soon as you started giving the directions, I knew exactly which place it was. When I was a kid, there was an old woman—Mrs. Wilson, I think her name was—lived in that cottage." She pointed at a small, stone house at the end of the road. "All the kids were convinced she was a witch who would turn you into a frog if she caught you. We'd ride our bikes as fast as we could past her house, shrieking 'Beware the witch!'"

Kit had a sudden image of her as a seven-year-old with scabby knees, blond hair streaming behind her as she pedalled furiously down the road.

"So, I hope you like Thai," Frances continued. "I've booked us into that place on Hellier Street."

"Sukonthai?" Kit whistled. "Very fancy."

"Too fancy?" Frances glanced at Kit, frowning as she turned the car around. "I just wanted to make a good impression."

"Oh, you've already done that." Kit grinned.

"Huh, so I could have saved us some cash and just taken you to the local chippie instead?" Frances joked.

"Hmm," Kit mused. "You would have lost points for every chip stolen by a marauding seagull, though."

"Dodged a bullet there, then," Frances replied, and Kit relaxed at how easy the banter was between them. This was a Frances that no one at the newspaper got to see. Funny, sharp-witted, with a gentle warmth about her that was totally disarming. She felt like a little kid who had discovered a treasure and was torn between showing it off to everyone she met and hugging it to herself as her own little secret.

The restaurant, when they arrived, was rather quiet for a Saturday night, with only half of the two dozen tables occupied. Kit was relieved to see that she knew none of the other diners. They hadn't yet talked about how they were going to handle the relationship at work. She suspected Frances had told Nick, but she wasn't close enough to any of her colleagues to share personal stuff like that. She had no idea how people would respond to the news that the chief editor was dating one of her reporters, although she was fairly certain there would be one or two who could make trouble for them.

The white tablecloths, subdued lighting, and soft gleam of brass cutlery created an elegant atmosphere that was only enhanced by the low buzz of conversations. The maître d' led them to a table for two situated in a cosy corner toward the back of the room, offering them each a copy of the menu once they were seated, then leaving them to consider their selections.

"There's rather a lot to choose from, isn't there?" Kit murmured. She was overawed by the extensive list of meals on offer, including a dizzying array of her preferred vegetarian choices, each one sounding more delicious than its predecessor in the list.

"I'll say," Frances agreed. "I invariably get so overwhelmed by all the choices that I fall back on one of my favourites. I may miss out on trying something new, but I've become quite the connoisseur of cashew chicken stir fry!"

"Clever technique." Kit grinned. "Is that what you're having this time?"

Deadline to Love 109

"Yep, that and a glass of their pinot gris." She looked up as a waitress approached, pen and pad poised ready to take their order.

Kit chewed her lip in an agony of indecision before finally settling on a basil and chilli tofu stir fry and joining Frances in a glass of pinot gris.

"Well, this is nice," she said as the waitress retreated after taking their order.

"You mean the restaurant? Or us having dinner together?" Frances asked.

"Oh, well, I was thinking the restaurant," Kit replied. "But yes, us having dinner is nice too."

"At least it's a step up from cold, leftover pizza," Frances said, her eyes twinkling.

"Hey, there's nothing wrong with leftover pizza." Kit laughed. "It happens to be one of my favourite things to eat."

"So, what other favourites do you have?"

"Erm, let's see. There's leftover pizza. Then leftover pizza and…oh yeah. Leftover pizza." She grinned as Frances sputtered with laughter.

"Okay, my turn. What's the last song you listened to?"

"David Cassidy's version of 'Bali Hai,'" Frances said. "I came across the album when I was unpacking. It was one of Mum's favourites, so I stuck it on the record player."

"Huh, right. Is it bad that I don't know who or what you are talking about?"

"You've never heard of David Cassidy?" Frances's expression was incredulous.

"Hey, Millennial here," Kit protested. "All I heard growing up was Alanis Morrisette, Smashing Pumpkins, and the Spice Girls!"

"Oh my god, you crack me up," Frances laughed. "You do realise I'm a Millennial as well? I'm not that much older than you."

"Old enough to have a mum who was into David Cassidy, though." Kit grinned. "Whenever my mum got nostalgic, she'd subject us to her Culture Club collection. Anyway, how is the unpacking going?"

"It's not." Frances rolled her eyes. "I've hardly had time this week at all."

"Need any help? I could lend a hand if you like. You could play that David Cassidy record while I'm there."

"Tempting, but I think we still don't know each other well enough for me to feel comfortable with you rummaging around in my undies drawer."

"Oh, I don't know," Kit replied. "We're almost halfway through our first date. One more and I'll be moving in with you."

Frances threw her head back and roared with laughter. "O my god, yes, that old trope! Although, to be honest, I'm sure we both know lots of women who have done it."

"Hmm, no comment," said Kit, squirming in discomfort. "Oh look, here's our food."

"What, wait, you?" Frances leaned forward, avid for details, ignoring the meal placed before her. "Do tell!"

"In my defence, can I just say I was very young and the house I had been living in had just burned down, and it just seemed logical for me to move in with my new girlfriend," Kit replied. "Now stop gaping at me and eat your dinner before it goes cold."

Frances grinned but did as she was told, and they ate in silence for several minutes.

"That was delicious, but I couldn't eat another bite," Frances said, pushing away the remains of her meal and picking up her wineglass. Kit chased the last few morsels of her meal around the plate before declaring she too was done. Frances eyed her empty plate.

"Impressive," she said. "Would you like to finish off mine for me? Or order dessert?"

Kit shook her head. "What say we drink up and get out of here? Dessert and coffee at my place?"

"An excellent suggestion." Frances beamed, gesturing to a waitress for the bill. When it came, she gave it a quick glance before sliding her credit card into the folder, ignoring Kit's protestations.

"My treat," she said. "You can pay next time. Shall we?" She pocketed her returned card and receipt, stood, and gestured for Kit to lead the way out of the restaurant.

CHAPTER TWENTY-EIGHT

Neither of them spoke during the short drive to Kit's house. Frances looked sidelong at the woman beside her. She seemed a million miles away, lost in her thoughts, a faint smile on her lips. Frances was dying to kiss those lips again. Would Kit get spooked if she did?

Before she could decide one way or the other, they arrived at Kit's place. A warm, yellow light that she hadn't noticed earlier shone from one window, casting a welcoming glow into the night. She followed Kit along the short garden path to the front door and into the tiny living room, where a small table lamp provided the only illumination. Frances marvelled at the shelves crammed with books that Kit had somehow managed to squeeze into the room alongside a settee, an armchair, and a coffee table, which were all oriented toward a small fireplace on the end wall. Several framed photographs hung on the walls; Frances drifted toward them for a closer inspection.

"Yours?" she asked, turning toward Kit, who stood in a doorway leading to what Frances guessed was the kitchen.

"Yeah," Kit replied. "Make yourself comfortable. Will espresso do you, or would you prefer something else?"

"Lord, I'd be bouncing off the ceiling if I had an espresso this time of night!" Frances laughed. "Does your machine run to lattes? I'll have one of those," she said when Kit nodded.

"Okay, I won't be long," Kit replied. She disappeared into the kitchen and Frances took the opportunity to study the photographs more closely. They were three black-and-white seascapes portraying heaving seas with dark, lowering clouds and rocky headlands.

Way better than my lighthouse, she thought as she moved to inspect the bookshelves. You could tell a lot about a person from the books on their shelves. Before she had time to form an opinion about what a Hannah Gadsby biography, a collection of Val McDermid's murder mysteries, and a copy of *The Tibetan Book of Living and Dying* said about Kit, she heard her approaching. Not wanting to appear to be snooping, she quickly sat on the sofa next to a sleeping cat.

"Marvin, I presume?' she asked when Kit reappeared carrying a plate of chocolate biscuits. "How's he doing?" She stroked his curved back, and he raised his head to blink at her momentarily before going back to sleep.

"Really well. Apart from the half-grown fur, you'd hardly know anything had happened to him," Kit replied. "I hope you don't think I got you here under false pretences," she went on, putting the plate down on the table. "Promising you dessert and only delivering some Tim Tams."

"Far from it," Frances replied, beaming. "They are my favourite. I used to love doing the Tim Tam Slam. I wonder if I still can."

"Eww!" Kit said. "A complete waste of a perfectly good Tim Tam *and* coffee, if you ask me. Speaking of which, coffee coming right up."

It only took a few minutes for Kit to return with two steaming mugs. Putting them on the coffee table, she seemed to hesitate, as if deciding where to sit. Frances half hoped she would join her on the sofa, but she sat instead in the armchair a few feet away. Reaching for a remote, she pointed it at a miniature music system in a corner of the room. Florence + The Machine's "St. Jude" flowed quietly from the speakers.

"Are you really going to dunk that in your coffee?" Kit asked as Frances leaned forward to snag a Tim Tam.

"Not if it puts a second date at risk," Frances replied, her hand hovering halfway between her cup and her mouth, a teasing smile playing on her lips. "To be honest, though, a latte is not the best medium. Too much froth to really get that perfect blend of chocolate-infused coffee. An espresso works better." She bit into her biscuit. Waving the uneaten half at the photographs on the wall behind Kit, she said, "Those really are very good. Very atmospheric."

"Thanks," Kit replied, reaching for a biscuit of her own.

"How'd you manage to make Cannington look so good?" Frances asked. "They are of Cannington, yes?"

"Yes." Kit nodded. "The trick is to shoot in winter. That's when the place is at its best. All moody, stormy seas, and glowering storm clouds."

"Not to mention Antarctic winds howling a gale." Frances gave a mock shiver. "I don't think you'd catch me out there at that time of year."

"Nor anyone else," Kit said. "Which is kind of the point. The shots don't really work if the beaches are teeming with people. I like my images to be deserted. Just the power of the ocean and its different moods."

"Well, you're doing a great job of capturing all that," Frances said. "I really like these pieces."

"So, what do you do when you're not working? Any interesting hobbies of your own?" Kit asked.

"Promise me you won't laugh," Frances replied. "I play the ukulele. Hey, you said you wouldn't laugh!"

"Sorry, sorry," Kit said, trying to wipe the grin off her face. "That was the last thing I expected. You didn't strike me as a 'Tiptoe Through the Tulips' type of person."

Frances let out a long-suffering sigh. "That Tiny Tim has a lot to answer for," she said. "But I'll have you know, it's a serious pastime. We have championships and everything."

"Seriously?" Kit asked. "Well, I shall mock no more. Now, can I get you another cuppa? A nightcap, perhaps?"

"No, thank you," Frances replied. "In fact, I really should be going." She stood, digging a hand into her trouser pocket for the car keys.

"You sure?" Kit asked, getting to her feet too. "You're not leaving because I laughed at your ukulele playing, are you? Because I promise not to say another unkind word about it if you stay a little longer."

"Nooo, I'm not leaving because you laughed at my hobby, although that was exceedingly heartless of you, especially after all the fulsome praise I heaped on your photography," Frances replied, a broad smile on her face taking the sting out of her words. "No, I'm leaving because it's getting late."

And if I don't go now, I may never leave.

The unspoken words hung in the air between them. The atmosphere thrummed as they stared at each other and it took Frances all of her willpower to not pull Kit in close and kiss her.

"Good night," she said instead, brushing Kit's cheek with her hand, then turning and walking on shaky legs to her car.

Once inside the car, she sat staring at Kit's silhouette in the doorway. She seemed to stand there for an age before stepping back and closing the door. A moment later, the light in the cottage window went out, and Frances was left sitting in darkness.

"Fuck!" she muttered, twisting the key in the ignition and taking off in a spray of gravel as she spun the car in a U-turn and sped away.

CHAPTER TWENTY-NINE

Kit was having a shitty week. Again. And it was only Tuesday. Saturday night's date with Frances had been wonderful. She'd had a great time and had got to know her a little more. She'd almost stuffed things up right at the end. Almost caved in to her desire for Frances, but for once, her head overruled her heart. Apart from a short exchange of texts, they hadn't spoken since and were studiously avoiding one another at work. Which was as frustrating as hell because she craved Frances's company like mad.

She'd ridden to Port Haven on Sunday to photograph the town's little fleet of wooden fishing boats as a way to distract herself from thoughts of Frances. The ominous clouds that had imparted such an atmospheric mood to her images opened up on her on the ride home and she had been soaked to the bone.

The rain must have got into her Vespa's electrics because it refused to start Monday morning, and by the time she'd got an Uber to work, she'd been late. Which had earned her a reprimand from Clarrie.

Then there was Simon. She had thought he'd have gotten over their spat by now. But no. Yesterday afternoon he'd deliberately shouldered her as she passed him on the way to the staff room.

"What the hell's your problem?" she'd challenged him.

"You cost me half a week's pay," he had growled at her.

"Nah, mate, you did that all by yourself." She had prodded a finger into his chest. "In fact, if either of us has a grievance it should be me. Thanks to you, Frances and I have had to put up with people spreading rumours about us having an affair..." She'd glared at him, her eyes flashing, wondering if he'd had a hand in that. He'd had the decency to look somewhat shame-faced before slouching away mumbling something under his breath.

At work today she'd been under the hammer all day, trying to file three different articles before the afternoon deadline. And now she was being badly beaten by Hilary on the squash court.

"Geez, mate, you are really off your game tonight," Hilary said as Kit missed another simple return to lose the game. "Not that I mind, but...Gives me a chance to improve my win-loss ratio against you." She grinned at Kit, who gave her a rueful smile.

"Yeah, sorry, Hils," she said, picking up the ball and tossing it to her friend. "I've had a bad few days, is all."

"Let me guess. Would it have anything to do with a certain editor in chief?" Hilary asked as they made their way out of the court. "Have you mentioned Saturday's dinner party to her yet?"

Hilary hosted a regular dinner once a month for half a dozen or so of her friends and had suggested last week, once she had learned they were "on" again, that Kit bring Frances to the next one.

"Not yet, no," Kit admitted as she towelled her neck and face dry. "I'll ask her tomorrow night."

"Ooh, a second date!" Hilary gave Kit a teasing elbow in the ribs. "So, you managed not to scare her off after the first one, then? Going somewhere special?"

118   Lesley Dimmock

"Ha ha." Kit threw her towel at her. "I'm pulling out all the stops," she said, ducking as Hilary threw it back at her. "Taking her down to the foreshore for a kebab at Johnny's."

"Who says romance is dead?" Hilary laughed. She leaned in and gave Kit a peck on the cheek. "See you on Saturday, hon. You and your plus-one!" She winked as she walked off toward her car.

CHAPTER THIRTY

Kit stood at the edge of the seawall, shoulders hunched and hands shoved into her coat pockets, watching the waves lap at the sand below. Lost in thought, she was startled by the touch on her elbow and soft voice in her ear.

"Penny for them."

She spun around to find Frances smiling down at her, her eyes gleaming in the streetlight that illuminated the esplanade behind her.

"Nah, you'd be wasting your money." She smiled back. She was not about to admit that she had been standing there fantasizing about making love to her. She could feel the heat rising up her neck and was grateful for the semidarkness.

"Shall we?" She gestured with her chin toward Johnny's kebab van which was stationed fifty metres away, bathed in floodlights. "Nice coat," she said, nodding at Frances's red overcoat as they waited in line to order their food. "That colour really suits you."

"Thanks," Frances replied. "I'll tell you the story behind it one day."

They lapsed into silence as the line inched forward until, finally, it was their turn to order.

"One felafel and one lamb kebab, thanks," Kit told the skinny teenager working the register, handing him a twenty-dollar note, and receiving two foil-wrapped packages in return.

"Here you go," she said, passing the kebab to Frances. They walked over to the seawall and sat with their legs dangling over its side to eat their food. The lights of the Trelawney Hotel glittered off to their right, throwing shards of light onto the gently lapping water of the bay.

"We could go there for a drink, if you like," Kit said, balling up the empty bag her felafel had been wrapped in and wiping her hands on a napkin.

Frances shook her head. "I'd rather just walk along the esplanade, if that's all right."

"Of course," she replied, scrambling to her feet and holding a hand out to help Frances up. "What?" she asked when Frances giggled as she hauled her up.

"Are you really wearing Garfield socks?" Frances grinned, nodding down to where one of Kit's trouser legs had ridden up.

"Guilty as charged." Kit tugged her trouser leg back down. "So, what's your favourite cartoon character then?" she asked as they strolled toward the breakwater jutting into the sea.

"Oh, it wasn't really a cartoon, but I loved *Fraggle Rock*," Frances laughed. "I used to race home from school to watch it. My favourite character as an adult, though? Hmm…that would have to be Scooby-Doo."

Kit wasn't going to admit she knew as much about *Scooby-Doo* as she did David Cassidy, so she quickly asked another question.

"What's your star sign?"

"Capricorn. You?"

"Cancer. What about in the Chinese zodiac? Do you know what you are there?"

"No idea." Frances pulled out her phone and tapped at it for several minutes. "Ah, a rabbit, apparently. Intelligent. Skilful. Artistic. Sounds about right. When were you born? Ninety-two, wasn't it?" She tapped a bit more, then roared with laughter.

Deadline to Love   121

"Monkey! That's hilarious."

"Give me that!" Kit reached over and snatched the phone out of Frances's hand. "Huh, it says here we're smart, resourceful and curious people."

"And that you like reading all kinds of books," Frances said, taking her phone back. "That explains the eclectic collection I saw on your bookcases."

"So, what's on your bookshelves?" Kit asked. "You do have bookshelves?"

"Yes, I do." Frances nodded. "I like a lot of travel writing, especially about Asia. I've got everything William Dalrymple has written. His histories of India are fascinating. Fiction-wise, I read a lot of British crime. Peter Robinson, Ann Cleeves, Ian Rankin and, like you, Val McDermid, just to name a few. Anything else you want to know?"

They had reached the breakwater and, by unspoken consent, began retracing their steps.

"Are you out?"

"Ouch, you don't pull any punches, do you?" Frances turned away and stared at the sea for so long Kit thought she was not going to answer.

"I'm not not out," she finally said. "People generally assume I'm straight. I'm sure you get that too." Kit nodded at the truth of her words. "So, someone passing me in the street isn't going to think 'There goes a lesbian.' Not unless I'm walking hand in hand with another woman, that is." She grinned and slipped her hand into Kit's.

"Oh!" Kit squeaked in surprise, then tightened her hand around Frances's, rejoicing in the pleasure the simple contact gave her.

"One last question," she said as they arrived back at the food truck.

"Uh-oh." Frances tensed beside her, a nervous smile hovering on her lips. Kit grinned and gave her hand a reassuring squeeze.

"This one's easy, I promise." She slowed to a halt and turned to face Frances. "Would you come to a dinner party my friend Hilary is holding on Saturday?"

122   Lesley Dimmock

"I'd like that very much," Frances replied without hesitation.

"Great." Kit let out a little whoosh of air. "Okay. Right then. Well, I guess we should call it a night."

"I guess," Frances said. She moved to free her hand from Kit's, but Kit tightened her hold, pulled her closer, and gave her a long, lingering kiss.

"I still owe you a proper dinner," she murmured, turning on her heel and walking rapidly toward her Vespa.

CHAPTER THIRTY-ONE

Frances watched Kit disappear into the shadows bordering the carpark, a bemused smile on her face. That had been one of the oddest dates she had ever been on. It almost had the feel of a job interview about it, with all the questions, but it had been fun, too. Her favourite moment? When she had slipped her hand into Kit's. It had all felt so right, as if their hands belonged together. That kiss at the end had been pretty special, too.

She spent the journey home pondering that kiss and the fact it had been Kit who had initiated it. Was there any significance to that? Was Kit ready to move things along? Or was she reading more into it, and it was just a kiss?

She was still thinking about it the next morning as she readied herself for work. Well, it had been a really lovely kiss, so who could blame her. However, she needed to focus on other things. Like the nine o'clock staff meeting that she was going to be late for if she didn't get her skates on.

Clutching a tall macchiato from her new favourite coffee stop—a little, roadside van handily located just on the outskirts of Cannington—she hurried through the newsroom and into her office. She had ten minutes to catch her breath, drink her coffee, and review the various reports sitting on her desk before the start of the meeting.

A large, manilla envelope marked "Private and Confidential" caught her eye. She quickly tore it open and slid out its contents. Sent from the Human Resources Department at the head office, it was a copy of the organisation's policy on workplace relationships. She skimmed her eye over the covering letter, giving a crisp nod and setting it aside. It was basically confirming the advice she had received when she had spoken in person to the HR manager on Monday. Now all she had to do was find an appropriate time to talk about it with Kit.

She rapidly glanced through the rest of the reports, digesting their key points before gathering them into a pile to take with her to the meeting. She retrieved her phone and tablet from her bag and made her way to the boardroom, where everyone except the finance team was assembled and waiting. Taking her seat, she swept her eyes over the group, lingering for a fraction of a second on Kit, who sat at the far end of the table. Apart from a slight inclination of her head, Kit maintained an impassive expression. It gave Frances a little thrill that she was the only other person in the room who knew how they had spent their evening together.

"Right then," she said, banishing the memory of Kit kissing her from her mind as she realised people were waiting for her to start the meeting. "Thanks for your time this morning. So, first off, head office has confirmed the launch date for the website as Monday the fifth of March, so we have a little over two weeks left. Where are we on the building of the site?" She turned to look at Nick, who nodded at her.

"The architecture is all in place. Now it's just a matter of uploading content, fine-tuning the coding, and testing, testing, testing." He gave the room a wry smile. "We should have the sandbox version ready by Monday, so you all can go and play with the site, report any glitches, broken links, etc. Give us feedback on its look, navigability. All that stuff."

"That's great to hear," she said. "Thanks, Nick." Hands were being raised, and she could guess the reason. "For those of you who are wondering, a 'sandbox' is simply a testing environment. It's isolated from the system, so you can experiment without worrying about damaging anything." The hands went down again as she finished her explanation.

"Regarding the content," she went on, looking at Nick again. "Do you have enough feature articles to give users plenty to engage with at launch time?"

"Yes." He nodded. "But please keep them coming. We will need lots of new material so we can keep the site looking fresh."

"The calibre of the articles submitted so far has been really impressive," Frances said, looking around the room. "I want to thank all of you who have contributed so much great work already. Keep it up." She paused, took a sip of water, and shuffled her papers until she found the report she wanted.

"Speaking of great work," she said. "The community has really embraced the new-look print version of the *Clarion*. Circulation numbers are up for the first time in three years. The letters and emails we have received have been overwhelmingly positive. People are loving the expanded sports coverage. So well done on taking on what was quite a challenge." She looked directly at Simon Peters, who leaned back in his chair and smirked at her.

"The increased coverage of stories about the Indigenous communities has really resonated, and not just in those communities. And readers are really embracing the local focus in the arts and culture areas as well. Susan, I believe you also have some news for us?" She turned her attention to the advertising accounts manager.

"Oh yes." The woman pushed her spectacles higher up her nose and peered around the room. "So, as you can imagine, it was quite a shock to suddenly lose what was a large chunk of advertising revenue when we eliminated ads from the gambling industry. However, the team has been working really hard to attract new advertisers, and just yesterday we signed a deal with Serendip Dairy Corporation to take out a fifty-two-week banner ad on the digital edition and a weekly full-page ad in the print version."

There were approving murmurs from around the room. Serendip was one of the largest dairy companies in the region, but it had shown little interest in the past in advertising in the *Clarion*, preferring to spend its advertising dollars with the *Warrnambool Standard*. Signing such a lucrative deal was a serious investment in the *Clarion*.

"That's a real coup, Susan. Well done to your team," Frances said. "It's a good sign that our stance on the gambling industry is paying dividends. Right, unless anyone else has a good news story to share, then I think we are done." She looked around the room, but no one moved. "No? Okay. That's it then. Keep up the great work," she called out as everyone began filing out of the room.

Gathering her papers and belongings together, she followed them out and made her way back to her office. She had barely sat down when there was a tap at the door. She looked up to see Kit standing in the doorway, hands clenched at her sides and her eyes flashing in fury.

"We've got a problem," she growled, stepping into the room and closing the door behind her before Frances could say anything. "Simon saw us last night," she said, dropping heavily into the chair in front of the desk. "He's threatening to go to HR and report us. The little shit." Her voice quivered with anger.

Fuck, Frances silently swore. "What did he actually see?" Maybe they could spin this to be just a friendly after-work stroll.

"Me kissing you," Kit said flatly.

Or maybe not…

CHAPTER THIRTY-TWO

"Well, Simon will get no joy from HR if he does report us," Frances said. "I received this earlier this morning after talking with Veronica on Monday—"

"You've spoken to HR about us?" Kit's eyes narrowed.

"Not specifically about you and me," Frances replied. "Just in general. Anyway, have a read." She passed the letter over and waited while Kit absorbed its contents. "I did mean to show it to you at some point, but events have rather overtaken me," she explained as Kit handed the sheet of paper back to her. "Anyway, as you can see, we would not be contravening any company policies by being in a relationship with each other."

"Which we aren't," Kit said, her mouth a thin, tight line. "Well, we're not, are we?" she challenged as Frances's face fell.

"No, I guess not," she conceded. Kit was right. Two dates and a couple of kisses hardly constituted a relationship.

"I'm sorry," Kit said, her tone softening. "Simon's made me furious, but I shouldn't be taking it out on you. Geez!" She banged her fist on the desk, causing Frances to jump. "Last night was really lovely, you know, and now he's gone and spoiled it."

"It *was* lovely," Frances responded, resisting her urge to reach out and touch Kit's hand. Public displays of affection in the workplace were definitely against company policy, and the last thing she wanted was for Simon to catch sight of them holding hands and give him even more ammunition. "Don't let him get to you, okay? And remember, it's only two more sleeps until we get together on Saturday!" Her childish words had the desired effect as Kit grinned back at her before getting to her feet and leaving.

Once she had gone, Frances rested her head in her hands and massaged her temples. Despite appearing unconcerned, she inwardly worried about Simon's motives. What did he hope to gain by causing problems for her? Was he trying to get her sacked? And, if so, why? Perhaps he did not like strong women in leadership positions.

Well, tough, she thought, straightening her back and squaring her shoulders. She wasn't going anywhere, and Simon Peters needed to get used to that.

When the call came from Human Resources midmorning the following day, Frances was not surprised.

"Hello, Ms. Keating? This is Veronica Waters. We spoke on Monday?" The woman spoke in a brisk, no-nonsense manner, and Frances had barely confirmed her identity before she went on. "We have received a complaint from a member of your staff of an inappropriate relationship between yourself and one of your reporters, Kit Tresize. You are being informed of this in accordance with the policy on workplace complaints."

"I see," Frances murmured.

"The complainant has been informed that if any such relationship existed it would not contravene any workplace policies and that therefore no further action would be taken."

"Right. Okay. Thank you," Frances said, but Veronica had not finished.

"The complainant then made accusations against you of exhibiting favouritism." Veronica was being extremely careful not to reveal the identity of the complainant, but Frances had a very good idea who it was.

"What? How have I done that? Did he, I mean, they say?" Frances's head throbbed with an incipient headache.

"No, they were unable to provide any examples, and they have been informed that we cannot proceed without documented evidence of such favouritism."

"I see," Frances said again, running her free hand along the back of her neck, trying to release the tension there. "Is there anything I need to do?"

"It's not strictly necessary, but perhaps you could provide an account of just what your relationship is with Ms. Tresize." Veronica's voice softened. "Just for the record. And of course, avoid any PDAs within the workplace or fraternising with Ms. Tresize during work hours."

"Okay, thank you, Veronica," Frances said faintly before ending the call. Kit was right. Simon Peters really was a little shit. Sighing, she picked up the phone's handset and dialled Kit's office extension.

"Kit, can you come to my office for a moment?"

"Um, yeah sure. Five minutes?" Kit sounded guarded but arrived within the promised time.

"Come in. And shut the door, please," Frances said.

"Sounds serious," Kit said, a nervous smile plastered on her face as she complied with the request.

Frances gave her a brief smile and gestured her to sit.

"So, Simon—although no names were mentioned—has carried out his threat to complain about us to HR," she said, once Kit had settled herself in a chair.

"Why, that slimy little toerag!" Kit exclaimed. "It couldn't have gone well for him, though. He's been as surly as all morning."

"No." Frances gave a grim smile. "He—or I should say, the complainant—was told there were no grounds for the complaint. However, you ought to know that HR wants me to document the exact nature of our relationship. It will be a formal record. Are you okay with that?"

Kit stared at her for several long minutes before slowly nodding. "Yep," she said, standing and moving to the door. "In fact, I'll write one, too. Just in case someone decides to lodge a sexual harassment complaint on my behalf."

"Oh, you don't think he would, do you?" Frances ran an unsteady hand through her hair. Great! Another thing to worry about.

"Nah." Kit shook her head. "Just covering all bases." She gave Frances a wry smile on her way out of the office.

Frances groaned as her head pounded. A headache was the last thing she needed right now. She scratched around in her drawers, unearthing a half-used blister pack of painkillers, poking two out, and swallowed them, washing them down with a couple of gulps of water. With another sigh, she pulled her keyboard closer, opened a new file, and tapped out "Declaration of a Workplace Relationship." She stopped and stared at the words, wondering how to describe what was happening between Kit and herself. Because, as Kit had so bluntly pointed out earlier, they weren't really in a relationship. Not yet, anyway.

Ms. Kit Tresize and I have formed a bond. Nope, that sounded way too stuffy. She deleted the sentence and began again. *Ms. Kit Tresize and I are currently dating but are not in a formal relationship at this point in time.* Short and succinct, but what else could she say? She added her electronic signature and the date, saved the document, then sent it off in an email to Veronica Waters.

She cast a wistful glance in the direction of Kit's desk and crossed her fingers, hoping that with any luck she would need to update that declaration in the not-too-distant future.

CHAPTER THIRTY-THREE

Codifying her romantic involvement with Frances had been one of the weirdest experiences Kit had ever had. Maybe not as weird as that axe-throwing date she had gone on one time, but right up there. Actually, she wouldn't mind chucking a few axes at a certain sports reporter, given his malicious complaint.

She grimaced at her reflection in the bathroom mirror. Two new little furrows seem to have taken up residence between her eyes. Damn that Simon Peters. She shook her head. No way was she going to let him occupy any space in her head tonight, she decided. Nope, tonight was going to be all about her and Frances having a great time at Hilary's dinner party.

She shrugged on her scooter jacket over the white, open-necked shirt she'd chosen to wear with a pair of baggy, charcoal pin-striped trousers. She gave herself a final cursory check, gave Marvin a cuddle, and let herself out of the cottage. Arriving fifteen minutes later at Frances's place, she removed her jacket and helmet and shook her hair loose before walking down the short driveway to knock at the front door.

"Hello, come on in," Frances said, opening the door. "I'm not quite ready."

"Sure. I, uh…Hi," Kit mumbled, tearing her eyes away from the swell of Frances's breasts under the snug-fitting white singlet she wore and following her inside. She hovered in the hallway as Frances disappeared into her bedroom, only to reappear a few moments later.

"How do I look? Not too dressy am I?" She had thrown on a long-sleeved sea-green shirt over the singlet and left it open to hang loosely over beige slacks.

"Nope, you look great," Kit managed to say, her throat suddenly dry. "That shirt really brings out the colour of your eyes."

"You look pretty good yourself," Frances replied, running her eye over Kit and grinning broadly. "You ready to go?"

"Oh, uh yes." Kit suddenly remembered the jacket and helmet in her hands. "Can I leave these here?"

Frances took them from her, disappearing once more into her bedroom. She returned carrying a mini cross-body bag into which she slipped her wallet and phone.

"Oh, wait! I almost forgot!" she said just as they were about to leave. She hurried back down the hallway to the kitchen, coming back with a bottle of chardonnay.

"Will this be all right?" she asked, giving it to Kit.

"It'll be fine," Kit said, noting the rather pricey label from one of the premium wineries in the Rutherglen region in northern Victoria. "We should get going, if we don't want to be late," she said.

"Yes, right. Of course." Frances grabbed her keys from a little bowl sitting on the hall table and led the way out to her car. They said little on the journey to Hilary's, with only Kit's occasional direction breaking the silence between them.

"That's it, there on the right," Kit said as they reached their destination. Frances pulled over to the kerb and cut the engine.

"You okay?" Kit asked as Frances made no move to get out of the car.

"Yep, just a bit nervous." Frances gave her a crooked smile. "It's a bit daunting meeting all your friends en masse."

"You'll be fine," Kit reassured her. "They're a really cool bunch. Come on."

She slid her hand into Frances's as they walked to Hilary's house, giving it a squeeze as she rang the bell and heard footsteps inside hurrying toward the door.

"Kit! Finally! We were about to send out a search party!" Hilary said as she opened the door.

"Yeah, sorry about that," Kit said, hugging her. "I forgot about the roadwork on Bennett's Road. Hilary, this is Frances." She watched as Hilary raked her eyes over Frances with undisguised curiosity before breaking into a grin.

"Frances, so lovely to finally meet you. I was beginning to think you were just a figment of Kit's imagination! Come on through." She led the way down the hall and into a dining room where five other women sat around a large oval table that was set for dinner. Murmuring something about seeing to the meal, she left the room. Kit grabbed Frances's hand again and drew her close as all eyes fell on them.

"Everyone, this is Frances," she said, as they sat down. "Hilary's wife, Natasha." She gestured at the Indigenous woman on Frances's left. "Sue, Libby, Akari, and Ashley."

"Shall I put that in the fridge?" Natasha nodded at the bottle of wine Frances had placed on the table.

"Uh no, I'll open it if that's okay. Anyone else like some?"

"Sure, I'll have some," Akari said as everyone else demurred, indicating their already filled glasses.

"We're so excited that Kit has finally brought along a plus-one to one of these dinners," Ashley said once Frances had finished pouring the wine. "It's been years. Not since Cass—Oh, oops. Damn."

"Oh, babe," Akari sighed, giving Ashley a sorrowful look.

"That's ten demerit points for bringing up She Who Shall Not Be Named," Sue declared. "How many is that now, Ash? You're going to be doing the washing up at every dinner from now until Christmas at this rate!"

"Leave her alone." Kit laughed, coming to her friend's defence. "It's not her fault we all have a She Who Shall Not Be

Named. How's a woman supposed to keep track of who can and can't be mentioned, huh?"

"What about you, Frances?" Libby asked. "Is there a SWSNBN in your life?"

Before she had a chance to respond, Hilary entered the room bearing a large serving dish.

"Grub's up!" she announced, placing the steaming dish in the middle of the table. "Lamb biryani. Vego version on its way."

"I'll get it, darl. You sit down," Natasha said.

"Right, dig in. Help yourselves," Hilary said once her wife had returned with the second biryani and a plate piled high with naans.

"Oh my, that was delicious, Hils." Kit leaned back in her chair and gently rubbed her very full stomach. Hilary beamed as the rest of the group made similar appreciative noises.

"I hope you've all left room for dessert," she said, laughing as they all groaned.

"I'll help you with that." Kit got to her feet as Hilary began clearing the table. She followed her through to the kitchen, carrying a stack of dirty plates.

"Oh my god, Kit," Hilary said in a loud whisper as Kit began loading the dishwasher. "She is gorgeous! I can see why you couldn't take your eyes off her all night!"

"Yeah, I might be just a little bit smitten." Kit gave a sheepish smile.

"And she is so into you, as well!"

"You think?"

"God, Kit, Blind Freddy could see it! Geez, now get back in there and try not to mess things up."

"Me? Mess up?" Kit spluttered, but Hilary just grinned at her and gave her a gentle push toward the door.

CHAPTER THIRTY-FOUR

"That was a lot of fun," Frances said as she drove home. "I really liked your friends. They seem a great bunch of women."

"Mmm, they liked you too," Kit replied. "I think they're taking a vote right now on whether to grant you immediate membership to the Cannington Lesbian League. It's usually a three-month trial process, so you must have really impressed."

Frances glanced sideways at Kit. She was pretty certain she was joking, but it was hard to read her expression in the faint light of the dashboard.

"You're just kidding, right?"

"No, the league is real, trust me." Kit turned to her, her eyes dancing with amusement. "You get a badge and everything!"

"Now I know you're having me on," Frances said, trying to sound hurt but unable to repress a smile. She enjoyed the gentle ribbing Kit was always giving her. It reminded her not to take herself so seriously. Besides, seeing the way Kit's face lit up whenever she laughed was worth the teasing.

"Do you want to come in for coffee?" she asked, pulling the car into her driveway and switching it off.

"Yes, I'd like that," Kit replied.

"Cool," Frances said, then did a mental eyeroll. Way to sound like a thirteen-year-old! "Right then, shall we?" If Kit noticed how flustered she had become, she gave no indication as she clambered out of the Mini and followed her inside.

"So, what would you prefer?" she asked, leading Kit toward the kitchen. "There's coffee. Plunger only, I'm afraid. I could make tea. Or perhaps something stronger?" She filled the kettle, switched it on, and turned to face Kit.

"You," Kit said, hooking a finger into the front of her trousers waistband and pulling her close.

"Are you sure?" They were so close it would be a miracle if Kit couldn't feel the way her heart pounded.

"Am I sure I want you?" Kit's eyebrow arched sharply upward.

"No, I mean are you sure you want to take this further? I mean now." She stared intently into Kit's deep, blue eyes.

"I am," Kit nodded. "I've waited a long time to feel this way again about someone. I don't want to waste another minute. Do you?"

"No," Frances managed to croak out before pulling Kit into a heated kiss. Their hands fumbled at each other's clothing, desperate for the touch of skin. Frances pulled away, staring mutely into Kit's face before taking her hand and leading her into the bedroom.

Their lovemaking was frantic, urgent as they sought release from their hunger for each other, collapsing into a tangle of arms and legs once the initial passion was spent. They took it more slowly the next time, bringing each other to a more gradual, but just as intense, arousal and orgasm. Afterward, Frances drew Kit into her arms and let herself drift in the euphoric languor brought on by the sex.

"I would totally love some pizza right now," Kit murmured into her shoulder, rousing her out of the light sleep she had fallen into.

Frances brushed the hair from Kit's face and stared at her incredulously. "You're kidding, yeah? Cos, one, it's past midnight and, two, how on earth could you fit any more food in after that massive meal earlier?"

"Okay, so for starters..." Kit grinned up at her. "That massive meal was over four hours ago, and I have expended a considerable amount of energy since then. Secondly, you do know that even Cannington runs to all-night food delivery these days, right?"

"We are so not ordering in pizza," Frances said, untangling herself from Kit and climbing out of the bed. "I can do you a cheese toastie, though. Will that do you?"

"Ooh, yes, please. I don't suppose you'd stretch to a cuppa to go with it, would you?" Kit gazed up at her with puppy dog eyes.

She shook her head in mock exasperation before snatching up her discarded shirt, shrugging it on, and leaving the room. Once in the kitchen, she shook with silent laughter as she prepared the midnight snack. She had imagined many ways in which this evening could have ended, but standing butt-naked in her kitchen at one o'clock in the morning making a toasted sandwich after spending the previous couple of hours having amazing sex with Kit Tresize hadn't been one of them.

When she returned to the bedroom with two cups of coffee, Kit was fast asleep. She tiptoed to the bed and quietly put one cup on the nightstand next to her, then gently pulled the sheet up over her. She crept around to her own side of the bed and carefully slid in, turning to gaze at her sleeping face for what felt like hours before falling asleep herself.

The memory of the night's lovemaking flooded into Frances's mind as soon as she woke the following morning, A huge smile crept across her face, only to vanish when she turned her head to find Kit gone. She bolted upright in a panic. Had Kit fled, regretting their night of passion? Had it been too soon after all?

She was halfway out of the bed, her mind a frantic whirl of incoherent thoughts, when the door swung open and Kit walked in, wearing nothing more than her half-buttoned shirt, and carrying two plates holding last night's forgotten toasted sandwiches. Frances sagged back against the pillows in relief.

"You didn't think I'd done a runner, did you?" Kit asked with a knowing smile, passing her one of the plates.

Was she really that obvious?

"No, of course not," she said, as Kit climbed into the bed beside her. "Well, maybe a little bit," she admitted. She peered at the steaming sandwich on her plate. "Did you microwave these?"

"Yeah. I hope they're all right and haven't gone too soggy," Kit replied. "Not quite the breakfast of champions, but it seemed a shame to waste them after you went to all that effort last night to make them."

"So, no regrets then?"

Frances took a cautious bite of her sandwich, wary of burning her tongue on the hot cheese. Kit turned to look at her, a small smile tugging at the corner of her mouth as her eyes flickered over her naked belly and breasts. She felt herself flushing under the scrutiny but resisted the urge to pull the sheet up over herself.

"No, no regrets," Kit said eventually. "This all feels very right."

Good," Frances said, not taking her eyes off Kit's face as she scooted closer to her and began unbuttoning her shirt. She vaguely registered the sound of their plates falling to the floor as she gently pushed Kit back against the pillows and began a new exploration of her body.

CHAPTER THIRTY-FIVE

"What do you want to do for the rest of the day?" Frances asked, stretching luxuriantly in the afterglow of an entire morning spent making love with Kit. "The sun's shining. We could go somewhere."

"I don't think I can move," Kit said with a groan. "I seem to have lost all sensation in my legs."

"Fine, we'll stay here then." Frances smiled. "I didn't want to share you with anyone right now, anyway." She leaned over and kissed Kit, then rolled out of the bed, picking up the discarded plates and remnants of toasted sandwich. "I do need to go pee, though. I'll bring us back some coffee, yeah?"

"And food. Food would be good," Kit called out as she left the room.

She used the toilet, splashed some water over her face, ran a comb through her tousled hair, and studied her reflection. Her eyes shone back at her with a happiness she'd not seen for quite some time. She pulled on a cotton bathrobe that had been hanging on the back of the door and headed to the kitchen.

140   Lesley Dimmock

She switched the kettle on, spooned some Bells Blend ground beans into the plunger, then began rummaging in the pantry for something to feed Kit. She came across a ramen soup kit she had been meaning to make and decided it would do. She was going to have to seriously stock up on food if she was to keep up with Kit's appetite. Where did she put it all? There certainly wasn't an ounce of fat on her.

Within minutes, Frances had two steaming bowls of noodle-filled soup. She placed the bowls, along with two mugs of coffee on a tray she unearthed from a cupboard, and carried it all into the bedroom. Kit had pulled her shirt back on and was sitting up against the pillows, scrolling on her phone. She gave Frances a lazy smile as she handed her a bowl of soup and slid into the bed beside her.

"This smells delicious," Kit said, stirring her soup, then swallowing a spoonful of the broth.

"I'm just glad you stayed awake long enough to taste it this time," Frances said with a sly grin.

"Yeah, sorry about that. It was all your fault though. Totally wore me out."

"Young people today." Frances shook her head in a show of dismay. "No stamina."

Kit's only response was to stick her tongue out at her. They ate in silence for several minutes before Kit spoke again.

"You never did say last night," she said, "but is there a SWSNBN in your life?"

Frances looked at her blankly for a moment or two before remembering what the acronym stood for. She Who Shall Not Be Named. She slurped another mouthful of noodles before replying.

"There is, actually. Unfortunately. Dee Watson." Her mouth twisted in a grimace at the memory of her last lover. "She dumped me for one of my closest friends." She paused and took in a ragged breath. It had been over a year ago, but the whole thing still made her so angry. And still hurt more than she cared to admit. "Well, I thought she was a close friend."

She gave Kit a wry smile. "Just goes to show you never really know anyone, hey? Anyway, so yeah, Dee is my SWSNBN. But you know what?" she said brightly. "That's all in the past now. I'd much rather focus on the future." She cupped Kit's face in one hand and stroked a thumb over her cheek. "On you. Us."

"Us," Kit echoed with a fleeting smile that did not quite reach her eyes.

Frances bit her lip, cursing herself for going too far, too fast.

"I'm sorry," she said. "Talking of an 'us' is too soon, isn't it? God, I can be such an idiot sometimes!" She scrambled out of the bed, stood at the window, and stared out at the garden. Hot tears pricked at her eyes as the silence in the room lengthened. She'd never forgive herself if she'd messed this up now. The sheets rustled, and then she felt Kit's arms wrap around her and hold her tight.

"It's me who's sorry," Kit murmured against her back, her breath brushing against her skin. Frances turned within the embrace as Kit continued speaking, her eyes fixed on a point somewhere beyond Frances's shoulder. "The speed of all this is making me feel a bit edgy and, yeah, any other time I would have bolted by now, but…"

"But?" Frances stroked the hair back from Kit's face, and Kit's eyes shifted to meet hers.

"But…'us' sounds good." This time, the smile did reach her eyes.

CHAPTER THIRTY-SIX

Kit had ridden home from Frances's place in a bit of a daze. She had had no real expectations of how Saturday night would go. It was just going to be another date. A chance for her friends to meet Frances and for Frances to meet some of the other lesbians living in Cannington. But watching as Frances effortlessly charmed her friends with her easy wit and self-deprecating humour, she knew she did not want to wait any longer to be with this woman who made her heart sing every time she looked her way.

The sex had been incredible. Hot and intense, but tender too. She had woken in Frances's arms knowing she was right where she belonged. She would not have left at all, but the cat needed feeding.

She had spent the rest of Sunday afternoon and evening resisting the urge to jump back on her Vespa and ride straight back to Frances's cottage. She hadn't got much sleep, having spent most of the night reliving the events of the night before, and she had been less than enthusiastic when her alarm went off this morning.

But she'd made it into work on time and, after exchanging scowls with Simon Peters, was now tuning in to the morning talkback show on the local radio. Talk radio wasn't her favourite kind of programme, but she found it a useful way to discover which issues were causing a stir in the community and that she might need to cover. Sticking her earbuds in, she clicked open the radio app in time to hear the announcer introducing the first caller.

"Pastor Evans, from the Harvest Encounter Church. Good morning, pastor. What's on your mind today?"

"Perversion," a nasally voice hissed. "Filth and perversion on the streets of Cannington."

Kit rolled her eyes. These religious types were always getting worked up about something or other. He was probably going to go on a rant about people wearing skimpy swimwear again.

"Really, pastor?" the announcer said in a tone that suggested he was rolling his eyes as well.

"Yes. Harlots and hussies practically fornicating in public."

Kit's skin prickled with sudden apprehension. She grabbed her tablet and hurried across the newsroom to Frances's office.

"You have to listen to this," she said, bursting through the door and slamming her tablet down on the desk. Frances looked up at her in mute surprise, but said nothing as Kit unpaired her earbuds and the pastor's voice streamed into the room.

"…women kissing in plain view, with no shame."

They exchanged horrified glances, then continued staring at the screen.

"And now the homosexuals…" The pastor drew the word out—hommo-sexxx-you-alls—in a voice dripping with bile. "Now the homosexuals have taken over our newspaper."

"Okaaay, thank you, pastor," the announcer said, cutting him off as an ad for carpets began playing. Kit wordlessly closed her tablet, shutting off the programme.

"Oh my god," Frances whispered, her face white with shock.

Kit felt sick. She glanced out into the newsroom and groaned. Half a dozen people stood staring at her, at *them*, their faces mirroring the shock and disbelief roiling through her own mind. She sank into one of the chairs provided for visitors, at a complete loss for something to say. Silently, she reached across the desk and entwined her fingers with Frances's. What did it matter now, if anyone saw? And bugger the ban on PDAs. Frances needed comfort.

"I can't believe I've just been outed on radio," Frances said in dismay.

Her expression suddenly hardened, and Kit swivelled her head to see what had caught her eye. Uh-oh. Simon Peters was strolling nonchalantly through the newsroom, a smug expression on his face. Kit scrambled to follow as Frances leapt to her feet and stormed out of the office.

"You're fired!" she roared as she approached Simon. "Pack your things and get out of my newsroom now!" The entire office fell silent as everyone watched the drama. Kit was standing close enough to Frances that she could feel her trembling with fury. Simon's eyes darted from Frances to Kit and back again.

"You can't do that," he said, jutting his chin out belligerently. "I got rights."

"I said, 'Get out.'" Frances's voice was low and loaded with menace. She turned her back on him and marched back to her office, slamming the door behind her. Kit crossed her arms and glared at Simon.

"You heard her," she growled. "Get your sorry arse out of here, you little piece of shit."

"Do I have to call security?" she went on when he didn't move.

His jaw worked, as if he was going to argue, but then his shoulders dropped and he turned away. She followed him with her eyes as he cleared his desk, pushed back past her, and slouched out the door. A hubbub of voices erupted as he disappeared. Kit walked back to her desk on suddenly shaky legs, ignoring the looks of concern her colleagues were giving her. She only realised as she sat down that she had left her tablet in Frances's office. Kit glanced across to it, but Frances was on the phone and did not look up.

Her mobile phone began buzzing with incoming messages to WhatsApp.

WTF? That was Hils.

OMG! Poor Frances. Sue

OMG! What's going on? Akari.

There were several more in similar vein.

Christ, had everyone in Cannington been listening to that wretched program this morning? Kit tossed the phone back onto the desk, too tired to respond right now. What she really wanted to do was take Frances home and hold her in her arms until this whole nightmare went away.

CHAPTER THIRTY-SEVEN

Frances's whole body was shaking as the door slammed behind her. While she felt justified in her anger, she was also horrified by, and ashamed of, the outburst. She had sounded just like her father out there in the newsroom.

I am nothing like him. Nothing.

She sank into her chair and took a very slow, deep breath before reaching for the phone.

Her first call was to Richard Deacon, the CEO of MediaScope, the company that owned the *Clarion*. He needed to know about her public outing, so the company could prepare for any fallout that might occur.

"Thank you for giving us the heads up." Richard's deep, warm voice instantly soothed her rattled nerves. Her anger subsided, leaving her drained and exhausted. "I don't need to tell you that you have our full support," he went on. "We can postpone the launch date. Give you some breathing space."

"That's very thoughtful," Frances said. "But I don't think it will be necessary. Are you still willing to come down and officially launch the site next Monday?"

"Just try and keep me away," he chuckled, ending the call.

Next up was Veronica Waters. The human resources manager listened in silence as Frances related the events of the morning.

"Right then," she said, brisk and businesslike. "As I understand it, Mr. Peters was still under probation?"

"That's correct," Frances replied.

"And his sacking had nothing to do with his making a complaint against you?"

"Not at all. Although I believe it was the lack of success with that complaint that led to him going to Pastor Evans."

All Frances could hear was the clacking of a keyboard on the other end of the line. Finally, Veronica spoke again.

"Okay, so you were within your legal rights to fire Mr. Peters. Normally, you would be required to give him a week's notice. However, the legislation allows for a week's salary in lieu of that notice."

"It'll be worth it just to be rid of him," Frances muttered once the call ended. Her next job was to call a meeting of the editorial board. Within minutes, Susan, Clarrie, Nick, and Brendan, the paper's chief financial officer, all trooped in, each wheeling their office chairs. They arranged themselves awkwardly around her desk and waited for her to speak.

"As you have all no doubt heard, Simon Peters has been fired," she said. "I'm sorry that leaves you without a sports reporter, Clarrie." She gave him a rueful smile, but he shook his head.

"It's okay. I can cover it until we get a replacement." His voice was gruff and he had trouble meeting her eye. "I'm the one who should be sorry," he went on, bunching his fists on his thighs. "I was the one recommended him for the job."

"Don't beat yourself up about it," she said. "You weren't to know he'd turn out to be a homophobic little troublemaker. But we do need to deal with the trouble he has caused."

"If I can interrupt," Nick said, waving a sheaf of papers he had brought with him. "I think you need to look at these. They're the printouts of all the emails that have been pouring into the Letters inbox this morning. I'll just read them out, shall I?"

Yes, because what I need right now is a massive dose of homophobic vitriol, Frances thought. Out loud, all she said was, "Okay, let's hear it." She sat back in her chair, closed her eyes and braced herself.

"Okay then." Nick cleared his throat then began reading. "'What a shameful act. Pastor Evans should be ashamed of himself.' A bit repetitious, but heartfelt, I'd say," Nick said. Frances opened her eyes and looked at him. He gave her a wink and kept reading. "'Low act, man. It's 2024 ffs.' 'Oh noes, the lesbians are taking over!' Sarcastic, rolling eye emoji. 'Piss off, pastor.'" He stopped reading as everyone began giggling. Frances managed a weak smile as the apprehension at the imagined onslaught of abuse dissipated.

"They're all like that," he said, smiling. "This one's the best. 'If it takes a lesbian to turn the *Clarion* into a decent newspaper again, then I say, bring on the lesbians!' Here, see for yourself."

Frances snatched the pile of paper from him and skimmed through them. Nick was right. There were hundreds of messages and almost all of them were positive. It was an outpouring of support that was entirely unexpected.

"You're Mick's girl," Clarrie said softly. "Of course, people are going to rally around you."

He's not the hero you all think he is, she wanted to shout, but bit back the words. Now was not the time. For the first time in a very long time, she was grateful for her father's hero status.

"Right," she said after a few moments, her voice wobbly with the effort to not cry. "Take an entire page and print as many of these as you can. Negative as well as positive. You choose which ones, Nick. I want to avoid any accusations of bias." She shuffled the papers together and handed them back to Nick. "And the staff?" she said, back in control of her voice. "How are they taking it?"

"Most of them are outraged," Susan replied. "Not about you being a—a lesbian," she hastened to add. "They're furious that someone would try and blacken your name like that. Is it true, though, that you are…" Her voice trailed away and she flushed in evident embarrassment.

"A lesbian?" Frances finished for her. "Yes, it is." She gave a wry smile. "I guess I should thank the pastor for doing me a favour," she said. "He's saved me from having to constantly come out every time someone asks me if I'm married or where's my husband."

"No, but they might start asking if Kit Tresize is your girlfriend." Brendan spoke for the first time.

"Jesus, Brendan, what the fu—" Clarrie turned on him.

"No, it's okay," Frances interjected. "It's a fair comment. Especially after all the rumours that have been swirling around the past month. Those rumours were untrue, by the way."

"Wait a minute," Susan interrupted, a confused expression on her face. "Are you saying Kit is gay as well?"

"How did you not know that, Susan?" Brendan asked with a bemused smile.

"Well, how was I supposed to tell?" Susan said defensively. "It's not like she looks like…Oh, stop it!" She lapsed into a bewildered silence as Brendan and Clarrie laughed. Frances smothered her own grin at the woman's discomfort.

"So, was it you and Kit the pastor was referring to?" Brendan asked. "You know, when he talked about two women kissing in public."

"Believe it or not, Brendan"—Frances couldn't stop the note of irritation from creeping into her voice—"there are more than two lesbians in Cannington!" Her annoyance faded as Brendan gave her a sheepish look. "But yes, he was talking about Kit and me." She knew she would have to tell these people the full story if she wanted their support.

"Simon Peters saw us down at the foreshore. He made a complaint to HR about an inappropriate relationship. And when that didn't get the result he was looking for, we believe he tattled to his pastor."

Her words were greeted with silence as each person digested the information.

"So, you and Kit *are* in a relationship then?" Brendan asked.

"We're dating, yes," Frances replied. "While it's not a problem as far as HR is concerned, can any of you foresee it being a cause of concern among the rest of the staff?"

More silence as they all thought about it.

"Well," Nick began, giving Frances a hesitant look before continuing, "from the 'sucking up to the boss' comments I overheard when the rumours about the two of you first began, I'd say it would be Kit who would cop the most flak."

"Kit's a tough cookie," Clarrie growled. "She won't take any crap like that. There's always going to be one or two who will bitch about something like this, but as long as she's not getting any special treatment from you, most people just won't care."

CHAPTER THIRTY-EIGHT

As Frances watched her team file out, her eye fell on Kit's tablet sitting on the side of her desk. Despite Clarrie's words about her being able to handle any crap aimed at her, Frances wasn't so sure. She was still skittish about the idea of the two of them being an "us." How would she react upon discovering others now knew about their relationship?

Only one way to find out. She picked up the tablet and made her way across the newsroom to Kit's desk, ignoring the stares that followed her progress.

"Kit," she said quietly, holding out the tablet. "I figured you'd want this back."

"Oh, right. Yeah, thanks." Kit took the tablet from her and dumped it on top of a pile of reports. "You okay?" She gave Frances a searching look.

"Uh huh," France gave a quick nod, her eyes darting around the room. She smiled grimly to herself as everyone within earshot pretended to be engrossed in their work while straining to hear their conversation.

"Come walk with me," she said. "There's something I need to discuss with you." While she kept her tone neutral, Kit must have picked up on the urgency behind her words because she got to her feet without a word and followed her through the newsroom and outside.

"What's up?" she asked as soon as they reached the footpath.

"Not here." Frances shook her head and crossed the road into the Botanic Gardens, slowing as she reached a bench under a Moreton Bay fig tree. She sat down and waited for Kit to catch up and join her.

"Jesus, what a morning!" she said, wrapping her hand around Kit's and taking instant comfort from the contact. She quickly filled Kit in on the outcomes of her various phone calls and meetings. "So, I think the damage will be minimal," she said. "There's just one more thing." She paused to take a deep breath. "I had to tell the editorial board about us."

"What?" Kit tore her hand free and leapt to her feet. "So now everyone knows we're dating?" Her eyes flashed with fury as she stared down at Frances.

"Not everyone," Frances replied feebly. "Just Clarrie, Susan, Brendan, and Nick."

"Oh, well, that's all right then!" The sarcasm in Kit's voice was impossible to miss. "This is un-bloody-believable. We're barely together and now every bastard and their dog knows our business! Christ!" She clenched her fists and threw her arms in the air.

"Kit, please. Just come sit down." Frances had never seen her so angry and it frightened her.

"No, I won't bloody sit down!"

Frances flinched as Kit yelled at her and tears sprang to her eyes. She dashed them away. She wasn't going to cry. She wasn't.

"Oh, Frances." Kit fell to her knees in front of her and reached for her hand, all traces of anger gone. "God, what kind of monster am I? Yelling at you like it's all your fault."

"You're not a monster," Frances said, stroking her hair. "Well, no more of one than me, anyway."

"What do you mean?" Kit's head snapped up, a confused expression on her face.

"The way I shouted at Simon this morning—"

"That was entirely justified," Kit protested.

"Was it, though? The mature, professional thing to have done was to summon him to my office and fire him in private. How many people do you think were intimidated by my show of anger? I acted like a bully. I acted just like my father."

"You're being too hard on yourself," Kit said.

"Maybe."

And too hard on my father? The thought swam unbidden into her head and sat there, an uncomfortable presence in the back of her mind.

"Anyway," she said, squeezing Kit's hand resting in her lap. "I get why you're so angry. I do. It's horrible having our private lives laid bare like this, but if we give in to our rage about it, we'll just end up tearing ourselves apart. And who wins then?"

"You're right." Kit sighed, gazing into her eyes.

"Of course I'm right," Frances grinned as she stood and pulled Kit to her feet. She enveloped her in a tight hug. "We'll get through this," she murmured, burying her face in Kit's hair. "So long as we stick together, we can get through anything."

CHAPTER THIRTY-NINE

Kit had been beating herself up all afternoon. She felt like a heel for lashing out at Frances the way she had. Seeing the fear flickering in her eyes had brought her up sharp. She was appalled that she could be the sort of person to do that to someone else. Desperate to go for a run and clear her head, she was relieved when she was finally able to escape the office. She would have just enough time for a run and get home to shower and change before Frances arrived. They had agreed that tonight, of all nights, was not one to be spent alone.

Once home, she quickly changed into her running gear. Pulling the back door shut, she slipped the house key down her sock and let herself out through the back gate to the narrow, sandy track that wound up through the sand dunes toward the beach at Marnoo Cove. The scramble up and down the dunes was the perfect warm-up exercise and as soon as she reached the firm sand just above the tide mark, she began a steady jog toward the distant spit of land that marked the cove's westernmost point. The sun was still high in the sky, but beginning its descent, and it sent shards of light bouncing off the water beyond the breakers that surged and sucked at the sand just to Kit's left. She could already feel the run, the sea, the breeze working their magic. As she ran, her mind emptied of all thoughts, focussing only on the rhythm of her stride and her breath. Within minutes, there was nothing but the pounding of her feet, the rasp of her breath, and the sounds of the waves. Time itself seemed to disappear as she lost herself in the pure sensation of running.

She felt better about herself once she had returned home from the run. And her body felt better for the exercise. She hummed to herself as she showered, thinking about what she would cook for Frances when she arrived.

She got dressed in a pair of sweatpants and one of her favourite T-shirts. It had faded to a nondescript greyish-white colour, its sleeves had long been ripped off, and its inscription could no longer be read, but it was soft and loose and brought back fond memories of the trip to India where she had purchased it.

Scrolling through her playlist, she chose a Rachel D'Arcy album and hit Play. The singer's husky voice oozed from the sound system. Kit had come across her in the *Endeavour* television crime series, where she appeared as a nightclub singer. Intrigued by her voice, she had Googled her and bought her album.

She had just finished spooning food into Marvin's bowl when there was a knock at the door.

"You planning on staying a week?" she asked, eyeing the large carry-all in Frances's hand.

"Very funny," Frances said, planting a kiss on Kit's cheek as she came into her living room. "No, I've got a little surprise for later on. Not that sort of surprise," she said when Kit waggled her eyebrows at her. "Is there somewhere I can hang my suit?"

Kit pointed her toward her bedroom. "You should be able to find a hanger in the wardrobe," she said. "I'll be in the kitchen when you're done."

"That smells good." Frances came into the room and slipped her arms around Kit's waist, looking over her shoulder as she stirred the onion and checked a pot of pasta that was slowly coming to the boil. "Can I help?"

"Sure, can you chop up that bok choy?" She gestured with a wooden spoon toward a chopping board on which a bunch of the Asian greens sat. While Frances chopped, she drained the pasta and tipped it into the frypan, then stirred in some soy sauce.

"That bok choy ready yet?"

"Coming right up." Frances brought the board over to the stove. Kit took it from her and added the vegetable to the mix, giving it all a vigorous stir. Once the bok choy had wilted, she turned the heat off and spooned the food into two bowls.

"Take a seat," she said, gesturing to the little kitchen table pushed against a wall. She slid one of the bowls in front of Frances.

"My signature dish," she said, sitting opposite her. "Stir-fried bok choy pasta. Actually, it's my only dish. Well, that and pizza."

"Why aren't I surprised by that?" Frances grinned before taking several mouthfuls of the food. "Mmm, pretty good."

"Damned with faint praise," Kit murmured, smiling into her bowl.

Their mood was subdued and they ate the rest of the meal in silence. Despite making light of the day's events, Kit could see they had taken a toll on Frances. The spark had gone from her eyes and she looked pale and weary.

"Why don't you go through and relax?" she said, collecting their empty bowls. "I'll clean up in here and bring in some coffee."

"You sure? I can dry up, if you like," Frances said.

"It'll take me ten minutes," Kit replied. "Just go, sit down." She shooed her out of the kitchen and set to work washing up the dishes, saucepan and frypan, leaving them to air-dry on the draining board. It took her another ten minutes to make two macchiatos and when she carried them into the living room, Frances was sitting in the armchair, her head bent over a ukelele, concentrating on tuning the instrument's strings. She looked up as Kit slid one of the drinks across the coffee table to her.

"I thought I would play you 'Bali Hai.'" She smiled. "I've been learning it all week."

"That sounds like a real treat," Kit said, pointing the remote at the stereo and halting the music. She curled into a corner of the sofa and nursed her coffee as Frances bent her head over her ukelele once more and began playing. Kit listened, transfixed, as Frances sang in a low, husky voice, her eyes shining as she looked up at Kit.

"That was absolutely lovely," Kit said as the last notes faded away. "And such a sweet thing to do. I loved it."

"I'm glad," Frances said with a smile. "I was worried I was going to forget the words halfway through." She made to put the ukelele in its case, but Kit pleaded for another song.

"Go on, please," she implored when Frances hesitated. "Just one more."

"Okay. Anything to stop that soppy puppy-dog look on your face," Frances laughed. She closed her eyes for several moments, then began playing a more upbeat tune.

"Oh, I know this one," Kit said, her brow furrowing with the effort to name it. "Don't tell me. Don't tell me…Okay, tell me." She finally gave in.

"Heyyy, heyyy," Frances sang, quirking an eyebrow at Kit, whose face lit up with a grin as she recognised the opening line.

"Hey, soul sister!" she said, half singing along as Frances continued playing a few more stanzas of the song, before stopping with a final flourish.

"You really are very good," Kit said as Frances carefully placed the ukelele away and snapped the case closed.

"Thanks," Frances replied, reaching for her untouched coffee, and pulling a face when she discovered it was cold.

"Oh, I'll make you another one," Kit said, starting to rise from her seat, but Frances shook her head.

"Don't worry about it."

"In that case, why don't you come over here," Kit said, uncurling one leg and patting the space beside it. Frances crossed the room and wriggled her bottom in between Kit's thighs, stretching her legs out to their full length, dislodging Marvin from where he slept at the other end of the sofa. He gave her a baleful stare before springing to the floor and stalking out of the room.

"Oops, sorry, Marvin," she called after his disappearing tail as she snuggled back against Kit.

"Don't worry about him," Kit said, inhaling the apple-y scent of Frances's hair. "He'll get over it." She wrapped her arms around her, syncing her own breathing to the rise and fall of Frances's chest.

"I'm sorry this has been such a bloody awful day for you," she murmured, resting her chin on Frances's shoulder and slowly stroking one hand up and down her arm.

"Yeah," Frances sighed. "It was a shocker, all right. I can't help worrying what new disasters are in store for me."

"Nothing else is going to go wrong," Kit said, nuzzling her ear. "But if anything does happen, I got you, babe."

There was a beat of silence, and then Frances snorted.

"Did you really just say that?" she asked, twisting her head to look at Kit.

"Made you laugh, though, didn't it?" Kit smirked at her. "There hasn't been enough of that today."

"No, there hasn't," Frances agreed, brushing her lips softly against Kit's cheek. "Take me to bed."

CHAPTER FORTY

Kit didn't need to be asked twice. She led Frances into the bedroom and gently eased her clothing off before stripping out of her own clothes and tugging her down on to the bed. She cupped her breast in her hand and ran her thumb over the nipple. Frances groaned and reached for her, but she pushed her hand away.

"Just relax," she murmured, sliding one arm under Frances's shoulders and holding her close as she made love to her. Frances clung to her, gasping, as Kit brought her to orgasm, then broke out sobbing as she came.

"It's okay, it's okay," Kit whispered, holding Frances tight until her sobs subsided and she fell into an exhausted sleep. She lay awake for long hours and wondered what she had done to deserve the amazing, beautiful woman sleeping in her arms. Whatever it was, she vowed to herself to do everything possible to keep hold of her. The song Frances had played earlier may have just been a light-hearted attempt to lift the mood, but she really did feel that Frances was her soul mate. Was she in love with her? She hardly dared admit it to herself, but yes, she was. She hugged the thought to herself.

She must have eventually drifted off to sleep, but it felt like no time at all before she was awake again. She groaned and opened her eyes to find Frances watching her.

"You're so cute when you're asleep," Frances said, brushing the hair from Kit's face.

"As opposed to when I'm awake?" Kit growled, pulling Frances into a kiss. The sleep seemed to have done her the world of good. The tension had left her face and her eyes looked brighter.

"Umm, no. You're pretty cute awake as well," Frances said, tracing a finger along Kit's jawline. "I'd love to stay and enumerate all the ways in which you are exceedingly cute, but I'll be even later for work than I already am." She rolled away from Kit and out of the bed.

"Why? What time is it?" Kit asked, shamelessly ogling Frances's naked bum as she walked around the room collecting her discarded clothing.

"Eight thirty," Frances replied. "And I've got a meeting in an hour!"

"Right then, into the shower with you." Kit scrambled out of bed, crossed to the wardrobe where she retrieved a clean towel and tossed it to Frances. "I'll get the coffee on while you're getting ready."

"We would save a lot more time if we showered together." Frances gave her a suggestive smile.

"I doubt that very much," Kit replied, pulling on a T-shirt and following her out of the room. She heard the water in the shower start running as she programmed the coffee machine for an espresso. She had just poured two tiny cups when Frances came into the kitchen, towelling her hair dry.

"The house special," she said, handing over one of the cups.

"Oh, what's in it?" Frances asked, inhaling its aroma and taking a sip. "It smells divine."

"My secret ingredient," Kit replied. "Cardamom. Its spiciness really complements the coffee flavour, don't you think?"

"I do." Frances nodded. "I love it." She gulped down the rest of the drink. "I'd love to stay for another, but duty calls." She stood and wrapped Kit in a hug. "I'm sorry about last night," she said.

"There's nothing to be sorry for," Kit said, peering up into her face. "We need to stop apologising to each other, don't you think?"

Frances gazed at her for a long minute, then nodded. "You're right. Okay, I really must go. See you there?" She kissed Kit, then let her go and hurried out the door, carry-all bag in one hand and ukelele case in the other.

Kit watched her drive away, a pang in her heart. She would have loved to spend the whole day with Frances, taken some time to properly restore their battered spirits. They could have gone to Port Haven together, enjoyed a day by the ocean. But no, they had to go to work. She wouldn't even get to see her this evening as it was squash night. She was tempted to cancel, but that wouldn't be fair to Hilary. She was not going to be one of those people who ditched their friends when they started a new romance. Besides, Hilary was agog to hear all the latest after yesterday's fiasco.

She finished her coffee and went to have her own shower. Fifteen minutes later, she was on her way to work. She would arrive late, which would no doubt earn her another reprimand from Clarrie, but she didn't care. She had bigger things on her plate, right now. Like dealing with people knowing she was dating Frances. Yes, Frances had assured her only a handful of people knew, but it was inevitable that word was going to spread through the office.

"Late again, Tresize," Clarrie growled at her when she arrived at her desk. Then, instead of the expected lecture about better time management, he surprised her by wheeling his chair over to her and giving her a shrewd look.

"Everything okay?" he asked, concern clouding his eyes.

"Yep." She nodded, busying herself with booting up her computer. Never one to share her thoughts or feelings with her colleagues, she wasn't about to start now.

"Frances told me about the situation between the two of you," he went on. "Well, me and the rest of the editorial board."

She stared at him, wondering where he was going with this.

"Well, the thing is…" He cleared his throat. "The thing is you've got our support. My support. So, if anyone gives you grief about it, you just send them to me, okay?"

"Okay." She nodded again, flashing him a smile. "Thanks, Clarrie. That really means a lot. I really appreciate it."

"Right then," he said, pushing himself to his feet. "Try to get to work on time from now on, will ya?" He stomped away, dragging his chair behind him.

She was touched by Clarrie's words and his support. He was pretty old-school and talking about her sexuality was probably right out of his comfort zone, so it meant a lot to her that he had come out batting for her.

She settled down to working through her email inbox, shooting off quick responses where she could and flagging other emails for further attention. Once she had completed that daily ritual, she turned to prioritising the jobs that she needed to work on.

Try not to upset the town's homophobes, she jokingly listed as the day's top priority before jotting down a depressingly long list of the tasks that needed her attention.

The most urgent was to finish and file the article on council's plans to redevelop the brownfields site out at the old woollen mill. She wrote nonstop for an hour about the plans to turn the mill building into a cinema, event space, and dining precinct while its surrounding grounds would be rehabilitated into parkland and community vegetable gardens. She gave the article one final readthrough, then filed it for Clarrie's sign-off.

She was just doing some shoulder and back stretches when her phone buzzed with an incoming text message. She squinted at the screen. Frances.

How you going?

Good, she typed back. *How was your meeting?*

Ugh. Tell you about it later. Wish you didn't have squash tonight.

Me too. Tomorrow feels like forever away.

"I hope that's a contact at council you're chatting away to there," Clarrie growled as he stumped past Kit's desk on the way to his own. Guiltily, Kit put her phone down, waiting until the coast was clear to pick it up again.

Busted by the boss. Gotta go do some work.

She dropped the phone into a drawer and turned her attention back to her computer.

CHAPTER FORTY-ONE

Frances smiled as she put her phone down. The little text exchange with Kit had made her feel like a teenager, passing messages back and forth behind the teacher's back. Not that she had actually done that as a teenager. Too much of a goody-two-shoes for that. But she could totally imagine Kit doing it and then looking all innocent when caught red-handed.

"Who, me, sir?" She could hear her saying. "No, sir. I found it on the floor and thought Isobel had dropped it, sir."

The imaginary scenario gave her a much-needed laugh. That meeting Kit had asked about, on the other hand, was no laughing matter. She had spent over an hour with George Evans, the CEO of Serendip Dairy Corporation, trying to convince him to not pull his company's advertising from the *Clarion*.

"We're concerned about any backlash this company may suffer as a result of its association with your newspaper," George had explained.

"Which I could absolutely understand," she had responded, "if my newspaper was publishing a viewpoint that ran contrary to Serendip's ethos. But it's not, is it?"

"Er, no, but some of our customers may object to us advertising in a newspaper run by a, a…a gay lady," he said, his face bright red.

"But you're not that small-minded, are you, George?" She made an appeal to his vanity and it seemed to work as he squared his shoulders and straightened his back.

"Indeed not, Ms. Keating," he had rumbled. "Very well. We shall continue with our current advertising arrangement, but one whiff…" He held up a finger in warning. "Just one whiff of scandal and we will have no hesitation in withdrawing our support."

"Can't ask for fairer than that," she had said, getting to her feet and shaking his hand.

She had sent a fervent prayer up to whatever deities there might be that none of the *Clarion*'s other advertisers were getting cold feet as well. The last thing she needed with less than a week to go until the launch of the digital paper was a drastic drop in advertising revenue to send jitters through the MediaScope board members.

The rumbling of her stomach as she drove back to the newspaper had reminded her she had had nothing to eat or drink since that espresso at Kit's earlier this morning. She'd decided a souvlaki at Theo's would be just the ticket. It had been while she was eating there that she had texted Kit. The lift in mood their short chat had given her was just what she needed to face her next ordeal—an on-air interview with talk radio host Josh James. The station had rung wanting to know her reaction to the pastor's comments and she had reluctantly agreed to a one-on-one interview. Besides, it would give her an opportunity to promote the digital version of the *Clarion*.

The radio station was situated on a slight rise out on the eastern edge of town. The building was painted in the station logo's background colour of burnt orange, with the station name rendered in maroon and white across its frontage. Frances pulled in to a parking space in front of the entrance at the side of the building. Pushing open the heavy glass doors, she stepped into a reception area adorned with music-related posters and framed records.

166   Lesley Dimmock

"Hi, I'm Frances Keating," she said to the young woman at the reception desk. "I'm here for my interview with Josh James."

The woman clacked at her keyboard for several moments, then nodded. Picking up a handset, she spoke into it in a barely audible murmur, then hung up.

"Rachel will be with you shortly," she said. "Please take a seat."

She had barely sat down when a middle-aged woman, her greying hair upswept into an untidy bun and wearing a brightly coloured floral dress and Doc Martens boots approached her.

"Frances, lovely to meet you," she said, extending a hand in greeting. Frances struggled up out of the sofa, which seemed intent on swallowing her, and shook it.

"If you'll just come with me, I'll get you set up." Rachel's manner was friendly, but businesslike. Frances just gave a nod and followed her through a door and into the inner workings of the station. She had never been in a radio station before and took in her surroundings with a genuine curiosity. Several doors with unilluminated red lights above them lined one side of the narrow corridor they were walking down, while more music paraphernalia decorated the other wall.

"Studios," Rachel said, waving a hand at each door as they passed. "We rarely have more than one in use at a time." She paused outside the last door and peered through its thick glass window. An "On Air" sign glowed redly overhead. Putting a finger to her lips, Rachel carefully opened the door and gestured Frances to follow her in and to sit in a large executive-style office chair that was squeezed into one side of an enormous desk covered in a bewildering array of knobs and buttons. Rachel fitted a bulky pair of headphones over her ears and checked that the big, fuzzy microphone was at the right height for her, gave her a thumbs-up, and silently left the room.

A balding, heavily bearded man sat on the opposite side of the console, wearing his own pair of out-sized headphones. He gave her a brief smile while continuing to talk into another microphone for several moments, before sliding a knob along a track and removing his headphones, signalling for Frances to do the same. Standing, he stretched a hand across the console.

"Josh," he introduced himself, as she shook his hand. "We'll be back on air just as soon as these ads finish. First time on radio?"

"Just relax and lean in to the mike to speak," he said when she nodded. "Okay? Ready to go?" He sat back down and fiddled with some buttons.

"Good morning. You're listening to Josh James on Radio CA 973 and today we have a special guest, the *Clarion*'s new chief editor, Ms. Frances Keating. Many of you may recognise that name because, of course, Ms. Keating is the youngest daughter of local footballing legend, Mick Keating. So, how does it feel, Ms. Keating to return to your childhood town?"

Frances adjusted the bulky headphones over her ears and leaned in to the microphone. "Frances, please," she said. "To be honest, it felt a bit strange at first. I've been away for so long, but I've always loved Cannington and it is great to be back."

"And to come back to take on the same job as your father. That must make you proud, to be following in his footsteps like that."

"Well, it's been a long time since my dad was the editor here, so I'm not exactly following in his footsteps, but I am proud, and honoured, to be entrusted with running the *Clarion*."

"Which brings us neatly to Monday's events. It seems not everyone approves of you being the editor."

"Look, there's always going to be people who don't approve of my sexuality. Unfortunately, it goes with the territory. But I didn't expect to be publicly outed like that."

"Don't you think people have a right to know?"

"Why? What does my sexuality have to do with my ability to do my job?"

"Well, why don't we open up our lines and ask the listeners?" Josh said.

"Wait, what?" Frances stared at him in shock. "That's not what I agreed to!"

"You *are* on talk radio, Frances," Josh replied, his tone unapologetic. "Hello, listener. What do you have to say? Should a person's sexual choice be public knowledge?"

"Is yours?" Frances could have sworn the speaker sounded just like Kit's friend Natasha. "And it's not a choice," she went on. "When did you choose to be straight, hey?"

"Er, thank you for your call." Josh stabbed at a button to end the call. "Who do we have on the line now?"

"Absolutely we need to know," the male caller said, declining to identify himself. "How else are we to stop them spreading their agenda?"

Frances leaned in to her microphone to respond, but Josh had disabled it. She glared at him in mute fury as he took the next call.

"Hello, Josh. It's Beverley here. I'm a big fan of your show." The thin and reedy voice suggested an elderly woman.

"Why, thank you, Bev—" Josh began to preen but was cut off.

"But what you're doing here is almost as mean as what that horrible pastor did." There was an audible click as she rang off.

The next caller identified himself as John, a potato farmer.

"Personally, I want to know that the bloke I'm sitting next to at the pub isn't going to make a pass at me," he said. "But I don't reckon a person being queer means they're not going to be good at their job."

"Old Mick would be turning in his grave, his girl bringing shame to his name like this." Another unidentified caller.

How dare he? Frances wanted to shout at him. Instead, all she could do was clench her fists and glare at Josh James as he took another call.

"Hello, my name is Radcliffe Hall," said the next speaker. "And I definitely think we all need to know people's sexual orientation."

"Okay, do you have a particular reason for thinking that, Radcliffe?" Josh asked, while Frances did her best to smother the giggles that threatened to erupt.

"Well, how else am I going to find all the lesbians in this town and stop being so lonely?" 'Radcliffe' said, hanging up with a howl of laughter.

Deadline to Love   169

"We're just going to take a short break," a visibly rattled Josh said, cueing up a music track. Frances tugged off her headphones and got to her feet.

"We're done here," she said, turning her back on the programme host and stalking out of the studio.

"I am so sorry." Rachel rushed to her side as soon as she emerged. "I had no idea he was going to do that."

"Well, it seems to have backfired on him." Frances gave her a grim smile. "Looks like Cannington is a bit more progressive than he gives it credit for, doesn't it?"

She left the building without another word. Once she had reached the privacy of her car, she slid into the driver's seat and pummelled the steering wheel with both fists.

"Arrggghhh!" she yelled, releasing the anger that boiled through her veins at this latest ambush. Gripping the top of the steering wheel, she leaned her head on her forearms and closed her eyes. God, what other nasty little surprises lay in wait? She was beginning to regret taking on this job. Sure, she had known she'd be under intense scrutiny. She was a Keating, after all. But she didn't expect to feel so exposed, or, despite the gratifying level of community support, so alone. Well, okay. Not totally alone, she amended as Kit's face swam into her mind's eye. Knowing she had Kit on her side was just about the only thing keeping her going at the moment.

Her phone began ringing and she scrabbled in her bag to find and answer it. It was Kit. Did she have some sort of telepathic ability to know when she was thinking about her?

"Hey," Kit said. "I just heard about that dumpster fire of an interview. Are you okay?"

"I am now. Although, I swear, one more person comes at me with how wonderful my dad was, I'm really going to let them have it!" she replied, as a tear trickled from her eye. God, she never used to be this teary. What was making her feel so vulnerable now? The job? Or the fact that she was falling in love with Kit?

"Are you sure?" Kit asked, her voice filled with concern as Frances sniffled despite herself. "Do you want me to come over tonight?"

"I'd love you to, but don't you have squash?" She wiped away another errant tear.

"That's really why I was calling," Kit said. "Natasha rang Hilary and told her about the interview, so Hilary rang me. Told me the game was cancelled as you needed me more than she needed another chance to beat me."

Frances gave a hiccuppy little laugh. So, it *had* been Natasha on the radio. "Your friends are the best,' she said, her voice shaky as tears threatened again.

CHAPTER FORTY-TWO

Frances had got herself back under control by the time she arrived at the *Clarion* office. She checked the rearview mirror in the Mini and grimaced at her reflection. She had had a good cry once her call with Kit had ended. It had been cathartic and she felt better for it, but her eyes were still a little red and puffy. Nothing she could do about it now. Not that anyone noticed. They were all, weirdly, keeping their heads down, making no acknowledgement of her presence as she walked through the newsroom to her office.

"Oh!" A massive bouquet of flowers sat on her desk. It was easily the biggest bunch of flowers she had ever seen and must have cost its sender a fortune. She moved closer to read the message on the attached card.

From all of us, it simply said. She turned around to find the entire staff crowded around her door.

"Oh!" she said again and burst into tears. Again.

"Okay, everyone, give the poor woman some privacy," Enid said as she squeezed through the crowd and gave Frances's arm several soothing pats. As people began to disperse, she made her sit in the armchair and passed her the box of tissues that sat on a bookshelf.

"Can I get you anything, dear?" she asked once Frances had composed herself. Balling the used tissue in her fist, Frances gave her a wan smile.

"I suppose a stiff drink is out of the question?"

"I could send someone out to buy a bottle," Enid replied, an uncertain frown on her face. "Your father would have had one stashed away in his bottom drawer for moments like this."

"What, he was prone to bursting into tears as well?" Frances teased.

"No, silly! His emergency supply, he called it," Enid said. "Although, if you don't mind my saying…" Her voice dropped to a conspiratorial whisper. "He did seem to have an awful lot of emergencies."

"I don't think it's any secret that Dad liked his drink," Frances said, which was an understatement if ever there was one. "Anyway, no, I don't really need anything to drink. This"— she waved at the bouquet—"was a very kind thing to do. I'm really touched."

"You've had a horrid few days," Enid said. "We all just wanted to show our support. Would you like me to arrange it into some vases?"

"That would be great." Frances nodded, getting to her feet and moving to her desk. "And put them around the newsroom, so everyone can enjoy them."

Enid left the office, almost dwarfed by the flowers as she carried them away. No sooner had she gone than Kit materialised in the doorway.

"I suppose that was your doing?" Frances smiled up at her.

Kit shook her head. "Nothing to do with me," she said, leaning against the jamb with her hands in her trouser pockets.

"Do you have any idea how bloody sexy you look right now?" Frances said in a soft voice made husky with sudden desire.

"Glad to see you're feeling a bit better," Kit said with an amused smile. "I'd best be getting back to work," she went on,

Deadline to Love   173

straightening up. "You want me to bring anything with me tonight?"

"Just your pyjamas," she replied.

"I don't wear jammies."

"I know." Frances smirked at her.

Frances buried herself in work for the rest of the afternoon. Much of it involved the arrangements for next Monday's launch of the digital newspaper. She had been taken aback by a phone call from head office letting her know that the entire board of management as well as the CEO were now going to attend. While she appreciated the show of support their presence would signify, it meant she now had six more people to consider in the arrangements.

Nick Davies had sent an email out earlier in the week urging content creators to redouble their efforts to submit articles for the various sections of the news site and those articles had been pouring into her inbox for approval. By the time she had ploughed through a dozen stories covering topics as diverse as the role of AI in journalism, wild swimming, and a biographical sketch of a little-known local glassblowing artist, she was feeling more like her usual cheerful self.

A chorus of "Goodbyes" and "Nights" followed her through the newsroom as she left, which buoyed her even more. It felt like they were all one team now. She crossed her fingers and hoped it was a lasting thing and not born out of momentary sympathy for her public humiliation of the past few days.

When she arrived home, Kit was sitting on the front step, waiting for her. She had changed out of her work attire and was now wearing a pair of burgundy-coloured jeans with a matching waistcoat over a grey T-shirt. Her hair had been loosely pulled back into a low ponytail. God, Frances thought to herself, how does she manage to look so hot all the damn time?

"Get your glad rags on," Kit said, getting to her feet and dusting off the seat of her pants as Frances approached. "We're meeting the gang at the Zodiac Bar."

"The gang?" Frances echoed as she let them both into the house.

"Yeah. Hilary, Natasha, and whoever else they can rustle up." Kit followed her into the bedroom. "Hils decided we needed company rather than moping around by ourselves here."

"Moping around wasn't exactly what I had in mind," Frances said as she shrugged out of her jacket.

"Ha ha," Kit replied with a grin, sitting on the bed, and watching while Frances undressed. "She threatened to bring everyone around here if we don't go out. We're partying one way or another, it seems."

"Fine," Frances sighed, rummaging through her wardrobe for something suitable. "Will this do?" She held up a button-down shirt with a paisley pattern in pastel tones of pink and mauve. "And blue jeans? Dressy enough?"

"Yup." Kit nodded. Frances quickly got changed and dragged a comb through her hair. She tugged on her dark-brown RM Williams boots and declared herself ready.

"Very nice," Kit murmured, standing and pulling her in close. She cupped her hand around the back of Frances's head and kissed her. Frances gave a small moan as the kiss deepened and she wrapped her arms tightly around Kit, before breaking away.

"Are you sure we can't just mope around here?" she said, her ragged breathing making her voice hoarse.

CHAPTER FORTY-THREE

The Uber dropped them off at the entrance to the laneway that led to the Zodiac Bar. Kit slid her hand into Frances's and led the way down the ill-lit lane to a doorway illuminated with flashing coloured fairy lights. Each letter of the word "zodiac" in the sign above the door was picked out in stars joined together with lines to look like a constellation.

"I had no idea this place was even here," Frances said as Kit pushed open the door and they stepped into a small foyer.

"I think it only opened a couple of years ago," she said, holding open the inner door for Frances to walk through. "It's become *the* place for the local gay and lesbian community to hang out."

They stood inside the dimly lit space, waiting for their eyes to adjust. About thirty people milled around in various clumps and clusters. Kit peered through the gloom, looking for her friends.

"There they are." She nodded toward the back of the room. Grabbing Frances's hand again, she wove through the room to where Hilary sat with Natasha, Akari, Ashley, and Sue in several sofas arranged around a long, low table.

"God, we were all horrified by what's happened this week," Sue said as Kit and Frances sank into the sofa next to her. The other four women, squashed into the other sofa opposite them, all nodded and shot Frances sympathetic looks.

"Thanks," she said. "It's been tough, all right, but I've really appreciated the support I've been getting." She smiled at Natasha.

"Mate," Natasha said, flashing her a grin. "We all got to stick together and stick up for each other, hey? Now, enough of all that." She clapped her hands. "Let's get this party started! Who's having what?"

"I'll give you a hand," Frances said, getting to her feet and accompanying Natasha to the bar once the drink orders had been sorted. Kit followed their progress with her eyes, then flushed when she caught the rest of her friends smirking at her.

"You've really got it bad." Hilary sniggered. "You can't take your eyes off her for one second!"

"Can't blame her. Frances is hot," Ashley said. "Well, she is!" she insisted when Akari gave her a look.

"So, are you in lurrrve?" Hilary made goo-goo eyes at Kit. "Or is it just a bad case of lust? Please tell me you're at least doing the nasty together?"

"Oh my god!" Kit's face grew hot with embarrassment. "You are the worst friend ever." She picked up a cushion and flung it at Hilary, who caught it and fell back laughing.

"What's so funny?" Frances asked, as she and Natasha returned to the table bearing trays of drinks.

"Just Hilary being her usual obnoxious self," Kit growled, helping to distribute the various cocktails around the table. She slurped half of her Scorpio in one go, coughing as the chili-infused gin hit the back of her throat.

"Everything okay?" Frances gave her a concerned look.

"Yep," she managed to croak once she had caught her breath. "Come and dance with me." She tugged Frances to her feet as "Good Feeling" began playing, leading her to the tiny dance floor where four other couples were shuffling around to the music. She wasn't usually keen on dancing in public, especially with so few others on the dance floor, but tonight she just wanted to hold Frances close and dancing together was the perfect excuse.

"Are you sure you're okay?" Frances peered at her. "We can go home if you prefer."

"No, I'm fine. Really. You know they're all watching us, don't you?" she said. She could see them over Frances's shoulder each time they circled in that direction. All grinning and nudging each other with their elbows.

"They're just happy for you," Frances murmured. "Natasha said as much when we were at the bar. Happy for us."

The music changed as she finished speaking and her eyes lit up as the unmistakable sound of a ukelele began. Kit laughed as she recognised the opening bars of "Hey, Soul Sister." She spun Frances around in a twirl and had just caught her in her arms when they were surrounded by her friends, who all whooped and bounced around them, waving their arms in the air.

It was almost midnight by the time the seven women staggered out of the bar, giddy and breathless from hours of dancing. Kit had had one too many Scorpios and was feeling a little the worse for wear. Frances didn't look much better. Her eyes were slightly glassy and her usually sleek hair was mussed and sticking out at odd angles. Kit's own hair had come free from its elastic band long ago and now tumbled in unruly waves around her face.

"I haven't had that much fun in ages," she said once they had hugged the others good night and watched them noisily clamber into their respective Ubers.

"Heaps better than moping around at home," Frances agreed, her eyes twinkling as she pulled out her phone to check the progress of their own Uber.

"Hmm, bit of a toss-up, that one," Kit said. "I enjoyed dancing with you, though. You've got some really sexy moves."

178   Lesley Dimmock

A car horn beeped and a car pulled into the kerb, its driver leaning across the passenger seat and calling out Frances's name.

"God, I'm going to have such a hangover tomorrow," Kit groaned, leaning her head against the seatback and closing her eyes as the car took off. She hadn't planned on drinking so much, but when the bar manager discovered who Frances was, she had insisted on shouting their whole group several rounds of the cocktails of their choice. All that dancing had made her thirsty too, and she had unthinkingly downed every drink placed before her.

"I've got the perfect cure," Frances said, running a finger up and down Kit's thigh. She cracked open an eyelid and turned a bleary eye on her.

"I don't know that I've got the energy for that sort of a cure," she said.

"That's not what I had in mind," Frances laughed. "I was thinking more along the lines of an omelette and lots of buttery toast. Apparently, it's just the thing for a hangover. That and loads of water."

"Oh god, I don't think I could face the idea of food right now." Kit groaned again.

"How come you're so perky, anyway?" she asked fifteen minutes later as she slumped at the table in Frances's kitchen and watched her whipping up two omelettes.

"Second wind and a super-efficient metabolism," Frances replied, sliding an omelette onto a plate and pushing it across to her. "Eat."

Kit did as she was told, surprised to find herself wolfing down the food. She polished off the omelette and four slices of toast, while Frances looked on approvingly.

"Now, drink." She shoved a litre bottle filled with water at her. Kit tried to protest that she was too full and that she would be up for the rest of the night peeing, but it was a waste of effort. She dutifully downed the water, banging the empty bottle down on the table with a loud bang.

"Satisfied?"

"Yep." Frances nodded, slid off her stool and propelled Kit toward the bedroom. "Now you can sleep."

Kit's last thought before she fell into a dreamless sleep was that she would never get any sleep with the way her stomach felt full to bursting.

CHAPTER FORTY-FOUR

The launch date of the digital *Clarion* was mere days away and there did not seem enough hours in the day to get everything done that needed doing. The office hummed with a barely suppressed panic as everyone worked frenetically to not only create content for the website and get it uploaded, but also to ensure that the print edition went out each day.

Kit barely saw Frances, who was under more pressure than any of them, for the entire rest of the week. She had caught glimpses of her, looking harried as she rushed around the office urging staff to find that extra effort. The rest of the time, she had been locked away in her office, the telephone glued to her ear, no doubt in constant contact with head office, ensuring everything would run smoothly on the day.

By Sunday evening, when she had arrived at Kit's cottage, she had looked exhausted.

"Nothing a good night's sleep won't fix," she said, giving Kit a tired smile before slumping onto the sofa next to Marvin and kicking off her shoes.

"Can I get you anything?" Kit asked, hovering over her.

"One of those little espressos you make would be lovely," Frances replied.

Kit nodded and headed to the kitchen. She took a jar of green cardamom pods down from a shelf and shook four pods into her hand. Splitting them open, she tipped the seeds into her mortar and ground them before mixing them into a measure of ground coffee beans. She poured the cardamom and coffee mixture into the portafilter on her machine. Within minutes she had two cups of aromatic coffee. She carried them into the living room, only to find Frances sound asleep on the sofa.

"Oh, well. More for me," she murmured, settling herself into the armchair with a copy of the latest Val McDermid mystery. By ten o'clock, she was ready for bed. Frances had not stirred in all that time, and while Kit was loath to disturb her, she knew she would be more comfortable in bed.

"Wake up, sweetheart," she said softly, giving Frances a gentle shake. Her eyes fluttered open and she looked momentarily confused as she sat up.

"Come to bed," Kit said, holding a hand out to help Frances up. "It's getting late and you've got a big day tomorrow."

"Geez, have I been asleep all that time?" Frances groaned, glancing at her watch, as she followed Kit into the bedroom. "Some company I am. You should have woken me."

"You obviously needed the sleep," Kit replied, undressing and climbing into bed. "Besides, it was kind of fun watching you sleep and listening to you snore."

"Oh my god, I didn't snore, did I?" Frances gave her a horrified look as she slid into the bed beside her.

"Only a little, I promise," Kit replied. She turned off the bedside light, leaving the room faintly illuminated by moonlight. Turning back to Frances, she cuddled into her back, spooning her. She felt Frances's breath slow and deepen as she fell back to sleep. Kit cursed the two espressos she had drunk earlier as sleep refused to come to her for hours, only to wake in the middle of the night when she felt Frances shift and get out of the bed.

"Wassup?" Kit said groggily as she half sat up and blinked sleepily at Frances's shadowy figure as it moved around the room.

"Go back to sleep," Frances whispered. "I've been laying here awake for ages, my mind going a hundred miles an hour. I'm better off going home."

"Don't be silly," Kit replied, sitting up straighter, snapping on the bedside light and tugging Frances down onto the bed beside her. "Do you really think you'll get any more sleep at home?"

"At least I won't be keeping you awake as well," Frances said, stroking the side of Kit's face. Kit grabbed her hand and planted a kiss on its palm.

"That's sweet of you," she said, "but I hate the idea of you tossing and turning alone. Come back to bed."

It took a bit more persuading, but she eventually coaxed Frances back into bed and wrapped her arms around her again. This time she had no trouble falling asleep only to be woken in what felt like just a few minutes later by the alarm. Frances groaned as Kit groped for her phone and fumbled to shut off its insistent beeping.

"Come on." Kit gently chivvied Frances out of the bed. "Today's your big day. You don't want to miss any of it now, do you?"

Frances grumbled about "slave-driver girlfriends" as she threw off the duvet and stomped into the bathroom. Kit used the time while she was showering and dressing to brew some coffee, handing her a cup when she eventually reemerged from the bedroom.

"How do I look?" Frances asked, sipping at the drink and taking a bite of the toast Kit had also prepared for her. Kit ran an appraising eye over Frances's outfit, beige linen slacks and a matching jacket over a cream-coloured business shirt. Her feet were shod in her RM Williams boots, polished to within an inch of their life.

"Great," Kit replied. "Just like a successful editor. Now, go impress the management." She gave Frances a fleeting kiss and gently propelled her out the door. "I'll see you in an hour."

Kit watched from the doorway as Frances clambered into her Mini and drove away. Turning back indoors, she busied herself tidying up the kitchen before readying herself for work. Her stomach fizzed with nerves about the launch. She could only imagine how Frances felt.

When she arrived at the office, the place was in an uproar with people running madly about, shouting to one another as they worked feverishly to have everything ready in time for the ten o'clock launch. If she hadn't had a pile of work to do herself, she would have turned tail and run from the chaos. Instead, she steeled herself and ploughed into the fray, hoping she would at least reach her desk before someone spotted her and corralled her into helping out with their crisis. She had almost made it when Enid spied her as she hurried past, her arms filled with a massive bouquet of flowers.

"Ah, Kit dear," she said, thrusting the flowers at Kit. "Can you find vases for these and arrange them along the tables in the staffroom?"

"I. Er. But…" Kit tried to protest, but it was too late, Enid had already rushed off. Sighing, Kit managed to shrug off her satchel and dump it at her desk before heading into the staffroom. Someone had transformed the space into an elegant buffet from its usual utilitarian appearance of tables and chairs shoved into groups arranged haphazardly around the room. Long tables ran down either side of the room. One, covered with deep-blue tablecloths, was laden with glasses, cups and saucers, the coffee machine, and an urn. The other table had been turned into a giant antipasto board, with various cold meats, cheeses, olives, dried fruits, crackers, and breads artfully arranged on a long sheet of brown paper. Kit whistled in admiration as she dropped the flowers onto the kitchen counter and walked over for a closer examination.

"It's pretty cool, isn't it?" Caitlyn Brooks came into the room and wandered over to join Kit.

"Whoever came up with it is a genius," Kit replied, nodding. "And I'm so going to steal the idea!"

"I think it was Siena. You know, from the digital team?"

184   Lesley Dimmock

"Geez, how'd she even have the room in her head to think of this on top of trying to get the website up and running?" Kit wondered, shaking her head as she turned her attention back to locating some vases.

"You don't know where Enid hides the vases, do you?" she eventually asked Caitlyn after a fruitless search through all the kitchen cupboards.

"Oh, they're kept in the boardroom," Caitlyn replied brightly. "Want me to go and get some?"

"Would you?" Kit said in relief. This chore was already taking up too much of her time. "I don't suppose you want to take over here? Finish the job for me?"

"Sure, no probs." Caitlyn flashed Kit a smile as she breezed out of the room. Kit quickly followed her out, just in case she changed her mind, and hurried back to her desk. She had just enough time to finish one last article and get it to the digital team for uploading to the Opinion Page of the new website before all the speeches and ceremonies for the launch began.

She was doing a final proofread of the article when she was distracted by the sight of Frances bolting out of her office at a rapid walk, smoothing her jacket down as she hurried toward reception. The CEO and board must have arrived. A couple of minutes later, Kit's inbox pinged with a message summoning all employees to the staffroom. She sent her article off before making her way back to the room, into which all twenty-five *Clarion* employees were now jammed and trying not to crowd the table at which Frances was seated, flanked by several of the board members, while the rest stood self-consciously behind them. The tension in Frances's face betrayed the nerves she was feeling, and she appeared to be only half listening to what the man to her left was saying, nodding distractedly while her eyes skittered around the room. Kit winked as their eyes met, and she could see Frances visibly relax as her lips twitched in a tiny smile back.

At a signal from Enid at the back of the room that indicated everyone was present, Frances got to her feet. The movement instantly riveted all attention on her and the room fell silent.

"Right. Well, I'm not one for big speeches," she said, smiling around at the sea of faces gazing at her. "I just want to say thank you to each and every one of you for pulling out all stops to get this project off the ground. It took a massive effort, given the short timeline, and I'm immensely proud of you all for what's been achieved." She waited out their applause. "I'd now like to introduce the CEO of MediaScope, Richard Deacon, who gets to do the fun bit of launching the site." She sat back down to another smattering of applause as the silver-haired man sitting to her left got to his feet.

"Thank you, Frances," he said in a mellow baritone as he beamed at his audience. "Today is a really exciting day as we see the vision that Frances brought to us come to fruition." He paused as surprised murmurs rippled around the room. Kit was as taken aback as anyone to hear that the whole digital project had been Frances's idea. Asking why she'd kept that to herself and let everyone assume she'd got the job because of the Keating name was something Kit swore to take up with her once they were alone together.

"So, without further ado," Deacon resumed as he picked up a tablet whose screen was mirrored on the staffroom's large TV screen. "It gives me enormous pleasure to declare the digital *Clarion* launched!" He stabbed a stubby finger at the tablet's screen. There was a moment's silence while the site spun its wheels before displaying as live and published. A cheer went up amid enthusiastic applause.

"And now, please stay and enjoy this fantastic-looking spread," he said before turning to Frances and pumping her hand.

"Well done, Frances, well done!" He beamed as the rest of the board crowded around to add their own congratulations.

"Thanks, thank you," Frances murmured, as one by one they shook her hand before drifting off to find a drink.

"Here, you look like you could do with one of these." Kit put a glass of champagne into her hand and tapped it with her own glass. "Cheers and congratulations. You pulled it off."

"*We* pulled it off," Frances corrected her. "All of us." She glanced around at the crowd, now all laughing, smiling, and relaxing in the glow of the success of the launch.

"We've got a good team here," Frances murmured as she sipped at her drink.

"And don't you forget it!" Kit replied, her eyes shining with merriment. "Especially that star reporter who's been churning out all those brilliant articles. See, look at that." She turned Frances about to face the big screen where the "likes" on an article Kit had written about the ecological wonders of a local swamp were clicking over at a steady rate.

"See, everyone loves my work," she laughed.

"What's not to love," Frances murmured. "About your work. Or you."

Kit's eyes widened in shock. *Did Frances really just say she loved me?* For an interminable length of time, she stared at Frances, not sure how to respond.

"Ditto," she said eventually, a slow smile of delight spreading across her face.

CHAPTER FORTY-FIVE

All Frances wanted to do was pull Kit to her and give her the biggest, deepest, most passionate kiss imaginable. Her mouth twitched in amusement as she pictured the reactions of those in the room if she did that. There'd probably be more than a few scandalised faces, several inevitable blokey "Phwoars," a lot of nervous tittering at the sight of the boss locking lips with a woman, and possibly a few cheers, but Frances wasn't keen to find out. Not right now. It was one thing to have everyone know she was a lesbian. Quite another to so publicly declare she and Kit were in a relationship.

Instead, she surreptitiously brushed Kit's fingers with her own, gave her a slight nod, and walked away. She bid farewell to the board members in a daze, vaguely nodding and smiling, their words of congratulations sounding as nothing more than a meaningless hum in her ears. She had a ton of work to do, but all she could think about was the moment Kit had said she loved her. That gorgeous smile and the word "Ditto" played on repeat in her head, making it impossible to concentrate and causing her heart to skip with joy at every replay.

188 Lesley Dimmock

That joy turned to consternation when she caught sight of Kit, a tense, strained expression on her face, weaving her way through the office and disappearing outside. Her first impulse was to leap up and follow her out, find out what was going on, but she was saved from herself by the ringing of her mobile phone. It was Abby.

"Just calling to see how the big launch went," Abby said as soon as Frances answered.

"Yeah, yeah. It was good. No hiccups," Frances replied distractedly.

"But?"

Frances sighed. Abby knew her too well.

"Well, I kinda blurted out to Kit that I loved her and she said 'Ditto,' but now she's rushed out looking really upset and all I want to do is find her and see if everything is all right."

"You declared your undying love for her in the middle of the biggest event of your career? You sure don't do things by half, do you?" Abby chuckled. "But seriously, how do you 'kinda blurt out' that sort of thing?"

"I don't know. It just happened. One minute we were watching the site visit numbers clicking over. The next I was telling her I loved her. I know she said she did too. But now I think she's had second thoughts. I think I've scared her off. God, I'm such an idiot!"

"What makes you think she's running scared?" Abby asked.

"Well, she's just rushed out of here, looking really upset," Frances said again.

"Uh huh, so of course, it absolutely has to be about you, yeah? Maybe she got some bad news."

"You're right, you're right," Frances sighed. "I'm overreacting. It could be anything. Nothing to do with me. It's just that she's so incredible and the best damned thing that's happened to me in ages and I'm terrified of stuffing it up and losing her."

"Lordy, girl, you have got it bad," Abby chuckled. "Look, instead of sitting there scaring yourself with worst-case scenarios, how about calling her or sending her a text and seeing if she's okay?"

"You're right, again," Frances said. "When did you get to be this sensible?"

"Ha! Years of listening to you talking me down from my relationship disasters must finally be rubbing off." Abby laughed again. "Now, stop talking to me and go talk to Kit instead."

Abby had barely hung up before Frances texted Kit. *Is everything okay?* An agonizing ten minutes passed before her phone buzzed with Kit's reply.

Yeah, yeah. Some idiot's just backed over my Vespa. I'm just with the tow truck now.

Relief flooded through Frances that Kit's sudden departure had had nothing to do with her. She then immediately felt guilty for such a selfish response. Poor Kit. She loved that scooter.

Oh no, that's terrible, she texted back. *Anything I can do? Maybe a lift home later?*

"It's going to cost me an absolute fortune to fix," Kit grumbled an hour later as Frances drove her to her cottage. "And I still haven't paid off the vet bill from Marvin's attack."

"I could lend you the money," Frances suggested.

"Nah, that's okay." Kit shook her head. "Thanks, though. I'm hoping the insurance will eventually cover it. Do you want to come in?" she asked as Frances pulled the car up in front of her house and switched the engine off.

"No, I won't," she said, turning to face Kit. "I really need to just go home and crash out. Listen," she said, reaching across the gear stick console to stroke Kit's face. "I meant what I said earlier. I love you." Kit stared at her with those incredibly blue eyes, then nodded.

"I meant it too," she said.

CHAPTER FORTY-SIX

As Frances pored over the first report on the digital *Clarion*'s performance, she marvelled at how much they had managed to achieve in one short month. Daily site visit numbers were steadily rising, as was people's engagement with the online content. A lively online community of commentators was building and keeping the paper's moderators busy with the volume of their comments. The biggest surprise of the whole exercise had been the cookery column that sales team member, Barbara Martin, had created. Turns out, Barbara was an absolute whiz in the kitchen and people could not get enough of her recipes. Frances was also thrilled that they now also had three citizen journalists regularly contributing pieces on subjects ranging from the fortunes of the local football team to permaculture practices.

It was what she had envisioned when she had first floated the idea of a digital edition of the newspaper during her job interview—an online community actively engaged in topics and issues that affected and interested them. So far, the gamble had paid off.

"So, the good news," she said at that morning's staff meeting, "is that head office is stoked with our progress. The bad news? You're stuck with me for the duration."

Laughter rippled around the room and to Frances's relief, no one joked that if only they'd known all it took to get rid of their new editor was to ensure the failure of the digital newspaper project.

Well, almost no one. As she dismissed them and headed back to her desk, she caught the twitch of Kit's lips that betrayed that she had had that exact thought. Two months ago, she was certain Kit might have voiced the thought and meant it. But the website wasn't the only thing that had flourished over the past four weeks.

She hadn't expected to find love on her return to her hometown and certainly not with the apparently surly, truculent reporter she had managed to get offside on her very first day in town. She'd soon discovered that underneath that prickly exterior was one of the kindest, funniest, and most loving women she had met in a long time. The weeks she had spent with Kit had been some of the happiest of her life, even with all the stresses associated with bringing a digital newspaper to life.

"Knock, knock." As if thinking about her conjured her up, Kit stood in the doorway, her eyes twinkling as she gazed at Frances.

"Fancy some lunch?" she asked. "I heard that new café up near the post office does a mean halloumi burger." Frances's heart flipped the way it did every time she saw the light shining in Kit's eyes as she looked at her.

"Sure. Who can say no to halloumi?" she replied, tidying the papers in her hands, dropping them into her in-tray and moving out from behind her desk. She would have loved to plant a kiss on Kit's cheek, but they were still keeping their relationship under wraps. Although, she reckoned half of them had already guessed. Instead, she had to satisfy herself by giving Kit's hand a surreptitious squeeze as she led them both out of the office.

She was cautious about any overt displays of affection out of the office as well after that terrible affair with Pastor Evans.

While there had been overwhelming support for her at the time, and people now seemed to have forgotten about the whole thing, she really didn't want to expose herself, or Kit, to any other attacks. It may have been the twenty-first century, but Cannington still was not an easy place to be out. Part of her felt cowardly for being so circumspect and that she was contributing to the continuing invisibility of the town's queer community by not openly walking hand in hand down the street with Kit, as they would have if it had been Brunswick Street in Fitzroy. But, this was Marchant Street and Cannington and sometimes it just wasn't worth the hassle. Especially when time was short and they had a halloumi burger to chase down.

Word must have spread about the place, because the café was buzzing with chatter when they arrived. Almost all the tables were occupied and a long queue was waiting for takeaway orders. One little table jammed into a corner was empty, and Kit hurried over to claim it before anyone else could. Despite the café's busyness, they were joined in no time at all by a server bearing menus, a carafe of water, and two glasses. She cheerfully plonked everything down on the table, promised she'd be back in a couple of minutes, and rushed away again.

"Ohhh," Frances murmured as she pored over the menu. "So many delicious-sounding meals to choose from."

"I know what you mean," Kit replied. "I'm torn between the halloumi burger and the mushroom roti."

"Well, I came for the burger, so that's what I'll stick with," Frances said. "I'm not even going to keep looking at all the other yummy options. Otherwise, I'll just be flip-flopping between all the dishes I really want to try." She closed her menu with a determined snap.

"Oh, I do love a decisive woman," Kit said with a grin. "Uh-oh, the pressure's on now," she went on, looking up as the server returned, notebook in hand and pen at the ready. "I guess I'll go for the halloumi burger too."

"Well, at least we've got an excuse to come back again," Kit said, once the server had taken their order and returned to the kitchen. "I really want to try that mushroom roti one day."

Deadline to Love   193

"Yeah, and there's at least six more dishes that sound really tantalizing," Frances replied. "We're just going to have to have a weekly lunch date until we've worked our way through the entire menu."

"Good plan," Kit replied.

"I know, right?" Frances said. "It's just that sort of blue sky thinking and forward vision that got me where I am today!" She laughed as Kit rolled her eyes at her. "And," she went on, "it's why you love me."

"Well, I don't know if it's that or your sheer bloody chutzpah!" Kit spluttered, her eyes dancing with amusement. "But yes, I love you." Whatever else she might have said was forestalled by the arrival of the server with their meals.

"Oh my stars, this is bloody awesome!" Frances exclaimed, two bites into her burger. "I don't know what they've put into the chutney, but the flavour is spectacular!"

"Delicious, isn't it?" Kit grinned around a mouthful of her own burger. "It's going to give the Cove Café's masala toastie a run for its money as my favourite."

"Masala toastie?" Frances asked. "What even is that?"

"Oh, just the next best thing since sliced bread," Kit replied, grinning as Frances rolled her eyes at the play on words. "It's a toasted sandwich with a potato, peas, corn, and spices filling. So much more interesting than the bog-standard ham, cheese, and tomato toastie every café on the planet offers."

"I'll take your word for it," Frances said, her scepticism plain to see.

"No, really," Kit insisted. "It's amazing. Especially with a side of potato skin crisps. I can see I'm going to have to take you there, so you can discover for yourself just how awesome it is."

"Okay, okay," Frances grudgingly conceded. "I'll keep an open mind and try it. If only to shut you up about it."

Kit stuck her tongue out at her.

"Very adult of you." Frances smirked.

"It's why *you* love *me*," Kit replied. "My mature but playful nature." She balled her used napkin and dropped it onto her now empty plate. "Shall we head back?"

They paid the bill and made their way back down Marchant Street toward the *Clarion*'s office.

"I do love you," Frances murmured, entwining her fingers with Kit's as they sauntered through the Botanic Gardens.

"I know you do," Kit replied, tightening her own fingers around Frances's briefly before breaking the contact as they approached the newspaper building. "You know we're going to have to tell them all about us sooner or later, yeah?"

"I know," Frances sighed, pausing before they reached the front door. "Although it's probably the worst-kept secret, I don't really like the feeling that we're hiding something from them. I'll have a think about the best way to do it."

CHAPTER FORTY-SEVEN

The solution had been a simple one in the end. When that first after-work staff drinks had proved such a success, Frances had made it a regular occurrence, held on the last Friday of each month. It seemed the obvious occasion to announce that she and Kit were a couple.

"What do you think?" she had asked Kit, as they sprawled side by side on her settee, sharing a packet of potato chips and watching the flames flickering in the fireplace. It was only mid-April, but winter was making an early appearance; as soon as the sun disappeared, so did the day's warmth.

"So, this Friday, then," Kit had mumbled around a mouthful of chips. The staff drinks had been brought forward a week as ANZAC Day, one of the country's most important holidays, would fall on the last Friday this month.

"Too soon?"

"No." Kit shook her head. "Let's get it over and done with."

Now that the day had arrived, the way Kit had been tense and jittery all day made Frances suspect that she may be having second thoughts. She was feeling a bit nervous herself. It wasn't every day she got to announce to her staff that she was romantically involved with one of them. She cast her eyes around the boardroom, seeking out Kit and eventually spotting her chatting with Julie and Caitlyn.

"Ready?" she mouthed when Kit looked her way. Kit gave a jerky nod of her head. Taking a deep breath, Frances tapped a pen against her glass, smiling nervously as the fifteen or so people in the room turned curious gazes her way.

"Ah, yeah, thanks," she said, at a sudden loss as to how to proceed. "I, ah, the thing is…I just wanted. Well, Kit and I wanted—"

"What she's trying to say." Kit's voice rang out from the other side of the room and all eyes swivelled toward her. "Is that we're in a relationship. With each other, that is."

"About bloody time!" Nick Davies called out. "It's been killing me trying to keep that secret!"

"Like it was a secret!" someone else called out. The room erupted into laughter and Frances collapsed into a nearby chair, her knees buckling in relief that the little ordeal was over and there hadn't been any adverse reactions. In fact, no had seemed surprised at all. Worst-kept secret, indeed. A glass of wine was shoved into her hand and she looked up to see Nick beaming down at her. She took a huge gulp then jumped to her feet.

"Where's Kit? I need to see she's okay." She tried to peer around Nick, but at such close quarters, his height effectively blocked her view of the room.

"She's fine," Nick said. "That took a lot of guts to stand up there and say that." He perched on the edge of the table as Frances sat back down.

"She's the bravest person I know," she said.

"I was talking about you," he said, leaning in close. "After all the shit you've been through recently? To expose yourself like that again?" Frances squirmed under his steady gaze, embarrassed by the admiration in his voice. She was saved from further discomfort by Kit's arrival.

"You ready?" she asked, greeting Nick with a nod. "I just got a text from Hilary that they're at the Zodiac already."

Deadline to Love   197

"Oh, right, yes." Frances gulped down the rest of her drink and got to her feet. She gave Nick a big hug and followed Kit out of the room, her face reddening at the chorus of ribald comments and cheers that followed them.

Once they were alone in the deserted newsroom, she snagged Kit's arm and pulled her into a hug.

"Thanks for coming to my rescue in there," she said. "I had a complete brain fade and couldn't think what to say."

"Well, someone had to put you out of your misery." Kit grinned up at her. "Telling everyone our business was much less painful than watching you flail around. Come on, let's grab our things and get going. Everyone will be wondering where we've got to."

The gang, as they had taken to calling Kit's circle of friends, was in its usual spot at the back of the bar. Several armchairs had been added to the two settees, creating a semiprivate lounge area.

"You made it!" Hilary leapt to her feet and hugged them each in turn. "So, how did the big reveal go?"

"Bit of a nonevent, to be honest," Kit said, waving her fingers at Akari, Natasha, and Sue, who sat on the far settee alongside a new member of the group.

"Oh, Frances, this is Gillian. She's just come back from a three-month trip around India. We can't wait to hear all about her adventures." Kit grinned toward the woman.

Frances stared in shock as the woman rose to her feet. It had been twenty years, but she would recognise that mane of auburn hair anywhere even faded as it was from its former fiery glory. A dozen bangles slithered and clattered along the woman's arm as she extended her hand.

"Gillian? Gillian Porter?" she said faintly, giving her hand a limp shake.

"You two know each other?" Kit looked from Frances to Gillian.

"We go way back," Gillian said, her eyes fixed on Frances. "High school sweethearts, weren't we, Frankie?"

"Seriously?" Kit asked, her eyes wide in disbelief.

"It was a lifetime ago." Frances wrenched her eyes away from Gillian and gave a bark of laughter that sounded unconvincing even to her own ears. She sat down numbly, barely hearing when Kit asked her if she wanted a drink. Thoughts raced through her mind, tumbling over each other, none of them coherent, other than *Fuck, Gillian Porter. Beautiful, bewitching, wild Gillian Porter…*

She may have put on some weight and her wardrobe become a little more sober, but all Frances could see was the laughing teenager in her habitual ripped T-shirt, kilt-style skirt and Blundstone work boots.

"So, look at you," Gillian said, snapping Frances back to her surroundings. "My little bookworm's all grown up." Her brown eyes sparkled as she smiled across the coffee table at Frances. Her eyes drifted to a point over Frances's shoulder before she could reply. Turning her head, she saw Kit approaching with two tall cocktails in her hands and a quizzical expression on her face. Frances gave her a small smile as she gave her one of the drinks and sat down next to her. Gillian looked from one to the other, her eyes alighting on the hand Frances had placed on Kit's knee.

"You two an item, then?" she asked.

"Yes, yes we are." Frances finally found her voice and nodded, tightening her grip on Kit's knee.

"Nice," Gillian drawled. "You look cute together." She gave Frances a knowing look as she sipped from her drink. "So, I hear you've been causing quite a stir since you came back," she said.

"Ugh." Frances frowned and shook her head. "I'd really rather not talk about that. Tell us about India instead."

Frances listened, enthralled, as Gillian regaled them with tales of her travels. She was a good storyteller and Frances found herself hanging onto every word as she recounted some of her hairier misadventures.

CHAPTER FORTY-EIGHT

A mist had descended when Frances and Kit eventually left the Zodiac Bar, shrouding their surroundings in a greyish haze and causing their footsteps to echo across the near-deserted streets as they walked to Frances's car parked at the *Clarion* building.

"You were quiet tonight," she said, shooting a sidelong glance at Kit, who walked beside her with her hands shoved deep into the pockets of her overcoat.

"I'm surprised you noticed," Kit growled, her gaze fixed on the path before them.

Frances was taken aback by the vehemence in her voice and stopped walking.

"What's that supposed to mean?" she asked, her tone sharper than she had intended.

"You couldn't keep your eyes off her!" Kit whirled to face her, her eyes blazing with anger.

"Who? You mean Gillian?" Frances gaped at her.

"Of course I mean fucking Gillian," Kit snarled. "I may as well not have been there!"

"Don't be stupid," Frances said, instantly regretting her words, as Kit looked at her in fury.

"Don't fucking call me stupid!"

"I'm sorry." Frances held her hands up in surrender, trying to mollify Kit. "I shouldn't have said that. But I don't know why you're so upset. We were just talking."

"'Just talking.'" Kit mimicked her words. "What about? Your high school romance?"

Frances opened her mouth, then closed it again, flinching as Kit pushed her face up close to hers and stared at her.

"Oh my god," she gasped, stepping back. "You're still in love with her, aren't you?"

"No! Of course not! Don't be ridic—"

"Go to hell!" She quailed at the look of fury Kit gave her. "I'll find my own fucking way home!"

"Kit, wait!"

Confused and bewildered, Frances watched Kit disappear into the gloom. *What the hell just happened?*

She completed the journey to her car in a complete daze. Sliding into the driver's seat, she pulled out her phone and stared at its darkened screen for several minutes. She knew it would be futile, but she dialled Kit's number anyway. The phone rang and rang and rang before going to voice mail. Swearing under her breath, Frances called again. And again.

"Kit, please pick up. Talk to me," she said, leaving a final, pleading message.

Her vision blurred with tears as she drove home. How the hell had everything blown up so drastically? Was she really going to lose Kit? Over Gillian Porter?

Once home, she grabbed a glass and a half-empty bottle of Glenfiddich whisky from the kitchen and carried them into the living room. Using just the light coming in from the hallway, she poured herself a drink and sank into the sofa. Should she ring Kit again, tell her how much she loved her? Beg her to let her explain? But explain what? That yes, she still had feelings for Gillian Porter, but that they meant nothing?

Frances had been a little bit in love with Gillian almost from the first day she met her. She was a new kid at school, having moved with her parents from Melbourne when her father bought into a medical practice in Cannington. She had all the big city street cred the country kids around her craved. Josie's gang had tried to recruit her, but she had given them short shrift. No one had been more surprised than Frances when Gillian chose her to be her best friend. She had been completely captivated by the wild-haired seventeen-year-old, who seemed to navigate her way through a bewildering world with an ease Frances could only envy. Gillian had been her first girlfriend and they had lasted for six heady months before Gillian dropped her to resume a long-distance romance with her former girlfriend. She had never really got over her, just learned to get past the hurt of the rejection.

Seeing Gillian again tonight had brought up the excitement and romance of that first love. Gillian was just as captivating and beautiful as ever, but there was no way she was still in love with her. She just had to make Kit understand that. Understand that there was only one person she loved. But first, she had to get Kit to talk to her.

"Please, Kit," she said, when the phone again went straight to voice mail. "Please call me. I love you. I can't lose you. Not like this." Her voice cracked and she threw the phone aside as sobs racked her body.

She woke up late the next morning, stiff from a night spent on a settee that was too short for her to comfortably sleep on. Her mouth felt like the bottom of a bird cage and a blacksmith had set up shop in her head, banging away with his hammer. And no wonder. There was barely an inch of whisky left in the bottle. She groped around in the sofa's cushions for her phone, finally locating it wedged down the back. Still nothing from Kit.

She staggered to her feet, groaning as the room swam around her and the blacksmith renewed his efforts inside her brain. Gingerly, she shuffled into the bathroom and shook a couple of painkillers out of a bottle. Washing them down with a handful of water from the basin tap, she stripped out of her clothes and stepped into the shower. Turning the water to its highest settings, she stood under the scalding torrent for as long as she could stand it, her tears mingling with the water running down her face as misery overtook her.

She had been okay on her own. Not happy, but not unhappy either. Content with her own company. She probably could have lived for years like that. A quiet, safe life. But not now. Not now she had met Kit. She had brought colour and joy and a passion for life into her life that she now could not bear to lose.

Shutting the water off as it began to run cold, she towelled herself dry and padded into her bedroom to find some clothes. Looking at the overflowing laundry basket, she decided she had neglected the household chores for long enough. The past few weeks, given the option of vacuuming and laundry or spending time with Kit, she'd gone with the latter every time. She began a load of laundry then headed into the kitchen. What she needed, apart from a lot of coffee, was toast with Vegemite.

She was beginning to feel more like herself after her fifth cup of coffee. Rather than wallow in misery, torturing herself by constantly checking her phone, she set about spending the day giving her house a thorough clean. And housework was best done accompanied by music. She returned to the living room and squatted on the floor in front of a set of shelves holding her vinyl collection. What did she feel like listening to? Not lovelorn songs, that was for sure. She flicked through the albums, stopping as her fingers alighted on The Clash's *London Calling* album. She'd been a bit late to the punk music movement, but had discovered The Clash, along with Joy Division and Siouxie and the Banshees through the university's music shop.

Perfect, she thought, sliding the record free of its cover and setting it on the turntable. She cranked the volume up as the first strident guitar chords of the title song crackled through the speakers.

The housework was cathartic and for hours at a time she did not think of Kit as she dusted, swept, and vacuumed her way around the house. It was only when she paused between each task that Kit returned to her thoughts. Each time she paused, she had checked her phone and each time, her heart had plummeted as there was still no response from Kit.

By the time she flopped down on her sofa, exhausted from the day's cleaning, her dark mood had returned. Her phone had remained silent all day. She couldn't even leave a voice mail now because she had left so many messages already that she had filled Kit's inbox. She could text her, try and reach her that way, but what would be the point? She would just be giving Kit another way to ignore her.

She can't ignore me if I'm standing in front of her, can she? I should just drive over there, refuse to leave until she speaks to me.

Without stopping to think about the wisdom of this idea, she grabbed her keys and ran to her car.

CHAPTER FORTY-NINE

Kit's anger propelled her the entire three kilometres to her home. She slammed the door shut and threw herself down on the settee, then stood up again, wrestled her coat off and flung it to the floor before slumping onto the settee again.

"Fuck, fuck, fuck!"

A startled Marvin blinked at her, woken by her noisy entrance.

"Sorry, mate," she said, stretching an arm along the sofa to scritch his chin, the act going some way to defusing a little of her anger. But not much.

God, why did it have to be Gillian Porter? She'd had bit of an attraction to her when she first arrived in Cannington. It hadn't gone anywhere because, in Gillian's words, Kit "wasn't her type." It had taken a while for the attraction to die and they had eventually become good friends. Obviously, Gillian's type was taller and blonder than Kit would ever be, as her former crush now turned out to be the high school sweetheart of her current girlfriend. A TV soap opera couldn't come up with a plot twist like that!

Awkward was one word to describe how that had felt. She could have coped with awkward but as the night went on, she watched as Frances and Gillian fell into an animated conversation that seemed to exclude all around them. Watched and seethed and knocked back shot after shot of whisky.

She hadn't been drunk when she blew up at Frances. And she certainly had not been drunk when she saw that flicker in Frances's eye, that flicker that betrayed the feelings she had for Gillian.

Her phone buzzed, but she ignored it. It would be Frances again. She'd already rung three times, leaving messages to please call her. But, she was in no mood to speak to her right now.

She declined the latest call with a swipe and tossed the phone onto the coffee table. She scooped up Marvin and buried her face in his fur. Tears scalded her cheeks as her heart cracked open with pain. She really had thought that she and Frances had a future, that they could build, *would* build a life together. How was that now possible when Frances was still harbouring feelings for an old flame? Now all she felt was an overwhelming sense of loss. Of hopelessness. Marvin mewed and squirmed free when she squeezed him closer to her, twitching his ears in annoyance and staring balefully at her as she sobbed.

"You're right," Kit said finally, wiping away her tears. "I was a fool to think this was going to be happily ever after. I'm glad it happened now and not when I was even more emotionally invested." Marvin blinked at her sceptically before stalking out of the room.

She woke up Saturday morning feeling wrung out from too much whisky and too little sleep. She had no idea how she was going to get through the next few days. She would have jumped on her scooter and ridden down the coast, but the Vespa was still out of action, waiting on a part, so she was stuck here. Stuck with her miserable thoughts. And a bloody phone that wouldn't stop buzzing.

206   Lesley Dimmock

She grabbed it and tossed it into the fridge. At least there, she wouldn't be able to hear it. She should go for a run. That would make her feel better. She changed into her running gear, looked around for her phone so she could cue up her playlist of running music, before remembering where it was and why.

She decided putting up with it buzzing every now and again a small price to pay for being able to drown out her thoughts and retrieved the phone from the fridge. She slid it into a pocket and set off toward the dunes, driving her legs up the sandy slopes to the beat of Dua Lipa's "Physical."

She returned home an hour later, hot, sweaty, out of breath and exhausted, but in no better a mood. She downed a litre of water, then padded into the bathroom to strip off her wet clothes and stepped into the shower, trying to banish the memory of sharing the shower with Frances just a few days ago. She groaned as her crotch throbbed as she replayed the way Frances had brought her to an orgasm that had them both slithering to the floor as Kit's legs gave way. They had lain there in a tangle of arms and legs, giggling as water cascaded over them, before remembering they were meant to be getting ready for work.

She hung her head and sobbed as the hot water pounded her body. She didn't know what felt worse. Frances's betrayal? Or the hurt her absence created? She'd risked her heart once for Frances and discovered a beautiful, caring and loving woman, who made her laugh and filled her life with joy. Was she prepared to take another risk to keep all that?

The question haunted her all the rest of the day as she tried to bury herself in work. She had so many ideas for articles and so little time recently to develop them. By late afternoon, she gave up. Her thoughts and emotions were too scattered for her to properly concentrate. Pushing her laptop aside, she picked up her phone. Ignoring the notifications about all the missed calls, she dialled Hilary's number.

"Hey, mate," she said when her friend answered. "Are you and Natasha doing anything this evening? Can I come over?"

"Sure," Hilary replied. "We're just going to spend the night binge-watching *Gentleman Jack*. Everything okay?"

"I'll tell you when I get there," she ended the call and ordered an Uber. God, the sooner the Vespa was back the road, the happier her bank balance would be. She scooped up her keys as a car horn sounded outside.

"So I've totally stuffed things up with Frances," she said twenty minutes later, sitting sandwiched between Hilary and Natasha on their settee while they both hugged her.

"But, things were so good between the two of you. What happened?" Hilary asked.

"Gillian happened."

"Gillian? I don't get it. What does Gillian have to do with it?" Natasha chimed in, her confusion evident in her voice.

"Because they were lovers once and I just know Frances still has feelings for her. I completely lost it at her last night. Told her to go to hell." She leant forward, elbows on her knees and held her head in her hands. "I don't know how I'm going to fix this," she said mournfully.

"Mate, have you tried talking to her?" Hilary asked.

Kit shook her head. "No. She's been calling me all night and day, but I've been too angry to answer. But the calls stopped a couple of hours ago. She's probably given up on me. And who can blame her. I was so awful to her." She began crying, leaning into Hilary's comforting hug.

"Oh, Kit, mate," Hilary said. "You are such an idiot at times. Frances loves you so much. You'll work this out."

"You think?" Kit sniffled and scrubbed the tears from her face.

"I do," Hilary replied, her tone firm. "I also think that you're in no state to go home, so you're staying here the night. Isn't she, Tash?"

"But my cat," Kit tried to argue.

"He'll manage without you for one night."

CHAPTER FIFTY

Her car had barely come to a halt before Frances was out and practically racing down the short path to Kit's front door. She knocked at the door, mentally rehearsing what she would say, while waiting for it to open.

"I love you. I'm sorry. Please let me explain."

Her thoughts trailed away as she realised she had been standing outside a closed door for a good few minutes now. Frowning, she knocked again, calling Kit's name, then stepped back to look at the house and peer through a window. The sun was setting, throwing lengthy shadows, and if Kit were home there would be a light on inside by now. But the house was in darkness.

Her shoulders slumping, she trudged back to the car. Was she ever going to get a chance to fix things, or had she lost Kit for good?

"Christ, that doesn't bear thinking about." Frances shuddered as she turned the key in the car's ignition and drove away from the empty cottage.

Her own house did not feel much more welcoming when she walked in. Dark and silent, with not even a cat to greet her. Frances had never felt as lonely as she did right now. Turning on a table lamp dispelled the gloom and made the room feel a little more inviting. She plumped herself down on the settee and began scrolling through the TV channels. She wasn't a big watcher of television, but right now, getting lost in a mindless program was just what she needed. She finally settled on an old episode of *Escape to the Country*—the couple on the show were trying their hand at traditional basket weaving—and then ordered a chicken korma through Uber Eats. It was tempting to open a bottle of wine to drink with the meal, but this morning's hangover was enough of a deterrent. Besides, alcohol was not the solution to her problems. Instead, she added a pot of masala tea to her order.

Frances's fingers were itching to pick up her phone and text Kit. *Are you okay?* She wanted to ask. *Where are you? Can I see you?* But she knew it would get her nowhere. It would be ignored, just like every other message she had left until giving up earlier that afternoon.

Stan and Edna were going into raptures over the views of the Yorkshire Dales offered by the mystery house when her doorbell rang. For a nanosecond, she thought it might be Kit, but it was just a delivery guy with her dinner. Sighing with disappointment, she slumped back onto the settee and half-heartedly pried open the container of food. Tantalising aromas assailed her nostrils, and she was soon scoffing down a deliciously creamy korma. Her mood had brightened by the time she popped the last fragment of naan into her mouth and washed it down with the masala tea which, disappointingly, had arrived in a cardboard cup with a plastic lid instead of an actual teapot. It still tasted good, though. So much so that she decided she'd make sure she had a constant supply of masala tea in her pantry so that she could enjoy it any time she liked.

Stan and Edna were now chatting with the presenter about which of the three houses they had seen that they liked the best.

"Go for the mystery house!" Frances said, cheering when the couple did just that, then cheering again when it was revealed they'd put in an offer on it that had been accepted. She hated it when the show just ended without letting the viewer know the outcome. As the credits began rolling, she jumped to her feet, switched off the telly, and prowled restlessly around the room. Now what? It was way too early to go to bed. She felt too antsy to read or listen to music and didn't feel like talking on the phone to anyone. Abby would probably just berate her for being a bloody idiot. Her oldest sister, Samantha, didn't really "get" her sexuality, so there was no point talking to her, and Pat, her other sister, well, who knew where she was these days? Since turning forty several years ago, she had announced she needed to find herself and had upped and left her husband and two teenaged kids and disappeared to the subcontinent. She was probably sitting in some ashram in the Himalayas. Perhaps Gillian had bumped into her.

Ah hell. Gillian. Why couldn't she have stayed firmly in the past?

"I gotta get out of here," she murmured. Scooping up her car keys and grabbing a coat, she let herself out of the house and slid into the driver's seat of her Mini. Minutes later she was driving down the near-deserted streets of Cannington toward Tumbledown Point. It was a favourite spot of hers when she was a teenager, but she hadn't been down there since returning to Cannington three months ago.

The sound of her door slamming shut echoed around the empty carpark as she picked her way through the boulders that lay at the foot of the rocky outcrop marking the western boundary of Trelawney Bay. She settled herself against a pile of rocks that time, wind, and water had smoothed and rounded and let the hiss and roar of waves push Kit out of her mind and fill it with some serenity.

It was almost midnight when she finally stirred, stiff and chilled to the bone from the breeze that had been blowing off the water. People joked that the winds in these parts came straight from Antarctica, unhindered by any landmass in their freezing passage northward across the Southern Ocean. Pulling her jacket closer around her, Frances could well believe it. Getting into her car, she cranked the heater up and turned homeward.

CHAPTER FIFTY-ONE

"Frances Keating, you are a bloody idiot!"

Frances winced and yanked her phone away from her ear as Abby's shrill words threatened to burst an eardrum. She had eventually given in to her need to talk with her best friend and phoned her early Sunday afternoon. She put the phone on speaker and curled into a ball on her sofa as Abby continued to berate her.

"Kit Tresize was the best thing to happen to you in a long time, and you've gone and blown it. Big time!"

"I know, I know." Frances moaned. "How am I going to fix it, Abs?"

"You're not," Abby replied. "Well, not yet anyway," she continued before Frances could object. "It's too soon. Kit will be feeling too raw and sad and angry to listen to anything you say. She'll just slam her heart shut against you and then it really will be over for the two of you."

Frances hated to admit it, but she knew Abby was right. Picking up the phone, she took it off speaker mode and tucked it up to her ear.

"How did you get to be so smart at all this relationship stuff?" she asked, curling her legs back up to her chest.

"I dunno," Abby replied. "Must be all the experience I've had crashing and burning every relationship I've ever been in." She was laughing, but there was an edge to her words.

"Aww, come on, Abs," Frances said. "Not all of the breakups were your fault. That Gabby, for instance…"

"Oh look," Abby interrupted. "That one had warning signs written all over it right from the start. I mean, 'Gabby and Abby'? Puh-leeze! I blame you for that one. You know I'm a sucker for anyone with dreadlocks. You should have stopped me from even approaching her."

"Yeah, right." Frances snorted. "Like anyone could stop you once you've set your sights on someone!" She smiled at the sound of Abby's laughter, her mood lifting. Abby always did make her feel better.

"Anyway, enough about me," Abby said. "I know it's going to be tough, but you have to resist the urge to patch things up with Kit right away. Give her some space."

"Okay." Frances sighed. "I'll try. It's going to be hard, though, seeing her at work. I'm dreading seeing her around the office."

"Hmm," Abby mused. "At least that's one golden rule of relationships I've never broken. And I seem have broken most of them. 'Don't get involved with work colleagues.'"

"Now she tells me," Frances grumbled into the phone. A peal of laughter and a singsong "Good luck" was all the reply she got before Abby cut the connection.

After spending the rest of Sunday worrying about how her first encounter with Kit would go on Monday, when she arrived at the *Clarion* office Frances's nerves were wound so tightly, she feared she would snap in half. She didn't think they could be wound any tighter, but as minute by agonising minute ticked by without Kit making an appearance, the tension cranked ever higher until she couldn't bear it any longer. She was about to make a dash for the bathroom so that she could have her meltdown in private, when Enid buzzed through with a reminder that the staff meeting was starting in five minutes.

"Arrrgghhh!" Frances screamed silently as she replaced the handset. "For fuck's sake, Keating! Get a grip! You're a thirty-eight-year-old professional woman in charge of a newspaper. You can do this!"

Standing, she smoothed her jacket down over her hips, took three deep breaths, plastered what felt like a very unconvincing smile on to her face, and strode into the meeting room. Her heart hammered uncontrollably as she scanned the room, looking for Kit, and then lurched in, what?—relief? Disappointment?—when she saw she wasn't there.

That initial relief—if that's what it was—didn't last. She could barely concentrate on the reports being presented for constantly expecting Kit to walk through the door at any moment.

She had worked herself up into such a fever pitch of anticipation that when Kit did finally make an appearance, it was almost an anticlimax.

"Sorry, sorry. Couldn't get an Uber for ages," Kit muttered as she slipped into the room halfway through Susan's sales report and took up a spot standing against the wall just to Frances's right. Frances slid her eyes sideways at her, but Kit just gave her an expressionless nod before turning her attention back to what Susan was saying.

Could have been worse, Frances thought to herself. *No death ray stares, at least.*

CHAPTER FIFTY-TWO

She was just going to go to work, like it was any other ordinary Monday. Which of course it was. She'd go to work, slip in behind her desk, get on with her job, and pretend that nothing at all had gone wrong in her universe.

Never mind that she'd spent the whole weekend curled up in a miserable ball of hurt and heartbreak that not even Marvin's determined nuzzling could ameliorate. She'd barely eaten for two days, refusing all Hilary's enticements. Not even a slice of her chocolate lava cake could tempt her. She had been subsisting on the cups of tea that were the only thing she could muster the energy to make and the occasional Jatz biscuit.

Nope. She was determined that as far as her workmates were concerned, everything was just tickety-boo in her life.

And then, of course, she had had to wait forever for an Uber and by the time it showed up, she was late and the staff meeting had already started and now everyone was staring at her and probably wondering why she looked like her cat had died. Which, thankfully, he hadn't, despite being totally neglected over the past thirty-six hours.

Kit could feel Frances's eyes on her, but she was damned if she was going to give the woman the satisfaction of seeing how much pain she was in. It took all her control to maintain a passive expression on her face as she glanced at Frances and gave her the barest of nods. The pang of longing she felt at the sight of her was so intense, though, that it was all Kit could do to not flee the room. She tried not to fidget from one foot to the other as the meeting went on for a seemingly interminable length of time. Finally, it was over. She bolted for the safety of her desk.

"Are you okay, Kit?" Julie's voice was full of concern as she arrived at their pod a few minutes later.

"Yeah, yeah," Kit replied. "Just a bit of a headache, is all."

"Looks like someone had too much of a good time over the weekend!" Julie laughed as she settled down on the other side of the screen that divided their workstations. Kit gave her a wan smile and forced a chuckle.

"Ha ha. Yeah," she said. *If only you knew.*

"Well, just sing out if you need anything," Julie replied. "I've got a veritable pharmacy in my drawer here. A pill for every ailment."

Got one to cure a broken heart? Kit wanted to ask. Instead, she pulled her keyboard closer and tried to focus on her bulging inbox. How could so many emails accumulate over a weekend? Sorting through, reading, and responding to them all got her through to the lunch break. She pushed away from her desk and stood. She wasn't hungry, but she decided a stroll outside in the sunshine would do her a world of good. And give herself a break from the oppressive hypersensitivity to Frances's presence which had made her tense and twitchy.

Once she was outside, her mood brightened immediately, and she surprised herself by being hungry after all. Not just hungry. Ravenous. Her usual lunchtime meal of a sandwich just was not going to cut it. Something greasy and fried, that's what her stomach was demanding. A toastie from the Nemo Café would fit the bill, but that was now a favourite hangout of Frances's, and she did not want to risk bumping into her there.

A felafel, then. She turned in the direction of Theo's Takeaway. Sure, this was another favourite of Frances's, but with it being further afield, she was gambling Frances would not venture there for lunch. She was right.

The felafel being far healthier for her than what her body demanded, Kit assuaged the craving for greasy food with a side order of chips. "That should do the trick," she murmured to herself, carrying the bag of food over to a small park and settling herself on a bench shaded by a massive jacaranda tree. While she ate, she tried to keep her mind free of any thoughts, particularly of Frances, but it was impossible. She couldn't stop wondering what Frances was doing. What she was feeling or thinking. There was a deep, aching hole in her heart that only Frances could fill, but she didn't know if she could let her back in. Wasn't sure she could take being hurt again.

Realising she had barely tasted the last few mouthfuls of her felafel, Kit shook her head free of all thoughts of Frances and focused instead on each bite, savouring the individual flavours and textures of the food. She supposed this was what was meant by mindful eating. In any case, it worked. For the five minutes it took her to finish her meal, she did not think about Frances once.

CHAPTER FIFTY-THREE

Burying herself in work the last few days had done nothing to distract Frances from thinking about Kit. It didn't help that she could see the top of Kit's head across the room every time she gazed out of her office window. Or that whenever Kit got up from her desk, she found herself surreptitiously tracking her movements, ducking her head whenever she glanced in her direction.

She had thought she'd been doing a good job of pretending there was nothing wrong, but Enid had picked up that something wasn't right. Not that she had said anything. She was just being extra solicitous, offering to fetch Frances coffee, bringing her slices of home-baked cake, reminding her to get outside and breathe some fresh air. She had even gone so far as giving Frances soothing pats on the shoulder every time they passed each other. People were beginning to notice and ask her if everything was okay.

"Yep. Yes. No, no one has died. It's all good. Really. That's just Enid being Enid," she'd say. "You know what Enid is like." And they'd go away nodding but still looking over their shoulders at her, unconvinced by her words.

Being in the same building as Kit, seeing her every day, but being unable to approach her, speak to her, was torture. She got what Abby had been saying when she had told Frances to give Kit space, but it had been five days since Kit had stormed away from her. They had been the worst five days of her life. Okay, maybe when her mother died was worse. But she had been a kid then. These were definitely the worse days of her adult life, that was for sure.

What was going through Kit's mind? Why hadn't she broken her silence? Had she really just given up on her? That thought sent her spiralling into despair.

She dragged her attention back to the report she had been preparing for the head office. It had already taken her far too long to write; her inbox was beginning to ping with emails from HQ asking when it might be ready, while expressing concern about her uncharacteristic tardiness in submitting said report. So, now she had to assure Richard Deacon—again—that she was on top of everything. That she had everything under control and that it was all going swimmingly.

"Everything except my love life," she muttered tartly as she fired off a soothing response to Richard's latest email. That done, she turned back to the report, which was no closer to completion than it had been thirty minutes ago. She had just started an analysis of the data on the newest sections of the website when there was a knock at her door.

"Yes, what is it?" she snapped, annoyed at the interruption, immediately regretting her reaction when she looked up and saw Kit standing in the doorway, a discomfited expression on her face.

"Oh, sorry. I can come back…" Kit made to retreat, but Frances waved her inside.

"No, no. Please. Come in. I'm sorry. It's just this wretched report I'm trying to finish."

"I really can come back," Kit said, still hovering in the doorway. "When it's more convenient."

"No, please," Frances repeated, her heart tripping at the thought that Kit was here to offer a rapprochement. If that was so, there was no way she wanted to miss this opportunity. "Have a seat. What can I do for you? Do you want a coffee? A tea, perhaps?" Frances knew she was gabbling, but couldn't help herself. She took a deep breath to calm down as Kit pulled out a chair and sat down across from her.

"No thanks, I'm fine," Kit said, a faint smile on her lips as if she knew what was going through Frances's mind. "So, the thing is," Kit began, shifting nervously in her seat as she spoke.

Here it comes, Frances thought, trying her hardest not to look as eager as she felt.

"I know we've just launched the new sections of the website, but I've had this idea…"

Oh. Frances's shoulders slumped in disappointment as she realised Kit was here to talk work. She missed half of what she said, only catching the last few words before Kit fell silent, a quizzical expression on her face as she waited for Frances to respond.

"Ah, yes, well. That sounds really promising," she hedged, hoping she didn't come across as not having a clue what the conversation had been about. Then she had a flash of inspiration.

"Why don't you outline the whole proposal and email it to me, so I can consider it in depth?"

"Oh, okay. Sure thing," Kit said, getting to her feet. "So, you don't think it completely daft?"

"No, not at all." Frances smiled, shaking her head. "But I look forward to reading more about it. Listen," she went on as Kit moved toward the door. Her heart pounded and her mouth suddenly dried up as Kit turned back and gazed at her, her expression unreadable. Frances swallowed. "I don't suppose you'd like to go get a cup of coffee? With me, I mean." The words came out in a rush, and she could hardly bring herself to look at Kit, fearing to see nothing but rejection and anger. It seemed to take Kit an eternity to reply and Frances's heart sank when she gently shook her head.

"I'm not saying 'no,'" she said. "But I need more time." With that, she turned and slipped out of the office.

Yes! Frances gave an exultant fist pump and spun her chair around in a full circle to celebrate. Then, feeling invincible, and before she could talk herself out of it, she grabbed her phone and rapidly tapped out and sent a text.

CHAPTER FIFTY-FOUR

How about now?

Kit's fingers hovered over her phone's screen as she pondered how to reply to Frances's text. She had been telling the truth when she told her she needed more time. But, to be honest, she had also been looking for an excuse to see her, and her idea to introduce a "long read" section to the website, where people could access lengthy, well-researched articles on a range of topics, had been a perfect opportunity.

The cheeky playfulness of the text was just one of the things she missed about Frances. Yes, her heart was battered and bruised, but it wanted Frances back. The hit of joy Kit had got from the few minutes she had spent in Frances's company just now was proof of that.

Okay.

She typed the word out and was about to hit Send but erased the word instead.

Sorry. Like I said. I need more time.

Deadline to Love   223

She stabbed the Send button before she could change her mind. Puzzled by her own perversity—didn't she want to get back together with Frances?—Kit chewed at her lip as she wrestled with the urge to take back what she had just texted and tell Frances instead that, yes, now was the perfect time to go for coffee. But she resisted, ignoring the twitching in her fingers as she resolutely focussed on outlining her proposal for in-depth articles.

"I'm still not sure why I turned her down," she said that evening in a phone call to Hilary.

"You know what your problem is, Kit?" Hilary replied.

"I'm sure you're about to tell me," Kit muttered.

"Uh huh," Hilary said. "You just don't know how to be happy."

"I do so!" Kit retorted, sounding a lot more childish that she would have liked.

"Sure you do," Hilary continued, ignoring Kit's eloquent rebuttal. "That's why you're sitting at home with the cat on your lap instead of off out having a drink with the woman who's head over heels about you."

Kit opened her mouth to say that was not true, but she *was* sitting at home on her own with Marvin curled up on her lap.

"So, what should I do?" she asked in a plaintive voice, not really caring how pathetic she sounded.

"Well, the obvious thing to do is to call her up and ask her out," she said. There was silence for a few moments before Kit spoke.

"Right. So that's going to make me look like an indecisive idiot," Kit grumbled. "I mean, I've just told her I need more time, and now you're telling me I should basically do the opposite of that?"

"Yep, that's what I'm telling you. You want to be happy, don't you?" With that, Hilary rang off, leaving Kit with one last question to ponder. "You going to choose pride or happiness, mate?"

CHAPTER FIFTY-FIVE

"Pride or happiness?" It was a question Kit pondered all night. Ultimately, she chose happiness.

"I mean, who wouldn't?" she asked Marvin. "A person would have to be an idiot not to, wouldn't they?" Marvin said nothing. Kit decided to take his silence as assent.

"And I am not an idiot," she went on. "But a person can choose happiness *and* need more time, can't she?"

Kit was not ready to think about what she needed more time for. Something was holding her back from rushing back into Frances's arms. She didn't know what it was, possibly a wariness of opening herself up to being hurt again, but she did trust her instincts, and she was going to listen to the little voice in her head that was telling her to take it slowly.

The trouble was, her heart had other ideas. She spent most of Thursday morning fighting the urge to simply rush into Frances's office and tell her all was forgiven. That she didn't care if Frances still had feelings for Gillian. That she just wanted to be with her. The only thing that stopped her was the fact that she did care. She cared a lot. That and the fact that Frances was out of the building, attending a series of meetings with the paper's board of directors, and wouldn't be back until late in the afternoon.

"Can't really complain," Kit grumbled to herself. "I did say I needed more time."

With her mother's voice echoing in her head with words to the effect of "Careful what you wish for," Kit pulled her keyboard closer and dragged her attention back to completing her "Long Reads" proposal. The sooner she got that done, the sooner she could get to work on churning out a few more feature articles. The bonuses she would earn from those would go a long way toward helping her meet Marvin's vet bills. She still owed nearly four hundred dollars and was keen to finally clear that debt. Thankfully, the insurance company had finally come through on paying for the Vespa's repairs. It wouldn't be long now before she could start saving for that new camera lens she had been hankering for, the one that would allow her to begin experimenting with shooting ultra wide-angle landscape images.

Visions of the photographs she could take spurred Kit on to finishing her proposal on adding a section comprising longer, well-researched articles to the website. She read her words through carefully, picking up a few minor typos and correcting them, and gave a satisfied nod.

"Call me biased," she murmured, "but that there's a compelling case. If I were Frances, I'd be convinced."

Opening her email client, Kit composed a short message to Frances, attached the proposal, and hit the Send button. She had no idea how long it would be before Frances decided about the new section, but in the meantime she had no other pressing assignments so there was no harm in starting work on one of the topics she had listed in the proposal as a potential article. Time spent on research was never time wasted in Kit's book. But first, as the grumbling noises emanating from her stomach reminded her, it was time for some lunch.

Standing in the queue at the nearby Eggy Café, Kit was toying with her phone, trying to decide whether to text Frances or not, when it buzzed in her hand and Frances's name lit up the screen.

Sorry, the text read, *I know you need time, and the last thing I want to do is push you, but can we please talk? x F*

The queue had shuffled forward while Kit had been staring at her phone. A tap on her shoulder dragged her back into the present moment, where the server was waiting patiently behind the counter to take Kit's order.

"Oh. Er. Um. I'll just have that and one of those," she said, pointing randomly at the sandwiches and cakes on display in the cabinet. She waved her phone over the payment gizmo and, clutching her two paper bags, made her way to a vacant table. She carefully put her phone to one side and inspected the contents of the bags. Luckily, the sandwich she had pointed at was meat-free. She ate it slowly and methodically, staring at her phone as she did so and putting off the moment when she would reply to Frances's text.

Eventually, when she had eaten the last scraps of the sandwich and licked the final crumbs of apple slice off her fingers, she had no more excuses for not responding to Frances's plea. She picked up her phone, weighing it in her hand while she thought about what that response would be. Her first reaction was to say "no," but… This was her moment to choose happiness. If she didn't, then perhaps Hilary was right after all; she really did not know how to be happy.

Okay.

Kit held her breath as she sent the text off. Seconds later, her phone pinged again.

Great! Brilliant! So, I should be back around 3 or 3:30. Shall we say Nemo's at 4?

Okay.

She deliberately kept her response cool and collected, something that obviously didn't bother Frances as her phoned pinged again and a GIF of Snoopy skipping in joy filled her screen. Kit snorted with suppressed laughter as she slipped her phone into her pocket, balled up her empty paper bags, and dropped them into a bin on her way out of the café.

Over the course of the next three hours, Kit had plenty of time to contemplate how she was going to approach the upcoming meeting with Frances.

Lead with your head, not your heart, she admonished herself. *Yes, it's all very well choosing happiness, but not at the cost of opening yourself up to more heartbreak. Go in with an open mind and a willingness to give her a chance, but don't let your emotions get on top of your common sense.*

Despite the pep talk, she was a bundle of nerves by the time she left the *Clarion* building for their rendezvous.

Cool, calm and cautious, she reminded herself. *Don't go rushing into anything.*

Cool, calm and cautious went out the window as the smile that Frances beamed at her from the back of the café made Kit's insides do a triple somersault. The day suddenly seemed much brighter. She gave a brief wave and wove through the intervening tables to where Frances sat.

"Have you ordered yet?" she asked.

"Yeah, I have," Frances replied. "Sorry, I wasn't sure what you felt like, so I haven't ordered you anything." She gave Kit an apologetic smile.

"S'okay." Kit waved her apology away. "I'll be back in a tick," she said, turning and heading back toward the counter. True to her word, it was only a matter of minutes before she was rejoining Frances and sliding into the chair opposite her.

"Hello," Frances said once she had settled. The warmth of her smile washed over Kit; she couldn't help but smile back.

"Hello yourself," Kit said in return.

Frances's smile faltered for a second or two at Kit's reserved response, but then it reasserted itself.

"You've got no idea how grateful I am that you agreed to this meet up," she said, leaning forward and stretching her hands toward where Kit's own loosely clasped hands rested on the table top. Kit jerked her hands backward, not ready for the physical contact.

"Sorry, sorry," Frances muttered, pulling her arms back and tucking her hands under the table. Before she could say anything more, the server arrived with her macchiato and Kit's tea. They sat in silence while the young woman deposited the drinks, pot, cup, and little jug of milk on the table.

"Thank you," Kit murmured, flashing a smile at the woman, then reaching for the teapot as she departed.

"You're not going to make this easy for me, are you?" Frances said as she watched Kit carefully pour tea into her cup.

Despite her resolve to be cool, calm, and collected, Kit felt a flare of anger at Frances's words.

"Easy? Why should I be making it easy for you?" Kit placed the teapot back on the table and gave Frances a hard look.

"You're right." Frances sighed. "I just thought that if you were wanting us to get back together, then you'd be a little more...I don't know..."

"Accommodating? Is that the word you're searching for?" Kit glared at Frances, then ploughed on before Frances could respond. "And I thought that if *you* were wanting us to get back together, then you'd be a little less...you know...in love with an old flame!"

"But I'm not," Frances said, leaning across the table. "There's only one person I'm in love with and it's not Gillian." She spoke in a hoarse murmur.

Kit took a long, slow sip of her tea, her eyes narrowed as she digested Frances's words.

"Okaaay," she said eventually. "So what was that all about Friday night?"

"Oh god." Frances scrubbed her face with her hands. "It was bit of a shock seeing Gillian after all this time. She was my first lover, you know? And seeing her, well, all those feelings came flooding back and, and...well I guess I got a bit caught up in the moment. But I swear to you, she means nothing to me now. She hasn't for a long, long time." She picked up her cup of coffee and took a sip. "Ugh! That's disgusting!" She pulled a face and got to her feet. "I'm going to order another one. Can I get you anything?"

Kit wordlessly shook her head. So, there was nothing between Frances and Gillian after all? The knot of anger in her chest loosened a little. It was still there, but not taking up as much room as before, and a flood of new emotions flooded into the vacated space. Hope, elation, but chief among them, confusion. Before she could make sense of the welter of thoughts and feelings swirling around inside her head, Frances was back and sliding into the chair opposite, a fresh, hot macchiato in hand.

"So," she said, giving Kit an apprehensive look. "Could we just start again?"

"Yes, please." Kit smiled and nodded. She really did not want to keep being angry at Frances.

"All right then." Frances paused to sip from her mug and gave a satisfied sigh before putting the drink down on the table and fixing her attention on Kit.

"Hello." She smiled. "It is so good to see you again."

Kit opened her mouth to object that they had seen each other every day, but she knew what Frances really meant, so she nodded instead.

"Yes. Yes, it is," she said. And then before she could talk herself out of it, went on with "I've really missed you."

"Me too," Frances said. "And I'm really, really sorry that I let everything become such a horrible mess."

This time, when she reached across the table and enveloped Kit's hands in her own, Kit didn't stop her.

CHAPTER FIFTY-SIX

"Don't let your coffee get cold again," Kit said after a few moments, gently disentangling her hands and gesturing toward Frances's forgotten drink, before reaching for her own cup of now distinctly cool tea.

"What? Oh, right. Yes." Frances shook herself out of the blissful reverie she had fallen into, daydreaming that everything was back to normal and that she and Kit could resume where they had left off. She sipped at her macchiato and marvelled at how well this reconciliation had gone. It had been bit of a gamble sending Kit that text. It could so easily have gone terribly wrong, pushing Kit even further away, but instead, it had paid off. Here they were, holding hands and Kit looking at her with real affection and smiling at her. Maybe now, they could get on with building their relationship, creating a life together.

"Hello. Earth to Frances!" Kit waved a hand in her face, a wry smile on her face.

"Sorry, sorry," Frances said. "I was miles away. What were you saying?"

"That I need to get back to work," Kit said. "I'm way behind on my stories since I've spent all my time writing up a massive proposal that the boss wanted straight away." She gave Frances a sly smile as she got to her feet.

"Oh right. Okay." Frances tried to ignore the wave of disappointment that washed over her as she realised the coffee "date" was coming to an end. She rose from her seat and followed Kit out of the café.

"So, can I see you tonight?" she asked once they had reached the footpath.

"Um. No. I don't think that's a good idea," Kit replied, sliding sunglasses over her eyes. "That probably comes under the 'Needing More Time' thing I mentioned the other day."

"Sure. Sure. I get it," Frances said, but she didn't. Not really. But she knew she had to respect Kit's wishes and not rush her, or she might lose her forever.

"This was nice, though," Kit went on. "I'd like to do that again one day soon. If that's okay with you?"

"Sure. Sure," Frances said again, not trusting herself to say anything more.

"I'll give you a call, yeah?" Kit smiled, then turned and walked off in the direction of the *Clarion* building.

Frances stood and watched her go until she couldn't see her anymore and then began her own slow trudge back to the office, berating herself for getting carried away with her visions of happily ever after. If she were really honest with herself, she'd admit how surprised she had been that Kit had agreed to the coffee catch-up in the first place. She should count herself lucky that Kit had done so when she could so easily have spurned the offer.

Instead, here she was, feeling sorry that Kit had rejected the invitation to see her again tonight, when she should really be celebrating the fact that they had made the first, small step toward (fingers crossed) getting back together. She was the first to admit that patience wasn't one of her strongest points, but if any situation called for it, then this was it. She would call on every ounce of patience she possessed if it meant winning Kit back.

Given how little there was left of the workday, it wasn't worth going back to the office, and, although she'd had a long day of meetings and the six-hundred-kilometre round trip to Melbourne and back, home held little appeal right now. Instead, she decided that, having put it off for long enough, it was time she went and visited the old family home. Of course, the place had changed hands many times since Frances had last lived there and she had no connection to it anymore, but still...

Despite a new coat of paint and an extension to the rear, 17 Poole Street looked the same as it always had. All the trees and shrubs that Frances's mother had planted were bigger, of course, and she felt a surge of happiness that none of the house's subsequent owners had cut down her mum's favourite fuchsia. It now filled the front corner of the garden, throwing shade over the small lawn, while the jacaranda tree towered over the back of the house, spreading its branches across the width of the property. She had loved that tree as a child, spending hours in the little cubby house that Mick had built for his girls. By the time Frances was old enough to climb up into the cubby house, her older sisters had outgrown it and it had become her private little sanctuary, a place she often fled to whenever her father's anger became too much to bear.

Of course, it had been no real escape as she could always hear her dad's voice bellowing from the house as he yelled at her mum. She would sit curled in a ball with her hands over her ears, but it was no good. His angry words couldn't be shut out. He had always known where she was too.

"Get down here and help your mother! Now!" He would stand at the bottom of the tree, hands on hips and shout up at her. She had been thirteen the last time he had climbed the rickety rungs nailed to the trunk and hauled her out of her sanctuary.

Frances shook her head to clear it of the unsettling memories. Starting up the car, she made her way out of Poole Street and drove toward the little house that was her home now.

CHAPTER FIFTY-SEVEN

Despite what she had told Frances about the ton of work she needed to get done, the last thing Kit felt inclined to do once she got back to her desk was work. She had spent the last fifteen minutes staring vacantly at her computer screen, willing the words to come, but to no avail. Instead, her head was filled with thoughts of Frances and by feelings of how much she had enjoyed their coffee...coffee what? "Date"? She was loath to use that word, but in truth, it was a date, wasn't it?

And as dates went, it wasn't the worst one she had ever been on. Sure, it was a little awkward at first, but Kit had to admit a lot of that was down to her own self-defensive prickliness. In the end, though, that had been impossible to maintain, not when her heart was leaping with the simple joy of being with Frances again for the entire time they had spent together.

So, what was with that whole "needing more time" thing she had come out with when Frances had suggested them seeing one another again this evening? More of that reflexive defensiveness. And it was nonsense, because what her heart was telling her was that yes, in fact, seeing Frances tonight was just what it wanted.

"Crap! I'm never going to get this article done," she grumbled to herself as she pushed away from her desk. Grabbing her phone, she headed into the staff room and punched in Frances's number. The phone rang and rang and rang again. Kit was on the verge of hanging up, when it was finally answered.

"Kit! Hi. Hello," said a rather harried-sounding Frances.

"Oh hey, Frances. Everything okay? I haven't called at a bad time, have I?" Kit said, already beginning to regret her impulsive decision to call.

"No, no, not at all," Frances reassured her. "I'm in the car and had to find somewhere to pull over. Took me so long, I thought I was going to miss your call."

"Oh right. Okay, so look. I, um, well…" As Kit fumbled for her words, two other staff members walked in, giggling together as they washed up their coffee mugs. Kit moved to the far side of the room and lowered her voice so as not to be overheard.

"Anyway, the thing is," she continued, *sotto voce*. "It turns out that tonight's not so soon after all." The words all came out in a rush, and Kit held her breath while she waited for Frances's response. The line crackled in silence for several heartbeats, and Kit had almost convinced herself the call must have dropped out.

"Hello? You still there?" Kit said, now really regretting she'd made the call.

"Yes, yes. Sorry," came Frances's breathless reply. "I dropped the phone. Really? Wow, I wasn't expecting that! Cool, so what were you thinking? You want to get a drink somewhere? I'm halfway home, but I can easily turn around."

The obvious enthusiasm in Frances's voice went some way to reassuring Kit that this whole call hadn't been a big mistake.

"A drink, yeah, that would be good," she replied. "The Zodiac?" Maybe that was a poor choice. "Or somewhere else?"

"No, the Zodiac's fine. I'll meet you there in say, twenty minutes, give or take."

Even though the bar was only a ten-minute walk away, Kit was too keyed up to hang around at the office waiting until it was time to leave. So what if she was early? She'd just have to fill in the time with a nerve-calming shot of whisky. She powered down her computer, stuffed her phone and tablet into her satchel, and left the building.

The bar was surprisingly busy, given it wasn't quite five o'clock. Kit wove her way past several occupied tables to the counter and ordered a dram of Laphroaig whisky. Clutching her glass, she made her way toward a small table off to one side of the dimly lit room and slid into one of its two chairs, positioning herself so that she could see the front entrance. She took a sip of her drink, closing her eyes as she savoured the smoky aroma of the single malt. One day, she would travel to Scotland and take herself on a tour of whisky distilleries, starting with those on Islay, the island home of Laphroaig.

Her daydreaming was interrupted by the ringing of her phone. Her heart lurched as she thought it might be Frances, cancelling, but it was Hilary and her heart lurched again as she wondered if she had forgotten a squash date.

"Hils, hi! How's things?" she said cautiously, taking another sip of the whisky. "We're not meant to be playing tonight, are we?"

"Nah, mate," Hilary replied. "I'm just calling to see how you're getting on after our chat the other night. Still sitting at home cuddling your cat?"

"For your information, Hilary Mason, I am in a bar, drinking a very fine Scottish single malt," Kit said in mock indignation.

"Oh gawd. I don't know what's worse. At home with your cat or out drinking alone," Hilary laughed.

"If you must know," Kit said, "I'm waiting for Frances, with whom I have arranged to have a drink, so no, I am not drinking on my own. Although, technically right now I am, because Frances has yet to arrive."

"Aha! So, you were listening to me," Hilary said. "Fantastic! I really am pleased. Now, don't go stuffing it up."

"Gotta go," Kit cut her off, having just spotted Frances in the doorway. "Talk soon," she said, hanging up and shoving the phone into her pocket as Frances approached, a 200-watt smile lighting up her face as she slid into the chair opposite Kit.

CHAPTER FIFTY-EIGHT

Despite having been to the Zodiac Bar several times already, Frances was having trouble finding Pelham Lane. They'd always walked or been dropped off by an Uber before, and from the driver's seat, it all looked unfamiliar. Having gone round the same block and ending up back on Marchant Street for the third time, Frances decided she'd have better luck on foot. Parking the car, she hurried along the street, following the little blue line in her map app and not really paying attention to her surroundings. So, she was a little taken aback when she found her path suddenly blocked by an elderly man very obviously the worse for wear from alcohol.

"Why, if it isn't Mick's girl!" he said, a sloppy grin spreading across his face. "Come and have a drink with us. Raise a glass to your old dad."

"Us" was a group of equally elderly and equally drunken men, sitting at a table outside the Waverley Hotel. Flustered by losing her way and worried about being late, Frances hadn't realised her route would take her straight past the Waverley.

She peered at the man who had accosted her, groping in her memory for a name.

"Reg, isn't it?" she said as recognition finally came to her. "Thanks, but I'll give it a miss," she said, trying to edge past the man. "I'm meeting a friend."

"Come on, just one drink," the man persisted. "Honour the bloke's memory. I'm sure your friend won't mind." His mates all made various noises in support, laughing amongst themselves as they swigged from their schooners.

Frances sighed. She wasn't in the mood for this. Didn't want a confrontation with these men. But she was already late and in danger of blowing what was probably her last chance of winning Kit back.

"Come on, girl," Reg said. "You don't wanna bring any more shame to his name, do ya?"

That did it. Anger fizzed through her veins as she stepped in close to the old man. He took an uncertain step back as she glared at him.

"You want to talk about shaming the Keating name?" she hissed. "Well, my father did that all by himself. I know you all think Mick was a great bloke," she said, glaring around at them all. "And sure, he was a champion footballer, but he was a right bastard at home. A shithouse husband and a shithouse father who made our lives a misery with his drunken rages. So, no. I won't be raising a glass in his memory, thanks all the same."

She stepped around an open-mouthed Reg, nodded to his equally nonplussed companions, and continued on her way, ignoring her shaky knees and trying not to worry about the fallout from her trashing her father's reputation. Right now, all she cared about was Kit.

Finally reaching the bar, she pushed her way inside, pausing for several moments to scan the room, her heart skipping in relief and a huge smile breaking out across her face when she spotted Kit sitting against the far wall.

"God, I could do with one of those," she said, nodding at the drink in Kit's hand as she sat down.

"Why, what's happened? Is everything okay?" Kit frowned in concern, looking around and waving to attract the attention of a passing server.

"No, no, it's all okay," Frances assured her, waiting until the server had taken their orders and left before launching into the tale of what had taken place with Reg and his mates.

"Bloody hell," Kit said when she had finished. "I reckon your name is going to be mud down at the Waverley from now on. And down at the football club. And over at the Chamber of Commerce. And...well pretty much all over town, really."

"I don't care," Frances said, a fierce expression on her face. "It's about time people heard the truth about good ol' Mick Keating." She took a sip of whisky, nodding in appreciation as its heat spread through her. "There's only one person whose opinion of me matters." She stared meaningfully at Kit. "My name's not still mud with you, is it?"

"No. No, it's not," Kit said, placing her glass carefully down on the table before going on. "I don't think it ever really was. I was angry with you. Felt hurt by you. But I never hated you. I never—" She stopped, looked away from Frances and picked up her drink.

"Never what?" Frances leant toward her, her gaze intent. "You never what?"

Kit turned to face her again. Frances's heart thumped at the intensity of her gaze. She swallowed, waiting for an agonising eternity for Kit to speak. Eventually, just as Frances couldn't stand the silence any longer, she threw back the last of the Laphroaig, thumped the empty glass back down on the table, and took a deep breath.

"I never stopped loving you. There. I've said it. Happy now?"

"Oh yes," Frances said, beaming. "Very happy indeed. So does this mean we're back together again?"

Kit gave her one of those lazy, slow smiles that she found so intoxicating.

"Yeah, I reckon it does."

Bella Books, Inc.

Happy Endings Live Here

P.O. Box 10543
Tallahassee, FL 32302
Phone: (850) 576-2370

www.BellaBooks.com

More Titles from Bella Books

Hunter's Revenge – Gerri Hill
978-1-64247-447-3 | 276 pgs | paperback: $18.95 | eBook: $9.99
Tori Hunter is back! Don't miss this final chapter in the acclaimed Tori Hunter series.

Integrity – E. J. Noyes
978-1-64247-465-7 | 228 pgs | paperback: $19.95 | eBook: $9.99
It was supposed to be an ordinary workday...

The Order – TJ O'Shea
978-1-64247-378-0 | 396 pgs | paperback: $19.95 | eBook: $9.99
For two women the battle between new love and old loyalty may prove more dangerous than the war they're trying to survive.

Under the Stars with You – Jaime Clevenger
978-1-64247-439-8 | 302 pgs | paperback: $19.95 | eBook: $9.99
Sometimes believing in love is the first step. And sometimes it's all about trusting the stars.

The Missing Piece – Kat Jackson
978-1-64247-445-9 | 250 pgs | paperback: $18.95 | eBook: $9.99
Renee's world collides with possibility and the past, setting off a tidal wave of changes she could have never predicted.

An Acquired Taste – Cheri Ritz
978-1-64247-462-6 | 206 pgs | paperback: $17.95 | eBook: $9.99
Can Elle and Ashley stand the heat in the *Celebrity Cook Off* kitchen?

www.ingramcontent.com/pod-product-compliance
Lightning Source LLC
Jackson TN
JSHW022308170425
82784JS00001B/2